KING OF THE SEA

KING

OF

THE

SEA

Derek Bickerton

Random House New York

All rights reserved under International and
Pan-American Copyright Conventions.
Published in the United States by Random
House, Inc., New York, and simultaneously
in Canada by Random House of Canada
Limited, Toronto.

Library of Congress Cataloging in
Publication Data
Bickerton, Derek.
King of the sea.
I. Title.
PZ4.B583Ki 1979 [PR6052.I23] 813'.5'4
79-4787
ISBN 0-394-50516-6

Manufactured in the United States of
America

9 8 7 6 5 4 3 2

First Edition

TO J.J.B.

KING OF THE SEA

ONE

THE STATION. I could begin with that. Less than two years ago I was living in this room in a wooden tower at one corner of the Dolphin Experimental Station. Out one window you could see the Pacific, and a couple of surf breaks, Concessions and Shark Hole. Out the other you could see the tall masts of sport-fishing boats jammed into a tiny harbor, and beyond them, the concrete towers of downtown Honolulu. In back of the harbor was a low gray building, like a jail. The tuna cannery. I got a small knot in my stomach whenever I looked at it, even though it was now illegal for tunafishers to kill dolphins, even though the boats that came in there were all local line-fishers, not the purse-seiners who had slaughtered countless thousands of dolphins. Tuna, I never ate it, never even gave it to the Station cat. The tuna industry was the Enemy.

However, the factory was still there, canning tuna, and what it didn't can got thrown back into the harbor and sucked out the harbor mouth by the tides, to Shark Hole. Shark Hole was called Shark Hole for the obvious reason. When I told people that we used to surf Shark Hole by night, Les and I, whenever there was a full moon, people used to look at me like that same moon had scrambled my brains. Walter especially. Because he was a local kid, part Hawaiian, he pronounced "full" and "moon" with the same vowel: "Eh, you guys go out there with the *fool moon,* ah? But you no can *fool the shock,* ah? Pretty soon he gon' get his *belly fool,* the shock!" And he would laugh like hell, he had a pretty macabre sense of humor, maybe that was what they killed him for.

Actually it wasn't dangerous at all, really. Most of the sharks there are nurse sharks, garbage eaters with blunt teeth that are good for cracking shellfish and not much else; one of them might have a go at you once in a blue moon, but not while there was anything easier around. You got the odd tiger or hammerhead, though, so you just had to watch yourself. And not do stupid things, like straddling your board with your legs instead of kneeling on it—letting your legs hand down, white in the water, natural sharkbait. I knew a guy lost a foot that way.

But then I can't remember a time, even when I was small, that I was ever afraid of the sea or anything in it. For as long as I can remember, I've been as much at home there as on land. True, that was before I met *orcinus orca* in his natural surroundings. But I anticipate.

THE PURPOSE of the Dolphin Experimental Station was to study the intellectual capacities of dolphins. You could tell that from the mere fact that it was called the Dolphin Experimental Station and not the Porpoise Experimental Station. Call them porpoises, and you commit yourself to the belief that they're no smarter than, well, "a smart dog" is the usual expression in the trade. You then study something called "porpoise behavior," which needs no more reflect intelligence than amoeba behavior or combustion-engine behavior. Call them dolphins, and you commit yourself to at least the suspicion that there might be more to it than that. Dr. Barry Levitt, Professor of Neuropsychology and principal investigator on the Station's current project, was located just a smidgen the right side of the line that divided dolphin-people from porpoise-people. For public consumption, he believed nothing at all unless the computer had printed it out exteen times. Off the record, he would own to the feeling that dolphins were as smart as, oh well, maybe "a smart chimp." Of the three grad assistants on the project, Frank, who was a born-again Christian with overtones of Tolkien and TM, thought they were Jesus Christ in flippers —not just smarter, but morally and ethically superior to poor old homo sap. Les and I fell somewhere between these extremes. But we all called them dolphins.

We had two dolphins, Mele and Lei. Both of them belonged to the species *Steno bredanensis,* and this was always a big turnoff for visitors, who had watched Flipper and had been to Marineland, and who knew, therefore, that a dolphin was a funny fellow with a built-in anthropomorphic grin. Stenos don't look like that at all. They have ugly humpbacked bodies covered in blotches, beaks like the front end of the Concorde or Bob Hope's nose, and hardly the vestige of a grin. But everyone in the trade, whether dolphin-person or porpoise-person, knows they are even cleverer and faster learners than *tursiops truncatus,* which is the commoner and more photogenic species you will have seen on TV.

When visitors came, whichever of us had drawn the chore of showing them around (Barry, for all his egotism, was too prickly with people to do this) would explain to them how these two dolphins, though of the same species, had quite different personalities, "just like people." Of course Lei was the one they dug; she would come to the side of the tank when you whistled, roll over, let herself be tickled, pretend to bite you, splash you with her tail, and otherwise react to you in a manner which was generally deemed appropriate, if a little on the forward side. Mele, on the other hand, hated strangers and would just swim round and round in circles in the center of her tank, no matter what you did to attract her. She had come to us as a discard from the U.S. Marine Corps Dolphin Program in Kaneohe, and Frank swore she must have been traumatized in some obscene military experiment. Only that, he thought, could account for her abnormal indifference to our kind. Keala came up with quite another suggestion.

I FIND IT VERY HARD, even now, to write about Keala. Of all the ties I had to earth, hers was the one that it was hardest to break, and her, perhaps, I hurt most in the breaking. And even now I feel guilty. That's laughable, really. Anyone who's done what I've done should have passed far beyond guilt by now, and yet when I remember how her face, flushed and open, would sort of collapse on itself when something hurt or upset her that she could not, brave as she was, strike back at . . . Enough of that. Personal feelings are irrelevant. I am, or was, a scientist of sorts, on a lowish level, and my only loyalty left is to the facts.

The facts are that I met Keala around six months before this story begins, that she was then a sociology major in her senior year, that it was only through her that I met Walter, her brother, and the rest of the Kealoha family, that I went with her for two months before we had sex together, something that was quite unprecedented—the two months, not the sex— and that I was then, just possibly, quite reluctantly, and against all my deepest principles, in love with her. Remember I was very young then. Or I'm very old now. I mean, one way or the other, there's a gulf between me then and me now too wide ever to be bridged.

We were looking at the tanks that day. The tanks had not been originally designed for dolphins. They were about fifty feet in diameter but only four and a half feet deep. Keala looked at me. That part of her that wasn't Hawaiian was partly Filipino; a mixture that often gives a wild, rakish beauty, reckless and ready for anything, mobile as the clouds to paint its owner's moods on, so I would tease her that no matter what she wished she could never hide her feelings from me. Now she was puzzled, irritated, ready to be indignant. "How they going to dive, in there?" she asked.

"They aren't."

"How come, they aren't? Dolphins *got* to dive. It's their nature."

"That's tough. They get well looked after. People with them all the time. Plenty to eat." And I explained to her how hard it was to get hold of a research facility that had proper dolphin tanks. We were lucky to have this one. Before it became a Dolphin Experimental Station, it had been a Turtle Experimental Station; the tanks had been designed as turtle tanks, for a practical project such as bureaucrats love and understand, to bring a great new Turtle-Breeding Industry to the Islands, only something went wrong, maybe the turtles got sterile from the copper sulphate they cleaned the tanks with, they tried to offer them to Pete Marcos the restaurant owner but after the first one Pete's clients got sick, or so the story went, and they were left to diminish through attrition. The last of them, grandfathered in, still inhabited a small enclave in the corner of Mele's tank. I watched Keala all the while I was talking and saw that she wasn't taking a blind bit of notice of me.

"You have any idea what proper tanks cost?" I asked her.

She ignored this. "You, Les, Frank, all of you always talking like how they're your friends, ah?"

"You mean Lei and Mele?—Sure. Sure they're our friends."

"Well," she said, her face flushed and her breasts heaving in a manner I found somewhat distracting, "suppose one guard in one jailhouse said, 'Eh, you know, all of these prisoners in here are my real good friends'. What you would say to that, eh?"

"I'd say he was a fucking hypocrite."

"Right on, brother." Her tone was sarcastic as hell but I still couldn't see what I'd said wrong.

"So what?"

"So what, he says! Look, Andy, you can't see that's the same —the same as you and them?"

THAT BLEW ME APART, for a while. Really, I'd never thought of it like that before. But the more I thought about it, the more

I realized that Keala had something. There's so much in life that we just take for granted without ever thinking about it. You hear people talking about wild creatures "in captivity" and how many times do you ever stop and think that the expression means exactly what it says? In Captivity. It seemed so natural—naturally!—for me to be walking round the tank and them to be in it. That's the way the world is, soldier. How absurd if it were reversed! But if it were reversed? I flashed on how it would feel to be trapped down there, under the Pacific, in some kind of air bubble no doubt, them prodding me with their beaks and arguing about whether I was as smart as a smart dogfish—but all loving the hell out of me, of course.

And then a lot of other things that I'd always sort of known, but never really seriously considered, began to appear to me in a new light. Like, every dolphin you see in a Marineland represents three that got caught. The other two are dead. People in the business don't care to admit it but it's the truth. Some fight so hard to escape, they die while being taken. Some go straight into shock. Some are so weakened by the trauma of capture that they die within days from trivial infections (although nowadays it's SOP to hit them with broad-spectrum antibiotics as soon as they reach their first "holding tank"). Some choke themselves "accidentally" on ropes, some throw themselves out of the tank, some just give up and stop their hearts. Those that survive are the pliable ones. They are the ones who obey, who do the clever tricks the kiddies so love to watch. What the fuck else would you expect them to do? Look at them down there entertaining the folks, any fool can see how happy they are to be here with wonderful us.

Just like it was with the slaves. Every slave on a plantation represented three that got caught. The other two were dead. Some died fighting. Some threw themselves off ships in mid-Atlantic. Some died from trifling ailments in the process that was known as "seasoning" (if there'd been broad-spectrum antibiotics in those days, Massah would have used them, natch). Some hung themselves or poisoned themselves, some just willed themselves to die. The survivors were the pliable ones, the ones that had learnt how to shuck. They clowned around, they hammed it up, they stepped and fetched it. Unhappy? You gotta be kidding! Can't you hear the way they're singing?

As those, so these. The slave on his plantation was better off than in the wilds of savage Africa; the dolphin in his tank was better off than in the shark-ridden Pacific. There were doubts as to whether the slave had human intelligence, or any intelligence; there were the same doubts about dolphins and they didn't even *look* human. "It's oppression," Keala said, with the resentment of another defrauded race behind her, and I couldn't argue with her. But what was I to do?

SHOULD I, at this stage, say a little of how I came to be where I was? I feel like a criminal on trial, debating whether to take the stand. If I tell you about myself, you will pick over my words for evidence that I'm insane—as I surely must be, to do the things I did. If I keep silent, I remain a faceless monster, alien, capable of anything. I'll take the first track. You do as you wish.

My parents were two singularly ill-assorted people. My father came from a long line of small-town New England bankers and doctors and merchants; my mother, from a family that passed themselves off as, and may well have been, French New Orleans gentry fallen on hard times. She was also very religious—Catholic of course—which I guess was what mostly held the marriage together once their first flush of mutual astonishment had worn off. My father had dropped out of Harvard Business School to do graduate work in anthropology at Chicago. Harvard had been his folks' idea, but he couldn't hack it, it wasn't *relevant.* Anthropology, on the other hand, was *about people.* In particular, it was about the kind of people that would never, until pigs flew, get to Harvard Business School. My father had White Liberal Guilt several years before it got fashionable. As an anthropologist, he had a distinct species of the genus. For hadn't Anthropology, in the nineteenth and early twentieth centuries, used all its prestige and scholarly authority to back up Racism? Well, he would do penance for that. He would show that Black People had souls and civilizations and cultures while the White Folks were still cracking one another's heads in the abyss of the Dark Ages.

So he became a sojourner in the tropical zones of Africa and the Americas, wherever blacks were found, first as a graduate student with a nonambulant baby (me), then on postgraduate fellowships, then on contract with the new universities that had begun to spring up in those exotic lands. And wherever he went, Mom followed. In fear and revulsion, not of black faces (for wasn't it precisely the sudden lack of these that had bankrupted poor old great-grandpappy's plantation?) but of Disease. Of beriberi, yaws, infectious hepatitis, sleeping sickness, blackwater fever. Her friends threw up hands in horror. You mean you're taking your *baby!* Corinne (that was her name), you're *insane!* Or so I was told long after the event; actually, I don't think she had any friends. In these re-enactments of those dramatic days, which as I recall Mom would perform any time up till my eleventh year (when she finally decided to give up on me), Mom would do the martyr's smile with which, she said, she had greeted these accusations. When she went to the altar, she told them with that smile, she had Taken a Vow. To go where He went, to be His bride and helpmate, in sickness and in health, in dysentery and beriberi, till death did them part.

Actually, Going Where He Went didn't include the Interior. The Interior, or the Bush as it was sometimes called, was something else. In the Interior, all bets were off, all contracts null and void: a land behind God's back, of Impenetrable Jungles and Unspeakable Rites. So it was understood that when my father, who as a Man—sex roles were sharply differentiated in my family—somehow had the power to penetrate the impenetrable, set off for the Interior (where, naturally, all the best and blackest culture was to be found), Mom and I remained in the Port.

All those tacky little colonies and ex-colonies where we lived consisted of an Interior and a Port. The Port was where you shipped out all the stuff you'd got from the natives for Low, Low Prices so you could sell it in the developed countries for High, High Prices. Consequently, the Port was westernized, up to a point; although it probably held more disease, more of the Unspeakable than any village in the Interior, there were suburbs where the toilets flushed and the drugstores sold Kleenex. The Port, needless to say, was always on the sea.

By the age of three, I was a powerful swimmer. Whenever I could escape from my mother's tender loving care, which was as often as possible, I seemed to head instinctively for the water. In part it was because I had discovered that by, or in, the water you can always find someone to play with. Of course there were kids in the white suburbs of the Port, but they weren't real kids—they were anemic worms in fancy white suits chased by black nannies with umbrellas. When you pinched them to check if they were real, they shrieked—they had that much sense, at least—and pains and penalties were visited upon you. The kids in the water were something else again. Pinch them and they'd pinch you right back. They were fun. They didn't have nannies, and they weren't scared; they were inventive, foul-mouthed, perpetually curious. They were black, mostly. It was years before I really noticed, but they were. They spoke all manner of barbarous tongues, and so, perforce, spoke I. I spoke Black Spanish, Ewe, Igbo, dialects of French and English that no Frenchman or Englishman could understand. Mom despaired of me. How would I ever get to a good Catholic school and university, talking like that? Associating with people like that? But there was nothing she could do about it. My father was always off into the Interior, and I could play Mom like a harmonica, even from real small.

Switching peer-groups every couple of years—every time my father moved to a new country—was more of a hassle than anything my parents ever laid on me. I was strong and tough, but I was never superstrong or supertough, and though the folkways of these countries don't really differ all that much, I was the wrong color and my hair the wrong kind. I needed that something *extra* to get instant acceptance, and that something extra was the fact that I could swim further and faster and dive deeper than any kid of my own age. Go up to some bunch of strangers on a wharf, all of them leering and prodding at me and shouting *mburuni* or *bakra* or whatever, and I'd challenge them to a race, using signs if need be or grabbing one and jumping in the water with him if that failed. Eventually they'd get the idea and I'd win. Always. They couldn't argue about that. I'd be in; grudgingly perhaps, but in.

Later, Stateside, some pro trainer saw me swim and spoke long and earnestly to my father. He said I had Star Quality. I could be another Mark Spitz. He'd train me for nothing, he said. He was so sure of my potential. Just take ten percent off the top when the Olympic prizes and sportswear endorsements started rolling in. My father passed this on to me. He didn't know from shit about any kind of sport but the man had impressed him and he wanted to give me the best chances. He was quite surprised and perhaps mildly pleased when I said no. I still don't know for sure why I said no. It's too easy to say I wasn't competitive. I am competitive, very competitive, in my own way. But somehow the idea of competition and the idea of swimming didn't go together. Swimming was something I did, in the first place, for social reasons—like I've told you— and in the second place, because I enjoyed everything about it. I loved the sea, its changes, the sense of wildness and freedom. What I was most afraid of was that swimming would be turned into work. I could just picture this big beer-bellied slob with a stopwatch in his hand, living vicariously the dreams of his youth and riding me like a warlock: eat this, don't eat that, practice, exercise, earlytobed earlytorise, double up there you lazy asshole, put some *guts* into it! No thank you.

So I didn't go in for the Olympics and I didn't become a second Mark Spitz. Tough shit. The kind of competitive I am, it would never have been enough to be merely the best. I would have to do things that had never been done before— things that no one but I could do.

AFTER A DOZEN or so years of living like this, a terrible thing happened to my father's career. There appeared black anthropologists. Always till then it had been Whitey's scene. Whitey told the blacks what their culture was, what it had been and what it ought to be. Then, out of nowhere, there were these big black dudes with doctorates from Howard saying, Hey, man, what is all this jive? What do *you* know about the Black Experience? You just a part of Institutional Racism, *bro* —just you get your white ass off of our turf, leave our culture alone! And no use him coming back with, How can you do this to me? I'm different, I'm liberal, I'm not like the rest of them! Because they would only answer, Sure, you're different. You worse! The rest of them take our time, our blood and our sweat—you trying to take our *Soul!*

Bad times in the academic circus, the late sixties. Beating of breasts and outraged indignation. Language never before heard in gatherings of scholars. For someone in my father's position, there were three ways to go. You could become a racist; you could play kissass to the Panthers; or you could pull out of the whole thing. Give him credit, he had the dignity to take the third course. Took him some time to extricate himself, but by the early seventies he was in Hawaii, where there were hardly any blacks but lots of other races, a nice climate, a soporific campus, and nearly six thousand miles of mountain, sea and prairie between him and the state of his birth.

Mom was happy because there were no Diseases and lots of Catholics. Women's Lib was but a cloud on the horizon, no bigger than a person's hand.

As for me, I was an anomaly. I looked like a *haole,* but I didn't talk or act like a *haole;* having spent almost all of my first dozen years overseas, I felt like an immigrant in my own country. Educationally, too, I was bizarre. Somehow in the mélange of schools I'd attended, or just by osmotic contact with the world through which I'd moved, I seemed to have gotten almost two grades ahead of other kids my age. In a couple of years I was attending college part-time. Try and think of a recipe for a misfit—you will hardly do better than that. And yet I wasn't, at that stage, at all. My position had its advantages. Belonging to no obvious cultural group, I could relate equally well to all of them. My reputation as a swimmer and, before long, as a surfer, plus a guarded tongue, enabled people to forget that I was indecently brainy for my age. Then in another couple of years there was sex and discos. I put the two together because they went together. If you're cool and good-looking, as I have to admit I was, you can cruise the Waikiki discos and score a different chick every night, forever, possibly, because with the tourists there are new faces coming in all the time. I didn't do that every night, it would have interfered with my surfing. Studying got fitted in where it could; I'd throw myself down with a book, and the contents would somehow sort of flash onto my brain, sorting themselves neatly almost without volition on my part. Nobody could figure how I could make straight A's and live the way I did. Misfit, indeed! No, I was hot shit then, around sixteen, eighteen, when I was using my mind just to survive and run on, before I began to really think about things.

I fell into the Station by purest chance. I graduated in my twentieth year, having majored in psych, and not having the slightest notion of what I wanted to become—except, perhaps, independently rich. Around this time things had gotten pretty rotten at home. For the first time, really, my parents had had to live together, there being no Interior into which my father could conveniently disappear. It had come as something of a shock to them to find they didn't really know one another at all. When they got to know one another, it came as a still bigger shock to find that they didn't like one another. They took a long time to admit to this, since both of them, in their different ways, were both highly moral and highly romantic. So there dragged on, month after month, a kind of guerrilla warfare of cutting remarks and pained silences and slammed doors in which disingenuous attempts were made by both sides to gain me as an ally. "Your mother seems to think . . ." "Why doesn't your father realize . . ." I wanted out, but I didn't want to have to pay rent. It was then that I heard Levitt was looking for someone who could program a computer and was prepared to offer, in exchange for this service, one of the dilapidated but livable rooms on the Station's premises. So, I enrolled in grad school and moved in.

UNTIL KEALA OPENED my eyes to the true relations between man and dolphin, I guess you could even say my life was idyllic. The Station consisted of a quadrangle set behind high palings, with the twin tanks in the middle and ramshackle buildings at either end. At the seaward end was a kind of wooden tower that looked as if it had been made at different times by drunken carpenters, at the top of which was my room. I would wake (if I hadn't been up late the night before) with the alarm clock hammering in my ears, and the sky barely lightening; rise, put on trunks, take my board (Les was a late sleeper and Frank didn't surf) and head out for Shark Hole or Concessions. At that time there wouldn't be anyone else out, the water would be like glass and I'd have the break all to myself. If it was good form I'd stay out maybe a couple hours. Then I'd come in, shower, brew coffee and fry up a few eggs on the hotplate in the Station's roach-ridden kitchen; by this time, the others would usually be about. We'd go check the notice board in the office, where Barry had a habit of leaving cryptic, chalked messages for us about the handling of the dolphins; whoever's turn it was to feed them would thaw out the fish, and we'd all socialize with them while they ate. But soon it would be time to get down to the serious business of the day, i.e. the experiments with the dolphins.

In the afternoon we usually had classes up at the U. I drove up in my Bug, a cherry '57 with original baby window plus the double headers and mag wheels I'd fitted myself when I reconditioned it; it was a point of honor to get it on campus and off again without paying and without getting caught. Then maybe I'd work in the library awhile and get back down to the Station towards sunset—which never varies more than an hour or so in our part of the world. I'd strip off, jump in the tanks and fool around a while with Lei and Mele, and then after that—well, whatever. Go with Keala to a movie or a disco. Go night-surfing with Les. Go up Kalihi and party with the Kealohas. Go down Kahala and hang out with the rich kids I knew from high-school days. Deal a little: Maui Wowie, Kona Gold, Thai sticks, a few Quaaludes now and then, nothing heavy, and never to anyone I hadn't known in high school. There's nowhere like Honolulu if you're twenty and into it. Yes, idyllic, you could call it. I guess.

You'll notice I've said nothing about the experiments in all this. That's intentional. At the time I thought very little about them. Although they took up most of my mornings, they didn't really take up much of my life, if you get the distinction. I just walked through them. I could do them half asleep. There didn't, at the time, even seem anything very odd about them. The way we did them was just the way one Did Science, period. After all, that was what we were there to learn. Ours not to reason why.

Not that there was anything cruel about the experiments. Even before the Enlightenment, I wouldn't have stood for any of that shit. So if you get your jollies from reading vivisection stories, skip the next few pages. They're very dull. Ditto if you're reading just to find What Happens Next. Maybe I shouldn't bother with it at all, but I really feel, in order to understand what went down afterwards, that you should have some kind of a reference point, some idea of what "research" meant and presumably still means to Professor Barry Levitt and doubtless thousands of his kind.

PICTURE ME SEATED at my computer. Color me keen, Anglo, with a heavy-surfer tan and sun-bleached surfer hair (the hair lighter than the face below it). I am a loyal member of the team that is working on Aural Discrimination and Short-Term Memory in *Steno bredanensis.* In plain English, we are finding out how well our dolphins can tell one sound from another, and how far their capacities will reach when you distract them with a variety of sounds and lengthen the time interval between them. You still may not think this has much to do with human-dolphin communication. Well, you are wrong. Barry was building up to that, but gradually, systematically, like a good scientist should. Only when he'd exhaustively studied all the cognitive and motor functions that are involved in communication would he feel ready for the big bust.

I type into the computer a string of digits, say something like

$$4 \quad 6 \quad 7 \quad 3 \quad 2 \quad 5 \quad 1$$

These digits serve as code-numbers for different classes of sounds—like, 4 is for warbling sounds, 6 for beeping sounds, and so on, each class has its code. What the computer then does is take each code number and look in its memory bank for the appropriate class. Having located, say, the class of beeps, it proceeds to select, randomly, just one particular member of that class—the three-digit code-number that represents a beep fractionally but recognizably different, in pitch and duration, from the rest of the thousand beeps whose codes are stored in the computer's memory.

When the computer has selected seven sounds, one from each class, it types back to me the codes for those seven sounds, thuswise:

$$496 \quad 622 \quad 803 \quad 357 \quad 209 \quad 551 \quad 975$$

Of course I have no idea what actual sounds these codes represent, and so much the better, in Barry's frame of reference, because the more abstract and mechanical it all is, the further divorced from any contact with fallible flesh and blood, then the more scientifically valid the results will be.

I now type a further string of digits:

$$2 \quad 4 \quad 7 \quad 2$$

The first digit means that this particular run will be match rather than nonmatch; that is to say, the dolphin will have to identify a given sound as being identical with one of a series that preceded it, rather than different from any member of that series. The second digit means that there will be a time lapse of four seconds between the last member of the seven-sound series and the single sound the dolphin is supposed to match, which we call the probe sound. The third digit means that there will be seven sounds in the series that precedes the probe (you'd think the computer could have figured that out from my previous set of instructions, but they're dumb assholes that have to be told everything twice). The fourth digit shows that we'll be playing the sounds from the right-hand member of a pair of underwater speakers.

Even if you're an Evelyn Woods graduate, all that takes only a fraction of the time you took to read about it. Which is just as well, because those instructions took care of just one run, and there will be several dozen such runs in the course of a morning's work. Each one to be typed in as a separate section of the program.

When I've finished typing the program, I give the *Go* signal. This causes the computer to begin feeding my instructions into a machine called a Wavetek. The Wavetek, which can reproduce, electronically, just about any sound there is, takes each of the computer's three-digit codes and converts it into the appropriate sound in the first series. Meantime Mele, or Lei, whichever one we are presently working with, and who has been sloshing around waiting, listens keenly to the seven sounds and, presumably, memorizes each one. Then comes the pause. She is just drifting, now, flippers idle, waiting for the probe sound. It comes. Like lightning, she dives and heads for a pair of underwater objects that look rather like inflated brake pedals. If she thinks the probe sound is the same as one in the series, she hits the right-hand pedal. If she thinks it's a different sound, she hits the left-hand one. If she's right, she gets a fish; either way, an electronic impulse from the pedal feeds back into the computer and tells it whether she was right or wrong. The computer files the information—it will come back to us, later, in the day's printout—and gets on with the next run.

I TRIED TO EXPLAIN all this to Walter Kealoha one afternoon, but both of us had drunk the best part of two sixpacks and I can't guarantee that I did it at all clearly. I should say something about Walter, for although in one sense he's peripheral to this story, he came to symbolize something that was important in my way of thinking. On the face of things, Walter was not the kind of friend an up-and-coming young graduate student should have had. He was, not to mince matters, a borderline sociopath and two-time Detention Home loser who'd graduated from glue-sniffing to reds and who now lived on welfare, supplemented by a little dealing (he was my main connection) and occasional hits on tourist rentacars in Windward-side beach-park parking lots. Moreover, true to type, he hated *haoles*, indeed the first time we ever met he had deliberately picked a fight with me which Keala herself broke up in a manner that became a family legend, told and retold till all the rough edges were honed off of it: ". . . an' 'en all of a suddin, Tita she come, she screamin' like one pigmobile onna freeway, she let fly widda purse, she *geev* om, brah, pow! pow! Da purse wen' bus' opin, all da junks wen' fly out, was like shotgun pellets, ah, an' da two guys, Walter, Andy, they so scare they wen' go hide unna da table, oh boy, suckin' unreal!'' Admittedly it would have ended there if I hadn't gone on going with Keala, if the other Kealohas hadn't liked me or at least been prepared to tolerate me; but we kept on running into one another, and gradually, through fences of shyness and caution, through cultural blinkers, began to see that we'd quite a lot in common. We were both totally opposed to authority. By this I don't mean we were rebels; rebels fear and hate authority or just want it themselves, whereas we were completely indifferent to it, civil disobedience came as natural to us as breathing, nothing you had to theorize about. On top of that, Walter, a tenth-grade drop-out who had been diagnosed at different times as hyperactive, dyslexic and MBD, was a whole lot smarter than some college teachers I have known. He did his best to disguise the fact, since it didn't fit his self-image of being the meanest shithead around, and yet I couldn't help feeling that he was mad at people for not recognizing it—his teachers in particular—even through his disguise.

When I'd finished explaining—we were lying in the grass

under the keawe trees at Pokai Bay, the sun growing hotter as it descended, everyone else on the picnic asleep or wandering aimlessly on the beach—he said, "Ass crazy, that."

"How you mean, crazy?"

"Well—ass not *natural,* ah?"

"For who? For us, or the dolphins?"

He raised himself on one elbow. "Eh, pass me one beer, I need om for wash down all this bullshit you tokking. Ah. Grassy ass, amigo." He squinted fiercely at me over the bottle, in mock seriousness. "You gon' tell me is natural, ah? You tok to one machine. Machine go tok back to you. He can tell you anyting you dunno? No can! He ony go tell you back what you wen' tell om awready! An' 'en you no unnastand om! Eh, brah, you more dumber dan da machine!" And he collapsed on the grass in delight at his own logic.

"I'm not talking to the machine. I'm talking to the dolphin *through* the machine."

"Like you tell, eek, squak, pow, beep, anna dolphin he press one pedal, ah? . . . Interestin' conversation!"

"Okay, okay, I'm not *talking* to it, I'm *communicating* with it."

"You communicating, ah?" He rolled the word round his tongue, making it sound like some esoteric sex perversion. "Heavy, ah? But I tot you was telling me jus' now, this guy whachacallom, the big honcho—"

"Barry."

"I tot you was telling me Barry like go find out how for tok to da dolphins?"

"Well—not exactly."

"How—exactly?"

"You saw that thing on TV the other night about teaching chimps sign language?"

"Huh? Oh, right, right." All the Kealohas could sign; the youngest brother had been born deaf.

"Well, Barry is going to teach dolphins the same way."

"They no can sign with their fleepers!"

"I know, you lolo, they'll use sounds instead of signs. But the principle's the same. First you figure out what a creature does best. Chimps can't speak, right, but their hands are nearly as flexible as ours. Dolphins are best at making squeaky noises. So you make up a language that has squeaky sounds instead of words—then you teach it to them. Simple."

Walter lay on his back, digesting this. Then he said, "I tot I read someplace dolphins get language awready?"

"Nobody knows that, for sure."

"You mean all you smart buggahs no can figure om out?"

"It's not that easy."

Walter spat. "Spose I meet one guy he no tok English—"

"You mean like you? You no tok English."

Walter laughed. "Awright, I tok peedgeen, but you know what I mean—I show om one beer, I tell, 'Eh, what that?' He tell, 'Podola'. Ass how I know 'podola', ass da word for beer in hees language. You dig?"

"Sure. And the floor of the ocean is littered with Bud bottles."

"Oh. I get it. They no more nothing, down there."

"Right. No objects. No artifacts, anyway."

"Get plenny fish."

"You'd get a long way on the names of fish. Even if they classified them the same way we do, which they probably don't."

"Hm." He lay there, turning it over in his mind. That was something else about Walter; if he ran up against something he couldn't understand, he didn't, like most Hawaiians—hell, like most *people*—just shelve it and forget about it, he'd worry at it till it made some kind of sense. "Crazy," he said. "For teach om some funny-kind make-up language, if they get one awready." Then he thought a bit more. "Maybe not so crazy." He laughed. "You teach om for tok, they no can say nothing that you no like hear!"

It struck me then, like a lightning-flash. Why things were as they were, why Science was arranged the way it was. It posed as a search for knowledge, but that was just a facade, a propaganda whitewash to disguise its real ends. It was really a search for control. Of objects, of the environment, of other species.

Ultimately, perhaps, of space, time and death itself. Last and most ruthless resort of a species running scared in a universe too vast and strange for its understanding. Control! Make Mother Nature sit up and beg! Get it before it gets you! That was what lay behind the flummery with the computer and the Wavetek. It was all beginning to make sense now. But it was still too vague and abstract for me to put into any form that Walter would understand.

There are some advantages in education, after all.

But it was Walter's insight that had sparked me. If you taught them to speak, they couldn't tell you anything that you didn't want to hear. Anything that was outside of your understanding, anything that might humble you or force you to a radical reappraisal of the world and your role in it. You could be sure that, like little computers, they would give back only what you put in. Garbage In, Garbage Out, the old programmer's saw . . . And those goddamn signing chimps! How much of their chimpishness could come through? How were they any different from the chimps that performed at Children's Tea Parties in zoos, all dressed up in blazers and flannel bags, pedaling kiddie-cars, spooning up ice cream, grotesque parodies of us? Man alone in a wilderness of mirrors. Who would break the glass?

"What you tryin' tell me," Walter was saying, "you no can unnastand dolphin language 'cause you dunno what they gon' tok *about.*"

"Well. Yeah, well, I guess that's a part of it."

"How you gon' find out that?"

"I wish I knew."

"Spose you go leeve wit' om?"

Communication with pidgin speakers like Walter—let alone with other species!—is not always a hundred percent. Plus you have to remember that this conversation took place shortly after the one with Keala, about slavery, so I read his remark in the context of that. I thought he said, "leave with them," because, trying to answer the question: What was I to do, now? I had come up with what seemed the only logical answer:

Release them! And this would have been a very radical step, involving not only fearsome logistics (anaesthetizing them somehow, rigging a block and tackle, swinging them onto some kind of stretcher or trolley, then hand-hauling them to the beach) but the end of a promising career in dolphin studies. Still, I was ready at least to contemplate it, and now, on Walter's query, I had a sudden, absurd vision of myself, Mele and Lei all swimming off into the sunset together, while an assembled chorus of surfers, snorkelers, scuba-divers, outrigger canoe paddlers and other water sportsmen sang some suitably uplifting anthem. I laughed.

"I not talking joke, ah."

"But I—oh, you mean *live* with them!"

"Ass what I wen' say, no?"

"Well. Uh. You got a point. Why not live with them? You mean in a tank?"

"Neh! Tank is like jailhouse!" He and Keala must have been talking, which surprised me, I don't know why, perhaps because I'd never seen them do anything in my presence except gossip or bicker over trivia—I felt suddenly, illogically jealous that they should have serious conversations I knew nothing about. "Try look," he said, "spose get one savage tribe you like study. What you gon' do, you gon' bring om to Honolulu put om in one cell? Nah, man! You gon' go leeve where they leeve, ah, you gon' study om in their natural surroundings. Right?"

"Right."

"Natural surroundings of da dolphin is da opin ocean."

"Condition Eight," I said.

"Come again?"

"There's this guy Lilly, John Lilly, he's maybe the guy you read that said dolphins could talk . . . Anyway, he listed eight conditions under which you might work with dolphins, and that was the eighth—the open ocean. But even Lilly said you could never really work there."

"When he say that?"

I saw at once how his mind was working. I tell you, this guy was sharp—in some ways.

"Oh, around—1964, I guess."

"So what, no more progress?"

Before I could answer him, Keala came in from the beach, stooping under the keawe branches and squealing in mock alarm as one of the thorns caught her. He turned to her with what looked like relief—he would never take these head-trips if there was anything else to do—and said, "Eh, where you was? I tot you was wit' Woody an' Mousie. Eh, you t'ink they gone an' . . ." He finished the remark with an obscene gesture, Keala laughed and pretended to slap him, and straight away they were off into their regular sibling routine. I did not join them. I had other things on my mind.

The Open Ocean. Condition Eight.

Could it be possible after all?

THE MAN TO TALK TO about Possibility was Les.

Les was big and hairy. Unlike Frank's—Frank came equipped with ponytail—Les's hair escaped in all directions. Like the hair of anarchists in nineteenth-century cartoons, the kind that wear cloaks and carry little round bombs that smoke. His clothes matched. I mean they matched his hair, for they surely never matched one another. He wore tanktops that people had left on the beach and salt-bleached cutoffs that looked like they'd withstood heavy shotgun fire. He wore his Long's Drugstore zoris till they fell apart on his feet, then instead of throwing them in the trash can he mended them with paper-clips and Scotch tape. They were more comfortable than new ones, he said. In a rare moment of humanity, Barry had stopped one morning, looked at him, and said, "Stanley, you know, you look a fucking mess." Les just grinned, he was a slow-moving, laid-back kind of guy, and he was pleased Barry had shown so much awareness of his environment, even if he still called Les by the name of his previous lab assistant. (That was close, for Barry.)

To know Les, you needed to look at his hands, not his

clothes. He had big hands, big fingers, they looked clumsy until he started to do things with them, like tease out the snags in a balled-up fishing line, then you saw that for all their size they were as precise as micrometers. He had patience, too. He practiced scrimshaw, an old whaler's art they were trying to revive around then, making intricate carvings in the ivory of whales' teeth. He could make you earrings out of a brace of Pepsi pop-tops. It was uncanny, the skill and delicacy of it, when you thought what a slob he was in other ways.

He was making himself a transistor radio out of the bits of two junk ones, heating up solder on the kitchen hotplate— when he wasn't surfing or working, he was always tinkering at something—the Monday evening after the beach picnic. Reluctantly he stopped what he was doing and put water on for coffee while I told him about my conversation with Walter and the lines it had started me thinking along. All the while he kept picking at his hair in a way that made you think he must have ukus in it, but that just meant he was absorbed. When I'd finished, he grunted, turned his broad back and made two cups of coffee. When he'd made them, he still didn't say anything. Like I said, he was slow-moving. He blew on the coffee through his hair till it was cool enough for him.

"What you've got," he said, "is a lot of problems. And when you've got a lot of problems, what do you do?"

"Give up?"

"You take them one at a time. What's your biggest problem?"

"That I'm not a fucking dolphin, whaddaya think?"

He frowned. Slow-movers hate impatience.

"All right. You're not a dolphin. What does that mean? What can they do that you can't do?"

I didn't answer. I could think of too many things they could do and I couldn't.

"You can swim, they can swim. You breathe air, so do they. They eat raw fish, well you can eat raw—"

"I can't swim for as long as they can, or as fast as them, or—"

He raised his hand. "One thing at a time! How long would you have to swim for?"

I thought about it. How long does it take to study a savage tribe? Multiply that by ten. "Years, maybe—"

"Ah, come on! Just to learn the basics."

"Well—months, probably."

"All at once?"

"You mean break it up into short spells? Yeah, I see what you mean. Yeah, you could do that. The spells couldn't be too short, though. An hour or two at a time, you'd never cover all their activities that way. Have to be through the diurnal cycle, several times, probably."

"Three or four times."

"At a pinch, yes."

Les smiled beatifically. "Now we're getting somewhere. You've just got to maintain in the ocean for three or four days at a time. How long can you swim for, now?"

"I don't know. I never tried."

"What's the most anyone can? Those guys in Lake Michigan, what was that, sixty hours? And that chick, what's-her-name, who swam to Cuba? Three to four days would be possible, then, right?"

"I'd say at about the limit of possibility. And don't forget all those geeks had little boats trailing them, bottles of orange juice and hot chicken soup—"

"But it's *possible!*"

"I suppose."

"Well, stick to that. We'll worry about details later. Now, speed. How fast can you swim?"

"I never timed myself."

"The best time for the English Channel is what?—around nine hours something, uh? And the Channel is twenty-two miles, direct, but you wouldn't go direct, what with the tide and current be more like twenty-five. Say, going on for two-and-a-half knots."

"They probably had a tail wind."

"Alright, two."

"For *four days?*"

"Ah, come on, Andy, you're the greatest, aren't you? If anyone can do it, you can do it, you know that."

I thought about swimming two nautical miles every hour for ninety-six hours. My mind blanked.

"It would still be nowhere near fast enough. Stenos can do twenty knots." Neither of us had mentioned it, we'd just tacitly assumed, since they were the smartest and the best species, that stenos would be the ones I worked with.

"They can do twenty knots, flat out," Les said, "when they want to or when they have to. Like you could do the same speed in a hundred-yard dash. They can't do that all the time any more than you can, why should they? They cruise at around four, five, usually."

"But they could get away from me any time they wanted."

"You couldn't study *any* creature if it didn't want you to?"

He was right, of course. In zoos, in tanks, in cages, maybe, but in their natural surroundings, never.

"You'll just have to make them love you," he said.

"There's still a gap of two knots or up."

"Right. That's just a technical problem. We'll come back to that. What other problems?"

"Food. Water."

"Sea's full of fish. And there's plenty liquid in their lymph glands."

"I suppose I catch them with my bare hands."

"Teach the stenos to fish for you."

He must have read my eye, for he said suddenly, "Hey! You're really serious about this, aren't you?"

I hadn't known I was; not until that moment. Till then I'd assumed it was an abstract curiosity: given x and y, could you z? But no sooner had he spoken than I knew he was right. It was a lot more than a game. If the thing proved halfway possible, I was ready to go through with it.

He turned this knowledge over for a while. "Okay, food. No problem. Concentrates, vitamins, you could carry four days' supply and not notice it."

"You can't take water in pills."

"Dehydrated water! Right. What's your minimum intake?"

"Two liters a day?"

"On land, maybe. In water you wouldn't lose that much."

I pointed out that you could get pretty dehydrated, just swimming. Yes, he said, but you were on the surface, where the sun's rays hit you. Stenos seldom swam on the surface—usually, a foot or two under it. But I would need some water, more than I could carry. I'd need some kind of distillation device. Perhaps a scaled-down electrodialysis plant, where the negative and positive poles would pull charged ions of H_2O through a membrane impervious to salts.

"All right. At the end of the four days, what do I do?"

"Come home, of . . . Oh-oh. You're somewhere way out in the ocean. Well, I still don't see what would be wrong with having a small boat tail you . . ."

I tried to explain to Les, as best I could, the whole rationale of participant observation. Of the Paradox of the Observer. Of how, if you're not careful, everything you need to find out is dissolved by the very means you use to search for it. If anyone wanted to learn about stenos the way I wanted to learn about them, he would have to become as much like them as he could, given the immutable conditions of the human form. To have a bunch of guys babysitting you, passing hot coffee and words of good cheer every few hours, would just reduce the whole thing to a farce; it would still be the great goggle eye of Sapiens, peering at those funny objects under the lens, a bit more uncomfortably perhaps (and therefore all the more virtuous-feeling) but fundamentally no different from what I wanted to avoid, what went on at the Station.

Les got the point. "Then you'll have to find some dolphins that hang out near the land."

"Stenos are pelagic."

"Tough shit. Try another species."

But this I was unwilling to do, and although this unwillingness was really a matter of sentiment, I found reasons to back it. "If I work from the land, they'll know I'm human, they'll have routines for handling me. The ideal would be if I could disguise myself as one of them. That's impossible, I know. But at least if I appear out of the blue—"

"Literally."

"Yeah, literally! They might not be quite sure what I was, they might accept me more easily."

Les looked sceptical. "You'd need a hell of a backup system for that. Like maybe a submarine or something. I think that's out. Look, why don't we go back to the swimming part." He liked a concrete problem, something he could use his hands on. He took a stub of pencil from behind his ear and began to doodle on the back of a set of old computer printouts, drawing chains of tiny dolphins leaping out of the sea. "It isn't that they're all that much more powerful than us. They only develop about two horsepower. So how come they go so much quicker? Three things. Shape. Skin resistance. Caudal thrust. Take them—"

"One at a time," I finished off in chorus with him. He ignored me. "Shape. There's not much we can do about that. Streamline you a little, maybe. Skin resistance is the kicker."

"I don't get it."

"Ever swim lengths in a small pool?"

"Not when I had anything better to do."

"Which length is the fastest?"

"The first, of course."

"Why?"

"You ain't tired yet."

"Bullshit. Think."

"Okay. Because it's calm, there's no waves."

"Where do the waves come from?"

"You make them yourself."

"Do Lei or Mele make them?"

"No. Shit, you know I never thought of that."

His smile, what you could see of it, loomed through his beard. "You go into a pool, you make waves, the waves bounce back at you from the side of the pool, you bull through them and make more waves, all the time they're dragging your pace down. Lei, in her tank, she don't make so much as a ripple. Why? It isn't just shape. Streamline a boat or a submersible as much as you like, you'll still get turbulence. Dolphins don't make any turbulence because their skin yields to the water pressure. There's a fatty layer under the skin that just gives, like a soft rubber. Should be possible to replicate that, nowadays, with so many synthetics about. Can't think why nobody has. It'll help with insulation, too. Cut heat loss close to zero. Whaddaya think?"

"Sounds fantastic."

"I'll check into it. There may be something on the market. Now. Caudal thrust."

"I don't have a tail."

"You sure? Well, we'll have to give you one. If you could get everything pushing from the rear, like they have . . . Your arms are just a nuisance, really, no way they're not going to make turbulence, thrashing around ahead of you." He began to draw, a weird, mermaidlike figure. "Suppose you had your legs in a kind of a sheath—"

"Sexy!"

"Shut *up!* How we have to swim now, they go counter to one another, and *that* makes more turbulence. You know, when you think of how we swim from a hydrodynamics viewpoint, it's crazy! Everything going in opposite directions. Now just imagine your legs are fused together, with big flukes attached to your feet—they'd pivot from the knees, up down, up down—"

"Just like a dolphin's tail."

"You got it."

"Tricky to learn, though."

"Practice. You can do anything with practice. Arms I don't know. A crawl would fuck everything. Maybe a dogpaddle . . . Listen, how about this, you keep your elbows up to your chest, forearms only, wrists bent facing forward, maybe webs on your fingers or even some kind of paddle attachment, that way you'd cut resistance and still get some extra thrust."

"Christ, it'd be like learning to swim again from scratch."

"Not quite. Anyway, you said you were serious, you're not going to crack at the first bit of difficulty, surely?"

Surely not. But we hadn't even considered the first and biggest difficulty we would have to meet; one that had nothing to do with the ocean at all.

I'VE MENTIONED ENOUGH about Barry Levitt to give you some inkling of what he stood for, but since his nature is crucial to the whole way this thing came out, perhaps I had better do him at full length. First of all, imagine the head of a rather large and angry lizard. Then try gradually to make it human, like in those drawing strips where one thing gradually shifts into another. Keep the wedge shape of the top of the head but add to it another wedge of short, black, slightly graying, tightly curled hair. Defork the tongue, but only literally. Keep the long immobilities punctuated by the sudden flurries of quick, darting movement. Remove the scales. There, you haven't had to change it all that much, have you?

Barry was good at his job in the way these things are measured. He ran a tight ship. His experimental designs were meticulous, virtually ruling out even the possibility of human error or faulty interpretation. His innumerable journal articles were dense forests of facts and figures, unrelieved by the least glimmer of wit or speculation; the brief paragraph titled "Discussion" that closed them made no claim which was not overwhelmingly supported by the data. He received large grants from federal agencies. He had been a full professor with tenure for a number of years and could have had deanships and chancellorships for the asking, had his tastes lain that way. They did not. His academic self was like the carapace of a turtle. Inside it lived another creature, myopic, permanently insecure, probably aged around seventeen. Like a turtle's—if I may vary my reptilian metaphors—the head of this creature would protrude from its shell, periodically, unpredictably, peer nervously about it for a while, maybe bite someone, then withdraw. I would have preferred it if the armor had been impermeable the whole time; you would have known where you were, then.

If it was possible to convince Barry that what I had in mind was scientifically respectable, then we would have no trouble getting the time and money that we needed. If he was not convinced, we were in Shit City without the train fare, because not only would he not support us, he would make sure that the bad word about us went out to all the dolphin-studying industry, and we would not be able to get support from anywhere else. It therefore behooved me to approach him with oblique care.

It was Barry's custom to hold with his staff what he actually referred to as "bull sessions." These would occur at irregular intervals, whenever some idiosyncratic clock in Barry's head told him it was time to update a rather puzzling category called "Human Relations with Staff," and were about as socially cheering as an invite from Rasputin the Mad Monk to come up to his place for a few vodka-and-cyanides. "Let's kick the ball around, fellas," he would say. This usually had the effect of causing a profound silence. Les would explore ears and nostrils in the hope of finding something to relieve the boredom. Sometimes Frank would come up with an opening like, "I've been thinking lately about Hawaiians," and then we'd hear a lot about ecology and Jesus. Barry's immobility would approach catatonia, and even Frank would eventually dry up, stopped by the total lack of positive feedback. Once I started to give Barry a rundown on how much of Waikiki was controlled by the Syndicate, but he asked so many naïve questions that I had to cut it off. Anything that wasn't work-related either bored or mystified him, so we usually stuck to that.

This time, we were talking about a phenomenon we'd noticed in this and a number of previous experiments with the stenos. It was a puzzling phenomenon because it seemed to violate the current scientific gospel. If you operant-condition any animal—that is, use a system of rewards to get it to reproduce a particular behavior, pecking or bar-pressing, say, on demand—your success-rate (the frequency with which the animal does what you want it to do) will rise in a gradual and steady curve to a peak where it will remain constant, as long as you do not try to extinguish the behavior either passively, by avoiding the stimulus that triggers it, or actively, by conditioning some competing form of behavior. Same even with more complex behaviors, like rats running a maze or our stenos matching different kinds of sound. The rat that has reached a certain level of success in maze-running should not fall therefrom; the stenos, once able to match sounds at ninety-five percent accuracy, should not drop back to near the level of chance. This is because, whether the behavior is simple or complex, Learning has taken place, and Learning is not optionally reversible, being engraved on the cerebral cortex in some way still beyond our wit to specify.

Trouble was, after a certain time, the stenos did drop back to the level of chance, and even below the level of chance. Luckily they did not normally do this until we had amassed sufficient data to prove that they *could* attain ninety-five percent accuracy on whatever task we'd set them, so this inconvenient fact never found its way into Barry's research reports. Still, it was annoying to have anything unexplained, and we were encouraged to toss such things around in our "bull sessions" in the faint hope that one of us might come up with a solution Barry could then use, without source acknowledgement, in one of his papers.

"Perhaps they get bored," Frank said brightly.

Barry's gaze flickered from me to Les and back again and his eyes gave an upward roll of despair before falling back into their saurian stillness. By which he meant, "Oh God, haven't I yet succeeded in drumming into your thick skulls that the greatest danger in this business is thinking about dolphins as if they were human beings?"

Frank was impervious to eye language. "At first they get hot, they like the problem-solving part of it—but then when they've solved the problem, you expect them to do it all over again. They can't see any purpose in it."

Barry's eyebrows rose. "Purpose, Andy?"

"Frank. He's Andy, I'm Frank."

"Frank," Barry said grudgingly. "Purpose?"

"Porpoise?" Les wondered. Barry ignored him.

"How long have *you* been doing tests, Frank?"

Frank blushed, which, fresh of skin, he did all too easily. "Well . . . since kindergarten, I guess."

"From kindergarten to Ph.D. Qualifying your life has been nothing but tests, and did you ever get bored with them?"

"Well, I guess, sometimes . . ."

"So bored you deliberately gave wrong answers?"

Frank blushed more and shook his head.

"And did you have any immediate reinforcement for getting them right?"

"My folks bought me a motorcycle when I graduated."

Barry paused a moment for the fatuity of this to sink in. "Well, the dolphins get immediate reinforcement, every time. Food. If they don't get it right, they don't get to eat. And you talk to me of 'purpose.' "

And Barry sat back with the air of one who has made an unassailable point. For once, I thought Frank was right, but I had enough savvy not to say so. Instead, I said, "Maybe it's not so much of a problem now, but I can see where it might get to be one in the next phase."

Barry's eyes hooded and he sucked in his cheeks; you've seen that tremor in a lizard's cheeks when all the rest of it's still. I don't know what that means for lizards, but for Barry it meant that he was interested but didn't want to let on that he was interested.

"It's no problem now because every experiment is different and separate—there's no build-up from one to the next. When you try to teach them a language it'll be quite different. Language is cumulative. You can't go on to the next bit unless you keep hold of the bit you just learned."

"We'll cross that bridge when we come to it," Barry said, but I could see from the continued twitching of his cheeks that he was worried by the possibility, however remote.

"Dolphins aren't chimps," I said pompously.

"True, but not transparently relevant."

"It's a much bigger bridge."

His eyebrows arched.

"He means," Les said, "that in all of that Premack and Gardner stuff, they were unconsciously relying on a lot they already knew about how chimps behave. Partly from observation and partly just from being a similar kind of species ourselves. Stuff about how and when it's okay to communicate and about what kind of thing. That's probably why they were so successful so quickly."

"Les is right," I said. "We can't just assume that there's a single scale of intelligence for all creatures. For land mammals, maybe, and then the chimp can learn because he's next in line to us. Sea creatures have so much that's different in their environment, their brains may have developed differently, so they're not on our scale, they're way off to the side somewhere."

"And this learning phenomenon could be some kind of by-product of that difference," Les added.

"This is pure speculation," Barry said. Speculation, the dirtiest word in his vocabulary.

"The learning effect isn't."

"And a lot will depend on getting everything right first time."

That gave Barry pause. He was in the process of drawing up a proposal for the language project; it was a big one, covering several years, costing several hundreds of thousands of dollars. If he made it, there would be big kudos, prestigious lecture tours, showers of dollars, media exposure (which he would both love and hate), the hushed respect and expeditious handling which anyone who is currently top of his tree receives (and he would love that). If he blew it, there would be awkward pauses, pitying looks, a progressive drying up of travel and research funds, a narrowing and hardening of all the arteries of his life.

"We know next to nothing about stenos in their natural state," I said.

"True. How do you propose to remedy the deficiency?"

"Les and I have been giving it some thought."

He looked sceptical. I knew it would be fatal to launch our project there and then; he would take each point as I made it and demolish the thing piecemeal. "Let me write it up as a paper," I said, "in the next few days. It's still pretty rough in parts. You'll probably spot lots of ways of improving it."

"All right," he said. "As long as you don't spend too much time on it. We can't afford any sideshows."

"Of course not. This'll be on our own time."

"Okay, then." He yawned, sign that serious business was over and serious play could begin. "Who wants to play the Moon Landing Game?"

He had this two-fifty-buck calculator he was always buying games for, printed programs you stuck into the back of it. In this one you were supposed to be in a lunar module on approach. Velocity and altitude flashed in red on the display panel. The gravity factor was five feet per second. You had six hundred kilos of fuel to burn. You could change altitude and velocity by punching out different volumes of fuel. The rules were the inexorable ones of space time and energy. Your opponent the machine was free from human error but, lacking human volition and craftiness, could not pull any tricks on you. Your aim was to arrive on the moon's surface with zero velocity, thus avoiding a symbolic splattering over the lunar landscape. The game fitted him like a glove. Reluctantly he let Les have a go, and I wandered out into the open, stripped to my trunks, and went into the tank with Lei.

It was nice to be with Lei after an overdose of Barry. But not as nice as it had been before Keala's revelation. Ever since that date, I'd been ill at ease with the dolphins. How did they really feel about me? Did they really see me as a jail screw, easier than some, no doubt, but never to be really trusted? When they nuzzled their silky skins against me, were they just tomming? The literature was full of reports, some gushing, others gruffly shy and embarrassed by any departure from "strict scientific accuracy," all of which attested to the love that dolphins bore for members of our species. For members of a

species that tore them from family and friends, that imprisoned them for life where there had been no vestige of a crime,
that deprived them of liberty, society, sex, that subjected them
to crazy experiments and made them perform grotesque
tricks? If they really felt love after all that then they must be
very low on the scale of intelligence; the lowliest rat will snarl
out his hatred and defiance of his captor. The only possible
conclusion was that they were intelligent enough to realize the
inevitability of their servitude, the impossibility of escape, and
to figure, as no rat or wolf could, that when you are wholly
within another's power, you can only gain some measure of
control over that other by pretending to love him.

So that all the time I rubbed Lei's smooth skin, whistled and
chirped at her, pushed away the beak that she persistently
thrust into my groin (and how, precisely, had she figured out
that that was where my penis was, if she'd never seen a man
naked, if she'd never seen humans making love?), I was distracted by thoughts of what she was really thinking. It was well
for the slave-owners that they never learned how they were
lampooned and ridiculed the moment their backs were turned;
the cruel accuracy of wit would have made them writhe in
shame. Was Lei, even now, satirizing each clownish move I
made, singing in triumph of the ease with which she'd de-
ceived me, and passing it all on for Mele's amusement, under
my very nose, in the clucks and whistles which she broadcast
to the other tank?

If I didn't learn their language I'd never know.

OF COURSE I SAID NOTHING about language in the paper I wrote
for Barry. The mere hint that I believed they might have something comparable with human communication would have
convicted me of scientific heresy—a heresy punishable by ex-
communication from all scholarships, grants or other sources
of academic income. I did, however, say a good deal about
"communication"—there could be no doubt that they had
some information exchange, albeit on an infrahuman level—
and about the fact, equally indisputable, that that communica-

tion was not a matter of isolated acts, but formed an integral part of their natural social behavior. That behavior, and the role communication played in it, was all I committed myself to studying. Thus, I argued, my aims were complementary to those of the upcoming language project: if both were funded, data from the one would feed into the other. Moreover, since all the work on the second project would be done by me, Barry's percentage effort as nominal P.I. would be minimal. Two for the price of one.

Then I hit a block. If I was really going to operate in mid-Pacific, the logistics were horrendous. I went back to the idea of a shore-based operation. After all, stenos, or some of them, did from time to time appear within sight of land. But they don't remain there for long, and sooner or later—almost certainly sooner—I was going to have to choose between breaking off and heading for home, or finding myself eighty or a hundred miles out with no food or water left. So I might just as well make it mid-ocean from the start and at least know where I stood, or rather floated (I was becoming aware for the first time of how much of our vocabulary is irrevocably bound to terrestrial living). But that meant, first, having a ship that was more or less permanently located in my general area, and second, a helicopter that would carry me to where the stenos were and then, after the three or four days that seemed at this stage the maximum possible observation periods, come back, pluck me out and carry me back to base. If that kind of backup had to be provided from scratch, the cost would run into millions. And nobody was going to provide millions to finance the harebrained schemes of a couple of grad students.

What we needed was to piggyback on somebody. Some organization that already had the equipment necessary and that was already using it, for other purposes, in the areas where I wanted to work. And, try as I would, there was only one organization I could think of that fitted the bill.

I knew what Les's reaction would be when I put it to him. I knew because, to a certain extent, it was my own. Just utter the words "military-supported research" in front of most college-educated people of my generation and they'll go off like steam whistles. Especially if they're into dolphins. Nobody in the business is likely to forget that in Vietnam dolphins were somehow conned or pressured into ramming Cong frogmen with CO_2 cartridges, causing their stomachs to exit via their mouths and their intestines via their assholes; which is the grosser, the mode of death itself or the fact that a friendly species was suborned into dealing it, I've never quite been able to decide. On the other hand, I've always had my own thinking, and always get suspicious of knee-jerk reactions. Anything that's hated by millions can't be all bad. And even if it were, you could always sup with the devil provided your spoon was long enough.

The U.S. Navy had a largish fleet of survey vessels, which would remain within the same area of ocean for relatively long periods. The larger among these vessels routinely carried helicopters. It was likely that there would be at least one of them in a suitable position for my work. Given their cooperation, the project could be carried out for little more than the price of the gas.

I laid all these arguments before Les.

His first reaction was what I'd expected: that I must be insane to even think of it. I got him calmed down a little, and went over the points very carefully. It wasn't really a question of pros and cons, I explained to him; there weren't, except on some rather abstract ethical level, any cons. And if we didn't get Navy support, we might just as well forget the whole thing.

"Then forget it," was Les's instant answer.

"Look," I said, "do you think there is any chance at all, even one in a thousand, if we could set it up the way we talked about it that I could find out how to communicate with them?"

His pale blue eyes blinked at me. He had thought mostly of the project as a technical exercise; its objective was something else again. "Yes, of course there's a chance," he said. "Probably a better one than that."

"To communicate with another species. For the first time ever. You don't think that makes it worth while?"

Les groaned. "You know what this is, don't you? It's the old debate about ends and means again. But you can't divorce one from the other, that's where the whole thing breaks down. The means distort the ends even while you're using them. I mean, Andy, for Christ's sake, you know what those bastards would do if they could learn how to talk to dolphins?"

"You think I'd tell them?"

Les just stared. He was an honest person.

"They're not even going to know that's what I'm doing. Any more than Barry. If we don't tell one we can hardly tell the other, can we?"

"Then why would they support you?"

"First, because it won't cost them much. Second, because even if I never saw a dolphin, just swam about on my own all the time, they'd learn a hell of a lot about human psychology and metabolism just from checking me out when I was through. Third, because in fact I'm bound to find out things that go on in the sea, things they've never had the chance of observing before, and they'll want to know all those things just in case one day one little fact might turn out to be useful to them. No, they'll buy this one as is, if we can only package it right."

Les shook his head. He still didn't like it, but he was a reasonable person, given time. Like, about ten days or so. Ten days in which he kept on tinkering with his designs, coming to me and asking my approval of this feature or that one, for once Les was into something, he was like a bull-mastiff, he kept on worrying at it, it wasn't in his nature to let it go. But every time he came to me I would say something like, "Yeah, sure, that's great, only isn't it a pity it's never going to come off because of your ideological purity." Then for three days he didn't say a word to me about it, and I thought, I've blown it, I turned him off it, the whole thing is through.

I don't know for certain what happened, because neither participant told me. As near as I can figure, at the end of the ten days Les was weakening, but he wasn't going to come over without a struggle. So he talked to Frank about it, hoping that Frank would strengthen his resolve. Apparently the reverse must have happened. Sometimes there's nothing more disconcerting than to hear one's own ideas expressed in a different kind of voice. Frank, of course, was more bitterly opposed to any entanglement with the military than Les was, but he probably came on so dogmatic about it that Les thought, "Christ, do I really sound that bigoted to Andy?" Well, whatever happened, when the three days were up, Les came to me looking a little shamefaced and said, "You know, I've been thinking, maybe I came on too strong about that idea of yours. Why don't you just go ahead, give it a try, see what they say? We're still not committed to anything."

"No," I said, "of course we're not." Of course we were, once the Navy had the project they could put someone else on it if we turned awkward, but it was a face-saver for him.

Frank gave in his notice the next day. He came up to Barry in the middle of the weekly planning session and said he would have to resign from the Station, his conscience wouldn't let him stay on in a place that had military research contracts. Oh, Barry said, eyes widening, he wasn't aware of any such. Frank explained. Barry looked at me almost with respect. It was the first time he'd heard of my intention to involve the Navy, and though I hadn't planned on his learning it this particular way, I wasn't altogether sorry. Although I'm sure we all irritated Barry in our different ways, I'd always felt Frank irritated him the most, and he was now able to contrast Frank's wild-eyed idealism with my level-headed realism. Indeed I realized suddenly that the naval connection would be a plus in getting Barry's approval: he always liked to broaden the base of his financial support, and there was the chance that he could invoke reciprocity to get hold of some of the secret Navy reports on dolphins that were something of a sore point among cetologists. I watched, inwardly gloating, while Barry made an oleaginous speech about regretting Frank's decision but respecting the principles on which it was based. Translated, it meant: "Glad to lose you under any pretext." A new wave of students was coming, short-haired and respectful, and he needed room for them.

I felt ashamed afterward about my gloating. Though I'd

never much liked Frank I hadn't disliked him either, and he'd certainly never done me any harm. I guess what most pissed me off about him was that he couldn't look at reality straight. He'd say things like, "You know, the old Hawaiians really had a deep respect for life," and we'd be standing right where you could see the notch in the Ko'olau Mountains where King Kamehameha I, with the help of European artillery, had driven the entire defending army of Oahu over a thousand-foot precipice. But then when the crunch came Frank had followed his conscience against his own material interest, and I can respect anyone who does that, no matter how much I may disagree with their reasons.

On balance, I guess, the episode upset me. We'd been a moderately contented team for all our griping. Now things had begun to change, and all as a result of my initiative.

It didn't seem a very good omen.

YOU CANNOT BE AS CLOSE to anyone as I was to Keala and still keep from them anything that becomes a part of your life. In fact it may even seem odd that I should have thought of keeping it from her. Don't you naturally confide all your most cherished ambitions to those you love? But some intuition warned me that this one would make trouble between us.

I'd driven her home early on this particular evening. She was then still living in the family house up toward the end of Kalihi Valley; it lay on a long, twisting, broken-backed road, littered with abandoned autos from the fifties and sixties, shaded by shaggy mango trees, loud even in the night hours with the crowing of cocks trained for fighting by old Filipino men in their yards. As it was so near the mountains, it rained there often, and I can remember, if not from that night then from many others, the heavy drips from the leaves on the roof of the Bug, and the rich, overpowering smell of mangoes that had been left to go rotten on the ground. There were lights in the house above. I said, "I wonder if Walter's home."

She turned, her hand already on the door, the lights from the house just penetrated the car enough for me to see she was frowning. "I don't think you should listen too much to what Walter say."

To fully parse that remark would take a fifteen-page paper on the Kealoha family and my relations with it. Very briefly, you must first understand how things are with Hawaiian families. They are very large, and they contain something of everything. The Kealohas currently had two preachers and three inmates of Halawa Jail. That didn't make any difference. Go to one of their family parties and you would see a preacher with his arm round a jailbird, both of them supping from cans of Oly and laughing like jackasses. I defy you to tell one from the other. It didn't matter to them because they were family, it didn't mean they condoned what the other did, but they didn't stop loving him for that, they could split the doer from the deed in a way few *haoles* can. Among *haoles*, you are what you do, no more than that; among them, you are who you are, what you do may be quite incidental. Keala was the good one in her immediate family (the preachers were uncles or cousins) and Walter was the bad one. Yet, no matter how they fought, they loved and respected one another, because the ties of blood were stronger than morality. For me, reared siblingless in a nest that had self-destructed (I still haven't told how that happened), this whole family syndrome was wildly romantic. And because I wanted to belong to it, to accept it and be accepted by it on precisely those terms, Keala's remark seemed to me an attempt at exclusion—an insistence that I, at least, obey the outer-world ethic, cleave to the good, shun the bad, and the hell with people.

"You think he'll lead me into temptation?" I asked her.

"Huh? No, Andy, I not talking about that. Is just he get some crazy ideas sometimes, ah, you don't wanna take notice of them."

"What's Walter been saying to you?"

"Oh, nothing. Some craziness you and he was talking last time we went out Waianae side. About living with dolphins, something like that. I mean Walter, what he know about that?"

"Just a dumb kanaka, huh?"

"You know what I mean!"

"I don't know what you mean. He had some good insights."

"Andy," she said, "don't tease me about this."

We'd had to have a pact about teasing. I love teasing people, especially people I'm fond of. Keala teased and was teased by her family and friends all the time—Hawaiians do this systematically and on principle, it keeps people from getting above themselves—but with me somehow it was different, she could never tell with me whether I was serious or fooling, and this uncertainty made her mad. So we had agreed that I would never tease her about anything serious, such as her desire to become a social worker; but there were problems even with that, since I somehow never learnt what's supposed to be serious and what isn't.

"I'm not teasing," I said.

"I think I rather you were."

"No, but listen, Keala," I said, placing my hands on her forearms, as if to restrain her from flight, "you know who is really responsible for all this, don't you? It's you."

"Me?"

"Sure. There I was, a happy innocent dolphin-tender, then you came and burst my bubble for me. Made me see it like it really was. Things have never been the same again."

"But you never even mention it again!"

"That doesn't mean it wasn't fermenting beneath the surface."

"I warn you, Andy."

"Warn me about what?"

"Teasing."

"Shit, that's just the way I talk! Keala, listen, I was grateful for you telling me that, it hurt, at the time, I felt awful about it, but it was the truth, and the truth can't hurt the righteous, can it? So what then? I can't do one thing and believe another, most people seem to but not me. So I have to do something that will change the ballgame. Like learning how really to communicate with them, not like in Barry's half-assed thing, but as an equal. If that's possible. I don't know if it's possible.

Barry may be right. They may be no smarter than smart chimps. All that squawking they do to one another may mean just 'Ouch! Wow! Help! Golly jeepers!' I don't think so. I have a hunch there's far more than that only we're too different and too smug to see it. But it's got to be proved, and I don't think anyone else can prove it. I don't really mean they couldn't, if they thought they should, it's just their heads aren't in the particular space mine is at."

Her response to this long speech somewhat amazed me. Without answering, she flung her arms about me and embraced me violently yet in a way that was far from sexual—that was almost like a mother embracing a child. I put my hands on her body and was surprised to feel it trembling.

"What is it?" I asked her.

"I don't know," she answered in a scared voice.

"You don't want me to do it."

"I feel something bad gon' happen."

"It isn't as risky as you might think. We're going to have everything worked out before I leave. If I leave. We have to get funded first. And there'll be months of preparation even then."

"It's not that. Not like you would get eaten by one shark or something. And not like I trying stop you from doing whatever you got to do, you know I never do that, ah, ever! Oh, Andy, I tell you I just don't know what it is!"

She was in a strange state. I had sense enough not to reassure her further, just hold her till the trembling stopped, stroke her hair and shoulders, while rain dripped on the roof and cocks crowed on the windy hillside. Child of reason though I was, some of her alarm leaked through to me. Because it was so clearly out of her control, it moved me more than any rational argument could have done. Many Hawaiians claimed second sight, I knew, and if I didn't believe in that, I didn't disbelieve in it either. But in a place from which reason could not have moved me, I was not about to surrender to the irrational. I was fully committed now. I'll tell you how I knew. I knew because, while I was holding her, I had asked myself:

suppose she refuses to see you again unless you abandon this, will you abandon it? The answer was, no. There was nothing in earth or heaven for which I'd abandon it now.

I WON'T WEARY YOU with a detailed account of the months that followed. You don't want to hear it any more than I wanted to live through them. I am not like Les. I think of an electrode. An electrode will sit there quite happily next to another electrode for years and years and if in all that time the nuptial spark never unites them, it doesn't give a damn. Me, I want that zigzag zap of electricity, like in the old Frankenstein movies, bazat!—right away. At the beginning of a journey I wish the end of it, at the end I wish the next beginning. Once I almost seriously suggested to Les that we build a time-destroying machine. It would function thuswise: say you had a hot date at seven and it was only midday and you couldn't maintain. You press the button, *shazam*, it's seven o'clock. Les recommended a course in the Tao and/or Zen. Horseshit. It's just differences in body chemistry.

Barry bit, just as I'd figured. Called me into his office, said I should have done this this way and that the other—his red-ink writing that looked like he was in training for a Lord's-Prayer-on-a-pinhead contest was all over the draft—and added, almost as an afterthought, "Go over it again and I'll see if we can't put it in." I went over it. Three more times. Barry even got into the habit of asking when the next draft would be ready. Meanwhile Les was trying all kinds of combinations of plastic and foam rubber and devising yet more ingenious life-support gadgets. It amazed me that an idle dream could, almost by inertia, acquire such robust life; it seemed to proceed now under its own momentum, and even if I were to drop out, I felt, it would still roll imperviously on. At last the proposal passed Barry's scrutiny, was typed up in the appropriate form and dispatched to the Office of Naval Research.

We got an unusually quick response from them. I think, in part at least, because they had been working on something very similar to Les's suit and suspected there'd been a leak.

One of the naval personnel who visited the Station periodically over the next few months questioned Les and me quite persistently about it; we called him the Skull, because he had a head more like a skull than any living head I ever saw, and was, I guess, Naval Intelligence, though what level of intelligence would suppose that, having had something leaked to us, we would play it right back to them, is something I leave you to guess.

The suit they finally evolved was a hybrid of Les's ideas and their own. It appeared, one fine morning, in the company of a whole cavalcade: a motor launch with mirrored brass and whipping ensign from Pearl Harbor, a couple of P.O.s, the Skull, Redding, a captain who seemed to be our regular liaison man, and a brick-faced old rascal with a voice like an airhorn introduced to us as Admiral Royce. First, the entire personnel of the Station had to take some kind of oath, administered by the Skull in monotone, that we would not divulge to any unauthorized persons any officially classified information on pain of the penalties authorized by Act of Congress No. Umpteen-twiddly-six. The good Admiral then delivered a speech which, while lacking in substantive content, seemed to discharge the symbolic function of welcoming us aboard. He then walked around me several times and made some remarks to the effect that I looked like a fine example of a typical young American (by which I think he meant I wasn't a Minority). Finally, we all boarded the launch and hightailed it for the open ocean, kicking contemptuous spray into the faces of all the yachtsmen and canoers off Ala Moana Park as we blasted by them at better than fifty knots. As we went, one of the P.O.s began unwrapping the suit.

It was a lot thicker than the conventional wet suit, yet, when you picked it up, it felt extraordinarily light. It was, in fact, porous, so that one's skin could breathe—but one would have to grease up before wearing it so as to avoid salt irritation—and made to yield to water pressure in much the way a dolphin's skin did. On the back of it, built into it, was something I at first took for an aqualung, and wondered at, since no such device could hold air for the periods I would be using it. In fact it was a booster engine, powered by electric batteries, that worked similarly to the propulsion systems of squids, pulling in water at the front and squirting it out in a strong jet at the rear. You couldn't use it all the time, the P.O. pointed out, the batteries wouldn't last, but you could get a few knots extra speed out of it in short bursts. The batteries must never be let to run down completely, since they powered two other gizmos —an electrodialysis unit such as Les had envisaged, and a device for shooting CO_2 cartridges into sharks (I flashed on the eviscerated frogmen of Vietnam, but the P.O. assured me, straight-faced, that these were a much smaller model). I could check the state of the batteries by means of an ammeter which, along with watch, compass and depth-gauge, was slotted into a wristband on the left sleeve of the suit. When the ammeter needle touched the red line on the dial—that was if nothing had already gone wrong—I would pull a zipper on my left shoulder, which would release a helium balloon, which would self-inflate and hoist a small radio beacon some fifty feet above the waves. It was amazing. They seemed to have thought of everything.

By the time I'd memorized this we were out beyond Steamer Lane where the big swells are. Here they cut the engine, and the launch began to drift up and down the faces of the swells. I noticed an unhappy look on Barry's face. Redding signed to me that it was time to suit up.

The suit was in one piece and you entered via a zippered opening in back from crotch to ankles, head first, gradually working arms and torso into position. The upper half of you was then completely encased except for a plexiglass bubble over your face, and you breathed through twin snorkels, one on either side of the helmet. When you'd gotten this far you had to go to the side of the boat, since, once the tail was fitted, you couldn't walk. Then it was just a matter of working feet and legs into the tail section, zipping up, and going over the side.

It felt weird at first. My legs were crushed together so tight

I was sure I'd get cramps (actually, I never did), and when I tried to move them they wouldn't obey me, they seemed determined to thrust in opposite directions and, of course, could not. For a few seconds I floundered, helpless. Then training took over. I'd been practicing for several weeks swimming in the manner Les had suggested, and although without the suit it was a pretty ineffective method, I'd managed to get the movements fairly correct. I struck out with my tail. The thrust of it amazed me, even without assistance from hands or motor. I moved like that for a while, just kicking, then brought my hands in. The hands of the suit had long ribs down the backs of each finger and extending several inches beyond the tips; between these, like the ribs of a fan, the suit's material was stretched in tight webs. I stroked with them, bringing them up close to my chest, no further than my chin, then digging them down and pulling them back like the paws of an otter. Now I was really beginning to move. I circled the launch, which was still drifting on the swells, then plowed under the surface and flipped the button that activated the booster motor.

Its effect was, indeed, electrifying; I seemed to be hurtling, at vertiginous speed, beneath the waves. That was subjective, of course—I probably was doing no more than six or seven knots—but everything's relative, and I was moving three times faster than I ever had in water before. I was so exhilarated I forgot to surface before breathing. Salt water poured into my plexiglass bubble. I coughed, gasped, choked. Instinctively I aimed up, and such was my speed that I breeched almost as a dolphin does, my head and shoulders rising clear of the water. I would have to work on that, perfecting the gradual rise-and-fall, "porpoising" movement by which the stenos could make good time below the surface turbulence and still breathe, as they did, on average once a minute. But that would take time. For the present I was anxious merely not to make an ass of myself in front of the grunts on the launch. So I remained on the surface and headed away from them as fast as I could.

Afterward the whole thing became commonplace to me, and

the sea yielded far different wonders, so it's a little hard now to capture the exhilaration I felt, just ploughing along, on that bright day, over and through the wavecrests that blew to spindrift against a stiff twenty-knot trade, blew into dazzling shards of gold and silver as they caught the light of the declining sun. The launch trailed me, engine churning sluggishly, about fifty yards astern and to my right. I could not outpace it, of course, but I could maybe play tricks with it.

I dived. That was scary, under power. You just went down and the water went blacker and blacker. A few fish, small ones, flickered across the blackness and then there was nothing. I wasn't scared about getting the bends because you only get them if you have breathed under pressure—if you breathe on the surface, the only limit on how deep you can go is the length of time the one breath can last you and the build-up of pressure on your eardrums (against which I was protected by my suit). I was a little more scared of rapture of the deep, nitrogen narcosis, because I couldn't remember if that was from breathing under pressure, too, or just happened anyway as your oxygen got used up. And, rapture or no, there was this crazy temptation just to keep on descending for as long as I could. I pulled out at one-fifty, so my depth-gauge said, and even that was almost too much, for a first try; I was choking and my lungs seared with pain when I hit the surface. The launch had passed me. I had another wild impulse, this time to turn and swim as fast as I could in the opposite direction to it, lose them altogether. Childish. I had no reason to run, then, nor anywhere to run to. I compromised, stayed in the same spot, trod water till the launch stopped and drifted again, its occupants peering about worriedly in every direction but the one in which I was.

I dived again, much more shallowly this time, and came up right under them, breathing, turning, raising my tail before they even saw me. I brought the tail down on the surface as hard as I could, drenching them, then dived clean under the launch. When I surfaced on the other side, there they were, solemn as owls in their dripping uniforms, Redding mopping at the Admiral's lapels with a white handkerchief. Only one of the P.O.s had a grin all over his leathery red face, which self-destructed as Redding turned on him. I put on power again and headed away from the launch.

Eventually they called me in, and eventually I could no longer pretend that I didn't hear their calls. I got dirty looks from Redding and the Skull, but their superior officer, once he had dried out, seemed inclined to treat my behavior as no more than the high-spiritedness natural to all red-blooded young Americans. After all, I had performed well, probably better than they'd expected, and after a couple of hours in the water I wasn't even blown or flushed, much less exhausted. I would need weeks of training, of course, to build up the endurance I'd need in the open ocean. But, as we headed for home, I don't think they were displeased with their bargain.

I don't know how Barry felt about it. His face was greenish and at a strange angle, as if only tension on his throat muscles was keeping his lunch down. Everyone tactfully avoided his eye.

IT WAS NEARLY FOUR MONTHS before I was judged combat-ready. By that time I could swim from Honolulu to Hilo, which is over two hundred miles, in under forty-eight hours. I wish I could convey to you the boredom of this feat. In the daytime it's not so bad because there are islands to look at, approaching and receding, boats to avoid by diving or judicious changes of course. In the night there's nothing but an occasional lighthouse that never gets any nearer. I'd recite all the songs and poems I knew and all the dirty jokes and even French irregular verbs and times tables. Or I'd try and reconstruct in detail the plots of the last ten movies I'd seen complete with dialogue. Then I'd look at the luminous dial of my watch to find that only another half hour had gone by.

Perhaps I should emphasize, for whatever significance it might have later, what a revolution in my habits this regime represented. I had reached this stage of life without ever, that I can remember, doing anything that wasn't Fun. If it wasn't Fun I didn't do it, and miraculously, every time, it turned out not to have been necessary to do it. Now, finally, I had found something for which it was worthwhile enduring hardship and monotony. But to pursue it thus meant doing violence to my nature, and I doubt very much if I realized, at the time, how much I was changing, or in what direction.

Anyway, that whole epoch is something of a blur in my memory now. There are only two occasions that stand out at all clearly.

The first was a windy afternoon in Manoa with a fine mist of drizzle blowing down from the Ko'olaus, when I went to visit at my father's house. I say "my father's," because it was my mother's no longer. Shortly after I went to live at the Station, she had discovered Women's Lib, and now saw that, after all these years of sacrificing herself for my father, she had never discovered her True Self. There she was with the menopause coming up and still no Identity! It was touching, even if ridiculous. And my father couldn't understand it. Any more than he could understand Black Power. He was no chauvinist pig, he was Mr. Nice Guy, who came home soberer than many judges and to whom it had never even occurred that he could screw around. "You Must Have Found Someone Else," he kept telling her; he would rather have had a flesh-and-blood rival than be cuckolded by an abstraction. But how the hell could she Find Someone Else, she responded, when she was still looking for Herself? Now she was in California, going to art school in a paint-stained dirndl and frizzy hair, looking, in the photo she sent me, ten years younger, while he, interminably editing the works of others (he had no heart for originality any more), looked, with his seamed face and stooping walk, at least a decade older.

The old wooden house, built by a Chinese near the ethnic cemetery, looked uncared for and about to be swallowed by the vegetation, anyway. The door opened promptly to my ring, and I found myself confronted by a large, flat, young, rather featureless female face, to which a spattering of freckles tried to give some interest.

"Oh," said this apparition, widening a pair of rather bovine eyes and twitching her head to throw back a long rope of mouse-colored hair, "you must be Andy. Richard's in the study, do come in."

I followed her into the familiar room, its window so over-hung by leaves that you had to burn lamps at midday. The grandfather clock, which had remained silent for months after Mom left, was now swinging a fresh-polished pendulum and giving out with its loud monotonous tick. My father, correcting galleys at his desk, turned as I came in, rose, and shook my hand with a vigor that accentuated, rather than reduced, the distance between us. His faded aloha shirt of yesteryear had been replaced by a number from Fly High Brothers, topped by a natty yellow vest; what was left of his hair had been artfully teased and sprayed to conceal as much as possible of his large, domed cranium. If I'd met him on the street, I'm not too sure I'd have known him.

"Andy, this is Rachel Moore, my research assistant. Rachel, this calls for a drink. Vodka tonic for you, right? See, I don't forget." What he meant was, I'm not senile yet. Rachel smirked complaisantly and went off to make the drinks with a switch of her hips that might have looked enticing had she weighed forty pounds less. "Well, how are things?" he asked.

I don't know what I replied. I was so furious I could hardly think, and all the more so because I knew perfectly well how illogical and unfair my reaction was. It wasn't any loyalty to Mom, for sure. In fact I think—or so I rationalized it—that I wouldn't have minded half so much, if at all, if he'd come straight out and said, "Hi, this is Rachel, we're shacking up together." It was that crap about "my research assistant," along with the coy looks they threw at one another when they thought I wasn't looking, that and the fact that it was so stereo-typed, all this May-and-December, prof-and-student shit, and perhaps above all, to add insult to injury, that he hadn't been able to find himself a better-looking one. Or at worst, a more sensitive one, because she seemed totally unaware of my reac-tion to her, and prinked, grimaced and did eyework at me as if she was the greatest sex object since the Venus de Milo.

I had not previously told him about my new project, at first because its fate was still uncertain, later because I feared it would only worry him. Now I told him the whole story. Rachel, nursing her Ripple, thought it was so exciting. He, at first, said nothing. I tried to intuit his reaction. Could it be relief? Finally he said, "It would be absurd to suppose you don't recognize the dangers."

"Of course."

"But there's at least one you may not have considered."

I must have looked pained. I didn't think there was anything I hadn't considered.

"You will be very much dependent on these creatures, for your safety," he said.

That was true. He was no fool. Couldn't have been, to sire me.

"Never forget," he said, "that they're a different species. And that, when you're in a corner, the only people you can rely on are your own kind. I made that mistake once, so I know what I'm talking about." This was the nearest I'd ever heard him come to speaking of his troubles with the Blacks, and I was touched briefly by this moment of—for him—intimacy, then chilled again by the thought that he could see my enterprise only in terms of something that had happened to him.

The silence that followed was filled by the monotonous ticking of the big clock. I wondered how he could stand to have it there measuring out what was left of his life. "You've had the clock mended," I said stupidly.

"Yes," he said, coming out of his own thoughts with a jolt. "I finally had it fixed." And, looking at Rachel's legs, "You can't make time stand still," he added brightly.

I don't have to come back here any more, I thought. Not if I don't want to. Not ever. I really don't have to. There was a deep relief in that thought.

The other scene was from the night before I left. We'd gone out dancing, Keala and I. Ever since the night in Kalihi she'd said nothing of the project; I thought she must have resigned herself to the inevitable, which just shows you how I underestimated her. That night she seemed unnaturally hectic and elated. I would have noticed it more clearly, and been more on my guard, if I hadn't been sharing the same kind of mood myself: scared and apprehensive, yes, a little, just about enough to get high on, as you can sometimes if the feelings aren't too intense.

We went to Spats and the Point After, so it wasn't until after three that we got back to the Station. We knew that in another three or four hours I'd be on my way, but neither of us was prepared to admit to ourselves or to each other that our time together was coming to an end, so we went on, determined to stretch time to its uttermost, making love with a kind of suppressed fury. I was thrusting deep inside her and practically on the point of coming when she arched her neck, turning her head away, and said, "I haven't got it in, you know."

She didn't need to tell me what *it* was. She was allergic to the pill, and always used an IUD. I froze rigid. I was so close, even pulling out I might shoot. I shut my eyes and deliberately thought about the most chilling, antisexual events. A bunch of mokes laying for me in an alley. A speeding bust with baggies in plain view. When these thoughts had sufficiently cooled my ardor, I withdrew from her.

"What you do that for?" she asked.

What did *I* do that for? "What did *you* do that for, are you crazy, do you want to have a kid?"

"Yes," she said.

"Why?"

She avoided my eye. Her hair had fallen across her face, she looked about six. "I no like talk about it," she said.

"Shit," I said, "you better talk about it. Christ, you could at least have told me."

"I did tell you."

"You did not."

"I wen' tell you I no get 'em in, ah?" Her speech always got thicker when she was agitated.

"Jesus, by a hair! If it hadn't been for my iron self-control it wouldn't have made any difference."

"No need I tell you. If I just kep' quiet, no way you gon' ever know."

"Until too late."

"Right!"

I was scared, no fooling. I could practically see the thing in the room, wrinkled, yelling, costing $65,000 to raise to college age, entangling me in all kinds of legal obligations. And yet she wanted it. And I had denied her. The second time. The first was the time I knew that my project meant more to me than she did. Would there be a third? Could it be that you could deny someone like that and still love them? Or was I just fooling myself and her? Was what I felt for her no more than a mixture of lust and affection? But then if love was more than a mixture of lust and affection, just what was it?

"I have to know why," I said. That, were I to have a gravestone, which seems highly unlikely now, should be my epitaph. "You could hardly have picked a worse time, you know. I mean, me going away and all. Besides this is something that involves both of us, not just you, we should have talked about it."

"That's why," she said.

"Why what?"

"You going away."

"You just lost me."

"Why I wanted a baby. In case you no come back, I still get something of you."

I'll swear, my heart turned right over. That thought would never even have occurred to me. But it was said so simply, so matter-of-factly, without any kind of dramatics or self-pity, that my whole soul reached out to her, not just my arms. "Look," I said, "Keala, never say that. It's not so. I'm coming back. No way you're going to get rid of me so easily as that."

"You think I like get rid of you, lolo?"

Most nights I would have said, yes, obviously, and gone on with mock accusation of unfaithful or even homicidal tendencies; tonight I did not.

She sighed. "Guess I was wrong, but."

"How you mean?"

"I no gon' make you, if you no like." And suddenly her head was down under the sheet, I felt the thick curls of her hair brush my groin, the pressure of her lips and tongue. And almost simultaneously I remembered, God knows why, the first time I had ever noticed her: in a vast lecture hall, one of those ghastly core courses supposed to make you into an All-Round Man, World Civilization or Intro. Philosophy or some garbage, and the instructor made a strange snuffling noise at the end of each sentence and in the middle of some of them, like a dog with rabies—I glanced up and behind, unable to believe that a hallful of my fellow-beings could watch this travesty without a trace of reaction (but they could), to see a face disappear behind a pair of hands, then reappear briefly, flushed like a peony, as if incredulous and wishing confirmation, then disappear again while the shoulders beneath it twitched in silent, incorrigible mirth, and I thought, "My God, there's a human person" before I thought, "But she's beautiful!"

I reached under the sheet, wound my fingers into her hair, and gently eased her away from me.

"What's the matter?"

"Nothing. You don't have to do that. I'll come inside you."

"Andy, it's okay. Really, it's okay."

"That's just what I meant."

I mounted her then, but this time it was different; there was no frenzy, I was possessed by an immense calm, the calm of heavens and oceans, I moved with slow and irresistible rhythm to the climax. If it took, it took. Let Nature take its course. I might regret it afterward, but at that moment, at that moment I regretted nothing, nothing at all.

LATER THAT NIGHT, after I had driven her home, or I should say early next morning, for the sky was paling over the rooftops, I came back through downtown; the streets were wet from the night's rain, deserted, even the trannies on Hotel Street had gone home, there was just one red-eyed drunk in a doorway sucking Greystone burgundy from his brown bag, and a few lights of riders who had early jobs; but still as it was, you could feel the new day coming in like a tide, and the immense calm and lassitude I felt gave way gradually to a sense, no longer of anxiety, but of rising excitement—the excitement that I'd always felt at the beginning of a voyage, or even on seeing the sea again after an inland trip, an excitement that had survived from earliest childhood unimpaired by experience and that seemed to share the sea's own qualities, its instability (that first dizzying lurch of a small craft as you cross the harbor bar) and its mutability (from doldrum calm to insane hurricane, cat's-cradling its currents over seven tenths of the globe) with an eagerness for come-what-may like that of little kids still unable to swim, hurling themselves from the end of a breakwater.

TWO

WHEREVER YOU LOOKED, the blue was unbroken. The sky, horizon to horizon, stretched bare of cloud; the sea, furrowed by long, regular swells moving southwest before the trades, was too glassy for whitecaps, and as empty as the sky—shipless, islandless. Only the sun, now falling westward, splintering on the plexiglass roof of the helicopter cabin, relieved the blueness, hurling out its slivers of gold light. The heat of the cabin, the thunder of the rotors and the infinity of blue space had between them just about hypnotized me; I was supposed to be keeping watch, but how could you keep watch, and what could there possibly be to watch for? In all that emptiness?

You can't know how big the Pacific is until you've flown over it. You take off from the Coast and highball into the jetstream a few hours, then there are islands; take off again, in another six or so hours there's more islands, and even at Mach .66 you're not through yet—the ocean goes on. But even that's not

enough. You're zipping too high to tell how fast down a narrow corridor of sky, and there's no scale, no familiar objects
with which you could measure it. It's only when you fly over
it real low, as we had been doing now for most of the day, low
enough to count waves, and realize that the area you've covered is still only a fraction of a fraction of one percent of its
total—then the vastness of it, and the loneliness, starts to eat
into your soul.

"I remember in 'Nam," Sam Beaulais said, "we was looking
for this VC cooch, an' it was kinda like this, in a ways, only
'stead of sea it was jungle. Green instead of blue. That about
the only difference."

"Did you find it?"

"Did we shit. So the ARV that was on board, they figured
this guy, the one they'd tortured to find out where the place
was was shitting them, see? So they flang him out. About this
height, we was, maybe a little lower. We never saw where he
hit. Goddamn trees done swaller 'im up."

"Bastards."

"Maybe. You ask me, they done him a favor, shape he was
in."

And Sam Beaulais shook his head solemnly. He had a lot of
head to shake. In profile, discounting color, it resembled one
of those fierce hatchet-blade heads you see on portraits of old
Indian chiefs. And was not that appropriate, he being descended, or so he had told me within minutes of our meeting
on Johnston Island, from Billy Bowlegs, the Seminole chief?
"Yeah, Bowlegs, the name oughta be by rights, on'y my great
gran'pappy, he musta thought it was kinda ridiculous or
sump'n, so when he was passin' along through Lou'siana or
some such place he pick up this Frenchy way of spelling, like
b-o-w is b-e-a-u in frog language, and 'leg' they pronounce it
'laig' in them parts, so was kinda close, see. Yeah, I'm a Seminole, a fightin' Seminole from Bracketville Texas. We was
never defeated. We leave Florida with our arms intact and go
fight the Meskins under Sam Houston in Texas." He looked
at me keenly. "I bet the way I talk you think I never been to

college, right?" I denied it, naturally. "Well I been to college. Texas A and M. Yeah, I'm an Aggie, all right. But I talk like I talk 'cause that's the way my people talk. What good enough for them, good enough for me."

It may have been true. You could never be sure with Sam whether he was telling the truth or just winging it, not to boast, but just because whatever it was sounded good at the time. Reality was his servant not his master. And somehow, for sure, he'd gotten to be a hot-shot chopper jockey, which is good going for any kind of Minority. But if he was Billy Bowlegs's scion by blood, old Billy must have been shooting out some pretty weird genes way back in the eighteen-thirties, because Sam was as black as the top of a stove, and, when he swung his Injun-brave profile into full face, had all the features to match it. "Sure," he explained, unabashed, when I hinted at this, "don't they teach you no history nowadays? There's pure African back there as well. All mix in with the Seminole. On account of some they fled slavery up there in Georgia, come down into the swamp country an' was like adopted into the tribe. That ain't uncommon in our people. No sir." Yet five minutes afterward, when I'd said something about "blacks" in a way which might have implied I considered him one of them, he said with great contempt, "Niggers! Lazy sonsa bitches. All welfare and pimpin'. Sons of slaves, and slaves is just how they ac'. Me, I'm a Seminole, a fightin' Seminole from Bracketville Texas, an' I swear to you the sun don't go down that I don't thank the good Lord that was how I was born!"

Right now we were low on gas, Sam said, and if nothing showed within another fifteen minutes we'd have to turn and head back to the *Farquarson*. The *Farquarson* was my base, a U.S. Navy survey vessel of the *Chauvenet* class, which was engaged in sonar-mapping and taking sediment cores from the Pacific bottom in an area roughly bounded by the International Date Line, the Tropic of Cancer, the 170th parallel of longitude and the 10th parallel of latitude. What the precise significance of this area was—whether it was particularly rich in mineral nodules, whether it straddled the route for an undersea invasion of America, whether it contained a second sunk nuclear sub like the one Howard Hughes fished for, or whether it was just an area nobody had gotten around to mapping yet—I never discovered, and no one I spoke to on the *Farquarson* seemed even curious about it, it was a job of work, that was all. But it was a good area for my purposes; not only was it one of the few areas in the tropical Pacific completely bare of islands, it was at almost any point (if you exclude a few atolls like Johnston Island) a thousand or more miles from inhabited land. The game plan was simple. The *Farquarson* had just begun the survey from the southern end; I would locate a steno pod somewhere to the north of it, that (hopefully) was territorial—nobody knew as yet how far a pod might range—and get adopted by it, and I should then (in theory!) never get so far from base that I would lose radio contact, indeed I should get nearer, as the *Farquarson* zigzagged slowly northward, and then further again, as it passed me and receded toward the tropics' rim, but that time was still several months away.

Sounds easy, when you put it like that.

Trouble was, I'd had one try at getting adopted already, and had failed. Abysmally. And I didn't, as yet, know why. Sam had dropped me with a pod about a hundred and fifty miles northeast of the *Farquarson* and left me there, as planned. The pod sniffed around me for about a half hour and then, as if on a prearranged signal, had turned tail and fled. Nothing I could do but put out my beacon and await pickup. It was deeply distressing. I wasn't used to not getting what I wanted. But worse even than the rebuff was the thought that it might be repeated, not just by one, but by every group of dolphins in the entire area. The whole project might simply prove impossible, either through some unknown deficiency on my part or through its very nature. And, quite apart from any loss to science, that would be a disastrous outcome to me personally, since I'd invested not just months of my time but all of my emotions in the project. To live with another species under conditions believed impossible for humans, to break the barri-

ers of communication between that species and my own—
these were ambitions that, once conceived, became impossible
to discard (not enough to be merely the best . . . but to do
things that had never been done before) or, if I were forced
to discard them, would leave a vacuum in my life that nothing
could fill.

I strained my eyes into the sun. We were heading almost due
westward, and the sun had already begun to decline, when we
turned to refuel it would be too late to make another run and
that would mean another fruitless day. I was willing for something to appear, so much so that when I saw a disturbance in
the water, at around two o'clock and way up toward the horizon, my first thought was, "No, you're imagining things."
That's all too easy when you've been watching long and hard
and nothing's showed; it's not hallucination exactly, the
human mind seeks always for patterns in things and just takes
scattered bits of random happenings and pulls them together
to make a vision. So a whitecap or two and a seabird hitting
the water and a couple of flying fish leaping would compose
themselves into a whole steno pod ploughing through the
ocean. Trying to keep any excitement out of my voice, I said,
"Could you take her about fifty degrees north of west, Sam?"

"Think you got something?"

"I don't know." I was trying to steer a heavy pair of field
glasses toward the exact spot. Not easy. Some breeze had risen
and the surface of the water was disturbed. Then a wave parted
and there was a high sail-like dorsal fin, and another; they
came arching up out of the wave as their owners breathed and
then vanished as they went down again. My heart lurched in
time with their movement. There was no mistaking them,
those strong barrel bodies with their pinkish blotches, those
high, bulging foreheads and the angle of their beaks. Stenos
all right.

"How you know they ain't the same bunch as last time?"
Sam asked.

It was a good question, and it stopped me cold because he
could well be right—they were a long way from the first sight-

ing but not too far for them to have moved in the intervening time. Then I thought, numbers. It's not easy to count from a distance, with them constantly diving and surfacing in no clear pattern, but there seemed to be no more than fourteen or fifteen of them. In the first pod there had been more than twenty.

"No," I said. "This one's smaller."

"You want down?" Sam asked.

"Sure thing."

Sam put the chopper on an intercept course. That was because it would be asking for trouble to put me down slap in the middle of them from some rattling machine. "Check your gear, son," he said with the change of tone which indicated that if he didn't necessarily respect me (and I doubt he respected anyone bar God or another fightin' Seminole), he at least respected the peculiar kind of insanity that would make me do what I was about to do now. Obediently, I checked that things like vitamin tablets and knife that weren't physically attached to the suit were all in their appropriate pouches, and that the suit itself wasn't entangled in anything else. Then I took the weighted end of the rope ladder that lay curled on the floor of the cabin and slung it out through the door. The rest of the ladder rattled after it and then snapped taut against the bolts that held it to the floor. By this time we were about a mile and a half ahead of the pod and dead in the path it would follow, provided, of course, that it did not change direction. The sound of the engine changed; we were hovering, slowly descending. I peered out the door, overcoming the slight giddiness that this always gave me, and saw the end of the ladder swallowed by a swell.

"You all set?"

I nodded.

"Then good luck, son, you gonna need it." We shook hands, awkwardly and solemnly, then I thrust head and shoulders into the suit, gathered up the rest of it in my left arm—for it would be impossible to descend the ladder with my feet inside the tail —and swung my legs over the side.

The machine had its nose into a twenty-knot wind and the ladder was blown out at an angle behind it. Between the buffeting of the wind and the downdraft from the rotors, it lurched and bounced crazily, and with only one hand free to grasp it, it was as much as I could do to hang on. Then, when I began to inch down, the paddle extension on the back of my hand kept catching on the rungs. I was so involved in the mechanics of my descent that the first swell took me by surprise, burying me waist-deep in water, and I had to pull back up a couple rungs to fix the tail part of me. Then all I had to do was wait for the next swell and let go.

The water took me a dozen yards from the ladder before I could make stroke one. Turning, I gave Sam a high sign, saw him wave acknowledgment and begin to haul in the ladder. Then I checked out my booster. Fine. It worked. I cut it immediately. Then I turned again and began to swim steadily in the direction from which the stenos should, in a few minutes, emerge.

I did not look back at the helicopter, and for a good reason. The first time it left me like that I had been almost overcome with an animal panic, which struck without warning the very moment the chopper lifted off. I was alone, I was helpless, trapped in the alien element, I would drown, I would never see human faces again. At least, that's how I rationalized it as it began to go away. At its peak, and it went from zero to peak on a count of one, I wasn't capable of even that much rationality, I was in the grip of pure blind fear, my whole nervous system a single long cry of "NO!" It may have lasted a minute or so—time has no meaning under such circumstances—and then ebbed gradually like the echoes of a cry slowly fading into silence; the disciplined routines of training took over. But I was still afraid that moment had somehow taken my edge, might even in some way have contributed to the subsequent failure, and I was determined not to suffer it again.

The change in the engine note told me when the helicopter had begun to rise. I still didn't look, I forced myself not to look until I could feel that the effort was doing more harm than the looking would, and by then the machine was just a speck, a speck that blazed like a star for an instant as the sun's slanting beams caught it, then turned leaden again, dwindled and vanished into the southeastern sky, where a low bank of evening cloud had already begun to form. As it vanished, I felt the fear again for a few seconds, but much less fiercely this time, there's little that doesn't fade with repetition. Thank God. Or alas. Or both.

I WAS GAMBLING that the stenos would come on without altering course, and I was lucky. I heard them before I saw them —a prolonged stammer of echolocation, like kids dragging sticks down iron palings, only so fast the individual sounds blurred. They must already have gotten a fix on me; I got a slightly spooky feeling from thinking how my unfamiliar image must swim already on the screen of their minds, like an image on a radar screen, only far clearer and more detailed. Then there came the first wild curving alarm whistle.

The first time, I'd gone swimming straight into the middle of them. That might have been a mistake: made me look too pushy. Now, I pulled a U-turn and dived, for I was blind to their world while on the surface. Instantly the view opened up, in that pellucid mid-oceanic water you could see for maybe fifty yards or more. And there they were, bunched, over to my left, about twenty yards away and now running parallel with me a couple of feet or so beneath the surface. Looking almost double their real size in the glassy green subaqueous light.

Stenos, as I've said, don't have the clean, slick lines of other dolphins; cramped in the confines of their tanks, Mele and Lei had looked cumbersome, almost ugly at times. But now, in their element, there was no hint of ugliness. The heavy rounded bodies spoke only of power, power and inexhaustible energy. They sailed along effortlessly, with barely a thrust of their great tailflukes. They were beautiful in their ease and wholeness.

I counted fifteen of them. They were bunched in a tight defensive formation, in two layers, the flippers of the upper layer would have touched the dorsal fins of the lower if their places hadn't been slightly staggered. Upper and lower layers rose to breathe alternately, interpenetrating one another, but without ever breaking formation, as if in some intricate dance. After the initial burst of sound with which they had greeted me, they had grown more silent, but sporadic squawks and fragmentary click-trains were still being exchanged among them. It was as if, having overcome their first astonishment, they were now discussing me in critical terms.

I made no move. It was essential that the first move come from them. So far as I was aware, there was nothing I could do to influence their choice, except, presumably, to maintain an unthreatening stance and read correctly any gestures they might make toward me. We proceeded thus, swimming parallel, for between ten and fifteen minutes—although I was so tensed up it seemed much longer than that. So long, indeed, it seemed that expectation was dulled, and their move, when it came, took me by surprise. One of them—they were still faceless and indistinguishable beings to me, at this stage— peeled off from the upper layer of the pod like a fighter plane peeling off from its formation and, wheeling effortlessly behind and beneath me, passed like a torpedo within inches of me, so close that the invisible wall of water thrown up by its passage forced me bodily aside. Then a second, this one unseen until the moment of impact, swung round on the opposite side of me so close that the edge of his tailfluke rasped against my thigh.

All of this happened so fast I could not have reacted to it, even if I'd wanted to. By the time my wits had reassembled they were back in place, and once again a stream of echolocation sounds was launched against me. Only now they were no longer merely locating me; again, this time much more strongly, I had the spooky feeling of being able almost, but not quite, to read their minds. For sound waves, unlike light waves, are not stopped by our envelope of flesh. Their sonar was going through me like X-rays; the shape of my skeleton, the branching tree of my nerves, the coils of my guts, the puddles of air in lungs and belly—all those parts of myself secret even to their owner—must now lie revealed to them as clearly as my outer form. If these stenos, who might never have come within sight of land, had ever encountered humans before, then all my elaborate disguise, I now realized, must be wasted upon them.

Again their sounds died to a sporadic chatter, and then, with the precision of a flight of waterbirds wheeling in a clear fall sky—if you had seen them move you would know why I can compare them only to flying things—they swung in an arc and came, all of them, directly at me. If you have seen dolphins only in oceanariums, obedient to some clown in tennis clothes, you cannot imagine the beauty and terror of that assault. I think I may have thrown my webbed hands in front of my face in a futile gesture of self-protection. No matter: when they were almost on me, their phalanx opened like the fingers of a hand and they passed by me, above, below and on either side, leaving me rocking out of control in the tumbled wake of their passage. Then, regrouping into their previous formation, they began to come at me singly. Each one would sweep in with beak aimed directly at my head or chest, deflecting only at the last instant so that the swordlike bills of bone passed by me, all but grazing the skin of my suit, while their smooth bodies bumped bruisingly against mine.

If they did me no injury it was not from lack of the power to do so. With those beaks they could have caved in my skull or breastbone as easily as you or I might crush an empty beer can. True, and I clung desperately to the knowledge, no dolphin had ever been known to injure a human, even under tortures of vivisection; but then I had done all in my power to make myself appear other than human, so that now, even after their sonar-scanning, I had no idea what my status might be in their minds. I could rely on no precedent because there was no precedent. I knew they could harass and kill sharks larger by far than I, and I knew that I could never bring myself to use my CO_2 cartridges against them, even in self-defense. If they wanted to kill me, there was absolutely nothing I could do to prevent them. But they did not want to kill me. They wanted to test me, I was almost sure that was what it was. They needed to know my nature, my strengths and weaknesses, whether I could be provoked. If I proved violent they could respond in kind, or more probably just shun me as the first pod had done; and if I proved docile . . . I realized then the importance of not appearing too docile. The timid young recruit always gets the hell kicked out of him by the old hands. If I were to succeed in joining them, I didn't want to do so at the price of being lowest man on their totem pole. So I began to strike back at them, not in any anger or panic, but with firm thrusts of my paddles and tail, not strongly enough to do them any injury, but with enough force to let them know that I had my own dignity and that, while they were entitled to impose this ordeal, they had better see that they kept it within reasonable bounds.

At first I thought I'd made a terrible, irreversible mistake. Their tactics changed suddenly. As I surfaced for air (which of course I'd been doing regularly, every minute or so, all the time this had been going on) my head bumped against something solid. There was a roof of bodies between myself and the air. I ducked, and hurled myself forward and up; the barrier was still above me. Back, and up; there it still was. My lungs began to flame. I battered blindly with my head, no longer caring whether I did damage or not, for this had stopped being anything you could call a game, it was a fight for mere survival now. The bodies remained intact, resisting me with their inert force. I felt my strength, already reduced by my struggle with them, pouring out of me like water from a sink . . . colored lights exploded behind my eyelids . . . exploded and went dark . . .

And then I was rolling on the surface, spray sloshing over me, gulping down great lungfuls of air, the sky open above me. Only something had happened to the sky. It was no longer the great arch of blue and gold I knew so well. It had darkened, thickened, congealed into a sullen gloom that was sucking up light like a sponge—

I was so disoriented that I thought one of two things must have happened, either a natural catastrophe or some derangement of my senses due to shock and oxygen loss. I had lost all sense of the passage of time; it seemed only moments since my meeting with the stenos, so absorbed had I been in my interaction with them. Actually, it had been late afternoon when I descended, and the better part of two hours had since elapsed, so that we were now, quite naturally, on the brink of night. Night! I felt a rush of joy and relief. For with the coming of night, my ordeal would surely end, as the Deep Scattering Layer began to rise.

WHEN MAN FIRST started to scan the depths by sonar, he found a strange thing. You could travel over an area of ocean, and the echoes would tell you there was no solid footing for hundreds or even thousands of fathoms down. Yet if you passed over that same area by night, echoes would come pinging back to you almost as soon as the sound probes were dispatched. Could the bottom have magically risen to within a few hundred feet of the surface, as this suggested? Obviously that was absurd. But it was some time before they figured out what was happening.

Near the surface, life is scattered, elusive. It thickens as you go down: creatures that shun the light and the fast-moving predators in the higher levels float in great drifts on the cold layers that the sun never reaches—squids, shrimp, jellyfish and swarms of yet simpler creatures. But when light is withdrawn each evening from the world, these creatures drift surfaceward, forming an almost solid layer a few chainlengths beneath the air. It's like a three-dimensional meadow undersea, from which sonar rebounds, on which stenos and other dolphins graze, every night. Already, one after another, they were losing interest in me. Already, one after another, they were surfacing, pumping in lungfuls of air, and then crash-diving, going away like bobsledders down an invisible mountain. Almost immediately they vanished from my sight, into water that seemed to darken even as I watched, as if someone were hurling in giant bottles of ink.

So volatile is the soul that, although only minutes before I had feared for my life with them, I was now almost panic-stricken lest I should lose them. I need not have worried. They had to surface for air, just as I did, and to maximize the depth of their dives they did not move much horizontally under the water: they rose almost in the place they had descended. But at first, rather than wait for them, I tried to dive after them, into the blackness. There was a small lamp set in the forehead of the suit that I could not afford to keep lit permanently, but could turn on at moments of need, and within the dim circle of radiance that it cast I could see the rounded shapes of the stenos hurtling down past me or already resurfacing, some-times with a fish or a writhing squid held trapped in the beak, which would be snapped and swallowed even while the steno was in full career. But the heavy action was at a depth which I could not reach without the risk of death and the certainty of sickening pain. Sometimes I would see small groups of shrimp or squid, spooked by the stenos, darting aimlessly about, and once or twice when a squid, with cold disks of eyes and a pulsating body within its aura of phosphorescence, blun-dered almost within reach of me, I would fight my nausea and make a grab for it. But even in shock it was more than a match for me: I felt like some blindfolded idiot at a country fair, snatching hopelessly at an apple swung on a string by his tormentors.

The stenos now ignored me completely. They were totally absorbed in their pursuit of food, for which they seemed to have no particular plan, nor, indeed, any need of one. The Deep Scattering Layer was beneath them, it was as endless as the sea itself, it could not run away any more than grass can flee a herd of cattle. They did not dive continuously. After a series of dives they would all rest, falling into a loose formation just below the surface. At these times, a continuous clicking, squawling and whistling would go on among them, as tantaliz-ing as the murmurs of talk from some late-night party over-heard by a sleepless wanderer of the streets. Could it be, after all, no more than some mindless mechanical chatter, as empty of meaning as the whistling of birds, as all the good porpoise-persons supposed? Chilled by loneliness, strangeness and the night, I had the fear that I might spend a lifetime watching them and still never know the answer.

That night seemed endless, worse perhaps even than the nights spent at sea during my training, for then I could afford to let my mind idle in neutral, while now it was searching constantly for understanding and finding none. If you have ever sat, on a café terrace, say, in a country where you spoke no word of the language and tried to make sense out of what you heard, you may have some inkling as to what I experienced —and you probably didn't do it for very long, because it gave you a headache, and was not very important to you, anyway. Long before the night was over, the pain behind my eyes was so strong I was tempted to abort the mission, there and then, and only my knowledge that a night pickup was virtually impossible, and only to be requested under circumstances of the severest emergency, prevented me from releasing my radio beacon. And yet that pain was only indirectly physical, was brought on by the sheer nervous tension of trying to solve the insoluble.

I think at times, in spite of it, I may have dozed a little, as I'd trained myself to do, not quite letting go, keeping just enough consciousness to rise and breathe, rise and breathe again, with the regularity of an automaton. Whatever the reason, I do not remember seeing the moon rise: suddenly it was just there, well above the horizon, close to the full. By this time most of the stenos were satiated, wallowing lazily just below the surface as they digested their meal. In the moonlight, when they surfaced, they were creatures of black and silver, with silver whirlpools around their heads, and then suddenly one of them leapt, his whole body from beak to tailtip clear in the air, waterdrops streaming from his belly like a cold white fire. I never before saw anything half so beautiful. He fell, and for a moment, after the smack and fountain of his fall, all was quiet; then another leapt, and another, until gradually, as the stars began to pale and the first livid grayness of false dawn showed in the east, the leaps grew ever more frequent until the whole face of the sea writhed under their rearing, plunging bodies. Sometimes as many as half the pod would be airborne at the same moment; sometimes the whole pod would chain-jump, one re-entering the water just as another leapt. Was it mere play that by coincidence fell into patterns, or was it disciplined? Or even a ritual of some kind? I didn't know. I didn't know anything. I couldn't leap. I couldn't dive. I couldn't match them at anything they did, except that I could mutter reassuringly to myself that *of course it can't be a ritual because ritual implies at one and the same time a spiritual awareness of the universe and the rational capacity to base a systematic series of outward observances, each having a symbolic significance, upon that awareness, and among all the species only ours possesses both characteristics.* There, at least that was the kind of thing my species was good at.

AS THE DAY DAWNED, I was able to recognize them as individuals.

There were, like I said, fifteen of them. They acted, in many ways, like a family, and at times I was tempted to conceptualize them as resembling one of the extended families that are still found in some human cultures, a family like the Kealohas, for example. You don't need to tell me what a pitfall this is. But it's a pitfall that can't, altogether, be avoided. You cannot see the world another species sees unless you yourself become a member of that species, and that, as I was to find to my cost, is something that lies far beyond the bounds of the possible. So if I sometimes seem to see my stenos in human terms, bear with me. There really isn't any other way, though we may fool ourselves from time to time.

The one that seemed nearest to a leader was the one I called Bull. Bull looked older than the others: his skin was a mass of healed patches from fights with giant squids and sharks, the rear edge of his dorsal fin was as frayed as an old flag in a hurricane. He was not the biggest or the toughest, though. That was Duke. But nobody messed with him. There was a pecking order, of a kind, in the pod, perhaps two pecking orders that didn't quite fit: who could snap at whom, and who could initiate sex with whom. The two orders both fluctuated over time, so weren't always easy to distinguish, but while at least two of the females occasionally snapped at Duke, neither of them, that I saw, ever snapped at Bull. And yet he wasn't the leader in any absolute sense. It was by no means clear, for instance, that he gave orders, even in the loosest sense. But then, did any of them?

That was one of the most puzzling things, at first. Decisions were being made about when and in what direction to move, when to start hunting food and when to stop, when to leap, when to play. Decisions, and quite a number of them, had been made, and instantaneously acted upon, during my hazing on that first evening, for example. On the analogy of any human group, you would have had to say that there was a decision-maker, or a small group of decision-makers, whose authority was accepted by the rest. And of course I couldn't know for sure that this wasn't happening. Like, when they all came at me together, it might be that a few seconds earlier Bull had said to them, "On the command, charge . . ." But I had a hunch, I can't say why, that this was unlikely. That if they did talk, it was not about things like that.

If I called Bull the leader, it was because he was the one nobody messed with, the one who swam at the front of the upper layer of the pod. Well, most of the time. Most of the time it was in formation, that is. For most of the time it wasn't in any formation at all, or else in the sleep formation, which is something else again. That sounds reasonable to you? That's how we, I mean our species, tackle any kind of problem. We look at the facts and see where there's anything approaching structure. Then we throw out the rest of the facts. We look at the facts on which structure can be imposed and see what happens most frequently within that structure. Then on the basis of that we make a Generalization, absolute and unqualified. Bull "is" "the leader." Make what you can of that.

But then if a leader has a second-in-command, whatever

authority the latter has, in human society, derives from the leader, not from his own self. So here's another place where human analogies don't fit. For if the steno pod had a second-in-command, that could only be Duke, and yet Duke held his place not as a gift from Bull but by virtue of his own qualities. Size, strength, speed, the most obvious, but other more abstract ones, too; the only one hinted at at this stage, visible in the livid scar of a huge squid's tentacle curling from beak to blowhole, was a courage bordering on rashness. No, he wasn't in any sense Bull's subordinate officer, nor was he the only alternative that human analogy might suggest—Bull's rival. The relationship between them, I was to learn, was something far freer and more shifting than either, containing mutual respect, and mutual wariness, and a continual playful testing of bounds, all muted and constrained within the matrix of the pod itself. And *that* is something still harder to convey than the one-on-one relationships, which is why I didn't begin with it, although it's so much more important than anything else that I'll have to try and describe it to you. In a little while. And a little at a time. For it was a long time before I understood it fully, even from where I was, right in the middle.

Next in size after Duke and Bull came three females. The largest and the most aggressive I called Sexy Susan, because she was into sex more than any of the others, she was the great initiator. Don't get the idea they were constantly balling. Dolphins in captivity, like chimps, do it more often than in the wild, and for the same reason: boredom. But they enjoyed sex and they were wholly free of any inhibitions about it, or about who should do what to whom. Male would mount male, female would thrust her beak into the ventral slit of male and female alike. And no shit about Privacy. Privacy doesn't exist in the ocean. There are no doors to close or bushes to slink behind. The water's clear enough to see through, or if not, sonar-probes will give away to everyone exactly what you're doing and who with. And you just don't sneak beyond sight or sonar range, because when they can't see or hear you, you can't see or hear them, and that means you've lost contact, you're cut off from the pod perhaps forever. And that's the only blasphemy, the only obscenity.

When I say Susan was the great initiator, I mean she made advances more often than any of the males. It wasn't a sexist society. Roles were not defined any more than physiology defined them: that's to say, when one sex has babies and the other doesn't, the one that's tied up with childbearing is always going to be to some extent at a disadvantage. For example, the one I called Pregnant Patsy always swam, during formations, on the lower level and near, but never at, the rear of the pod; the rearmost position was most often taken by Hester the Handmaiden, the third of the larger females, whose task, whether appointed or self-appointed, seemed to be to look out for Patsy in all eventualities. Patsy's, and to a lesser extent Hester's, behavior was docile and modest as compared to Susan's. But I wasn't with them long enough to know whether these were permanent traits or whether, at some other time, roles might have been reversed, so that Pregnant Patsy became Sexy Susan, and Sexy Susan, Pregnant Patsy.

Then there was Joker: smallest of the adult males but the most active, the highest leaper, the loudest splasher; who would steal fish from another's beak and, if challenged, hand it back with a parody of cringing deference; who would tease others into a frenzy but always dart off in time to avoid retribution; the only one I ever saw tailwalk, something that most stenos thought beneath their dignity, a trick for spinners and similar low species. And there was Mojo, Duke's dumb and faithful cohort, and the Loving Couple, the only male-female pair in the pod that kept together consistently, and then half a dozen stenos in varying stages of immaturity, the youngest hardly more than a year old.

I'M TELLING YOU all this as if it was revealed to me on that first morning. Of course, learning their characters took a lot longer than that. At first it was as much as I could do to distinguish them, because apart from Bull's tattered dorsal fin and Duke's squid scar, they didn't have much in the way of distinguishing features.

That first morning broke cloudy, with a heavy swell, gray, sluggish and ominous. I began to worry about storms. The position with regard to storms was tricky. Ideally, if it looked shitty I wouldn't be put down, but long-range forecasting still isn't all that accurate. If I could see signs of a storm coming, I was supposed to call base. If I left it too late, the helicopter wouldn't be able to take off and I'd have to ride out the storm. We didn't know if that was feasible. It was one thing we'd never tested, for the good reason that the only test was the real thing, and since, given luck, the real thing might never happen, there hadn't seemed any point in my risking my neck.

I looked at the sky, brooding and ugly. If I had any sense I'd call base now for a pickup. But I knew I wasn't going to call base. I still didn't know where I stood with the stenos. They hadn't accepted me, but they hadn't rejected me, either. Since dusk of the previous day they had seemed hardly to notice me. By now, at least, they must be used to me. If I just hung in there, they would sooner or later have to give me some sign as to how I stood. To leave them now would screw everything. I might never be able to relocate this particular pod, and even if I did, I had no guarantee that they would accept me a second time around. I would just have to take my chances.

The thought of struggling—worn-out, against countless tons of water, being flung helplessly about, helmet waterlogged, choking, feeling the last strength slowly ebbing, knowing the storm would outlast me and there was no hope of rescue—went briefly through my mind. I didn't dwell on it. That isn't hard, at my age. Death just isn't real when you're twenty-two. Or it wasn't then; now that Death and I have become better acquainted, it is real enough now. But not then. And drowning, I'd always been told, is the pleasantest of deaths.

The leaping had ceased now. The stenos were in loose formation and traveling roughly west by southwest. If "traveling" is the right word. "Traveling" gives you the impression of some kind of steady, purposeful progress. Theirs wasn't. If you imagine a bunch of first-graders out for a hike without a teacher, you may get some of the idea. They were constantly fooling around, chasing one another, getting into fake fights, darting to and fro and cutting loops and capers. Sometimes one or two would hang back until they looked like they were getting left behind; then they'd go racing lickety-split after the others. They dawdled and lollygagged, sprinted and cavorted, within the limits of their individual natures, of course—Bull acted most of the time like all this stuff was beneath him, while Joker and Susan were the flashiest pair of show-offs—and yet they never somehow deteriorated into a mere cluster of individuals, the pod changed shape as fluidly as a cloud but never shredded and dispersed as clouds do, it was as enduring as a rock in the center of the ocean, a moving rock. And there was something else about it that made it not like a grade-school picnic. One or two of them were always on the watch. It was a while before I caught on to this, because they didn't let it interfere with their playing around. And it wasn't as if there was any formal roster of watchmen. Whoever was furthest on the outside, that was his or her chore, it seemed to be tacitly understood, and from that one, for as long as he remained on the outside, you would hear repeated bursts of echolocation clicks fanning out into the open ocean beyond him. And every so often one of them, usually Duke or Bull, would make a complete 360 round the pod, pumping out click-trains all the way. It was all very casual, yet it gave the journey the air of a military patrol through unfriendly territory. And yet it was a picnic, too. Picnic. Patrol. You see how unhelpful human analogies are.

Any one of them probably was covering three miles to my one, but thanks to the manner in which they progressed I was still able to keep up with them without using my booster. Sometimes I fell behind them a little, but since their pace was so uneven, I soon caught up again. Sometimes I was within the pod and sometimes outside it. I thought that they were ignoring me still. Now I'm not so sure. They had tested me and I had shown neither anger nor fear of them. I had stayed with them all through the night's hunting. Now, as they displayed themselves and their ways before me, it was as if they were saying, "All right, now, you have seen us, this is how we are —if you like it, you can stay, if you want to; if not . . . well, the sea is endless, do what you please." And yet I could not have accepted this infinitely tactful and delicate offer, even if I had understood it, because I would not have known how to signal my acceptance, except by toiling doggedly along in their wake, hoping they would make some move, as I was doing now.

Then Duke, on one of his sweeps around the pod, curved sharply and came in beside me. Decelerating, he matched his pace with mine, and began to bump his side against me. But no longer with menace, as on the previous evening. All the time he was bumping me, a stream of sounds was pouring from him—squawks, clicks, whistles, rusty-hinge grating noises—a stream I knew somehow was no longer aimed *at* me, but *to* me. And, when you thought it over, that was only logical; because what, if some strange but not actively repulsive and possibly intelligent monster fell from the skies in your neck of the woods, would you do? Talk to it, naturally. Unlikely though it might seem that it would dig your lingo. At least it would know that you were intelligent, too, and not hostilely disposed.

But then the trouble began. A creature with arms can point at itself and utter its name, then point to you and try to elicit yours. Neither stenos nor any other species of dolphin can point their flippers at themselves. Any terrestrial creature can pick up objects, as Walter had realized, name them, and repeat the name until you get the message. Here was nothing to pick up, even a fish a steno would have to pick up in his beak, and since some sounds are made through the beak, another level of problems would appear. The more you thought of it, the more obstacles to communication loomed up, and yet that was all they were, obstacles—not one of them suggested that there was no one there to communicate with.

So I got nothing from Duke's message, not even the certainty that it was a message. He prodded me with his beak, as

one might rouse the attention of a particularly stupid or ab-
sent-minded child, and repeated the message, or perhaps re-
phrased it—when a string of sounds carries no meaning, it's
very hard to memorize, so I couldn't even tell if the sounds and
their order were the same or different. I patted his shoulder,
to show at least awareness and goodwill; I couldn't rub and
scratch him around the base of the beak and behind the eyes
as Lei loved to be scratched and rubbed, because the exten-
sions on my hands made it impossible to touch with my fingertips. I don't know if he got my message any better than I got
his, but almost immediately he plunged ahead of me a few feet,
stopped, waited, plunged ahead again. We were well to the
rear of the pod at this moment, and there was no mistaking his
body language: he was trying to get me to hurry up. But to go
any faster I would have required the booster, and I didn't want
to use that at a moment when any bizarre behavior might break
the tenuous link. Besides, I wanted to see how he would tackle
the problem.

Frustrated, he let himself drop back, behind me, then came
up beneath me and began to poke with his beak at where my
ventral slit would have been, had I been a dolphin. I suppressed an impulse to grab protectively at my groin; the suit
was thick and he wasn't pushing hard enough to do any damage. What he was trying to do was obvious, it's a favorite
dolphin game: one pushes his beak in the other's slit, the other
stops swimming and gets a free ride and a sex thrill at the same
time. Only this time, I'm sure, it was functional, not fun.

He got nowhere, there was nothing for his beak to lodge in.
But give stenos a problem and they don't give up on it. He
pushed alongside again, twisted his head up under my left
arm. His intention was obvious. I reached my arm over his
back as far as it would go, gripped as tightly as I could grip that
great, slippery body, and the moment he felt my pressure he
was off, headed for the center of the pod.

It was a symbolic act, I never doubted that from the first. I
was being formally invited to join them. Once I had been
drawn within the pod, all its members gathered round me in

a tight formation, pushing and nuzzling at me with their flippers and beaks; some, like Pregnant Patsy, rather shyly and hesitantly, others, like Susan and Joker, with boisterous energy. Only Bull, I think, didn't actually touch me, but glided benignly by with the aloofness proper to his station. Joker was the only one in whom I still sensed a little of the previous day's hostility. Swimming directly in front of me, he deliberately slowed down until his tail—which of course, unlike a fish's, was horizontal—came directly over my head, then pressed down with his tail when it was time for me to breathe, holding my head below the water. But as soon as the others realized this, they chased him away from me.

Within a minute or two he was back again. As with some flies, there was no getting rid of him, the moment your attention slackened, back he came. He did this trick two or three times before I came up with the answer to it, which should have been obvious: I wrapped my arms around the stem of the tail, between its broad flukes and his body, and pulled it down so I could get my head clear. Only, when I breathed, I didn't let go. He pulled away. I clung on. He began violently to waggle his body, trying to shake me off. But he could not shake me off. Almost all of a dolphin's power and maneuverability comes from his tail; immobilize that, and at once he's in trouble. He tried to bend his body back far enough to bite me, but could not. The others swarmed around, squawking and chattering furiously to one another, but no one made any move to try to help him. I figure they felt he'd only got what he deserved. When I let him go, he flashed off about a dozen yards in a single thrust and then turned, whistling indignantly. The others made derisive barking noises. You would almost have said they were laughing.

When I came to know Joker better, I understood that his behavior toward me, on that and a couple of subsequent days, wasn't really inspired by dislike. When I turned up, Joker was the clown, the butt of the pod. Perhaps every group needs a clown; perhaps to have someone you can ridicule is a need that transcends human or even mammalian existence, if a group is to be solid with itself. He made the most of that role, he hammed it, even, but I doubt whether he had originally chosen it, and I think he'd have liked to get rid of it, or at least show himself capable of getting rid of it if he so chose. Well, I was an obvious candidate for the role. If he could play tricks on me, make me look more ridiculous than I already was, and amuse the others in so doing, he would lift himself from clown to clown's entrepreneur. He worked hard on it, and if I'd knuckled under, for fear of alienating the rest of the pod, then clown I would have been. I had only instinct to thank for fighting against this fate, since at the time, you must realize, I had only the vaguest notion of what was going on.

But, bemused though I was, one thing was clear to me: I had won, not total acceptance, but a kind of probationary one that could be revoked at any time, doubtless, if I made a false move or simply if they got bored with having me around. I was tolerated, perhaps, much as the bright little cripple boy is tolerated by the bunch of big strong construction workers idling after their hard day, deigning for a while to be distracted, even amused, feeling maybe even a genuine if shallow affection but knowing that there is no responsibility, no bond, that when the chuckles change to cheekiness or tears they can simply get up and walk away. But I was tolerated. And that was all that mattered.

I WAS WRONG about the storm. As the day progressed, bruised and bulging clouds spread gradually into a wash of gray that covered the entire sky, the distance between trough and wave-crest lengthened and the crests themselves declined. But before that happened, the stenos' echolocation sounds were being answered from somewhere up ahead.

Within minutes, a second pod came into view, approaching us on an oblique course. Soon the two pods were swimming side by side, without mixing or abandoning their own formations. Whistles and long click-trains echoed from side to side, as if news was being exchanged. Suddenly, a steno from the other pod cut in on me, prodded me with its bill, bumped me with its high rounded shoulders. It was only then, I think, that I realized quite how traumatic my experience of the previous evening had been, for it went through my mind that, if I had to endure it again with every steno pod we encountered, I would simply have to give up. But luckily I didn't. There was a renewed burst of chattering and whistling from my own pod, and when a second steno from the other pod tried to do the same, Duke and Mojo fell in either side of him and hustled him away. Clearly they were saying: however odd I might appear, I was their property, and not to be annoyed or interfered with.

Within the next half hour or so, we met two more pods, and with each meeting a similar procedure took place. There were now something like eighty or ninety stenos milling around in the same small area of ocean, since some of the other pods were considerably larger than ours, and they had obviously not gathered there by chance. But how could they have concerted a meeting place where there were no marks to identify one? My first thought was that if the place was a regular one where they gathered every night, they would only require some inbuilt sense of navigation (mysterious enough in itself, but no more than birds have) in order to return there. But when, back on the *Farquarson,* I came to reconstruct my travels, it became obvious that they did not meet every night in the same spot, but that one resting place might be as much as twenty or thirty miles from the previous one.

However they located it, their pattern, on this first morning, was the same as on all subsequent mornings, although at other times the number of stenos might be greater or smaller. After a short period in which the pods mingled freely, the whole gathering fell into a kind of wheel pattern, with pregnant females and the very young around the hub of the wheel, the others in concentric circles, spreading outward. The outer-most were on watch, and did not sleep, or hardly; even as they drifted, motionless save for an occasional stirring of their great tailflukes, sporadic bursts of echo-probes came from them, checking that no shark or other enemy was approaching the sleeping herd. From time to time, without any perceptible signal, the watch would change, the outermost drift in toward the center and their place be taken by those in the next ring. The others slept, as much as dolphins can ever sleep: the higher nervous centers blacked out, enough motor reflexes kept going to lift them, every minute or so, to the surface in order to breathe. I couldn't sleep like that, not at first, anyway. I'd doze off and come to with a sickening lurch, under water, out of air, and have to hyperventilate to get myself out of it. That woke me up, sort of. It pissed me off too, because the need to sleep, I could foresee, was going to be the biggest constraint on the length of time I could spend uninterrupted with the stenos. Sooner or later, perhaps, I would be able to condition myself to float, rise, breathe and sink again quite automatically. Now there were just these flashes between black unconsciousness and scary wakefulness.

Later on, in early afternoon, the sun strained through the overcast and, having resigned myself to no sleep, I swam on the surface and watched the wheel, which seemed to rotate slowly and rock on its axis as the stenos rose and fell and kept up enough momentum to continue rising and falling. It was a dreamy, hypnotic motion, so that I drifted into a strange state, fully conscious, and yet somehow suspended in calm, a calm like that of sleep, as deep and as refreshing. And a great sense of joy invaded my soul. I can't explain it. There is the sense of lightness and elation in the heart that almost everyone, or anyone not lobotomized by reason, feels when dolphins are around, but I know that, and it wasn't that, it was something beyond that. It was like I'd been born in a foreign land, and after many years of wandering had returned, without realizing it, to the land of my ancestors—without knowing it, without recognizing the least detail of the scene, and yet, from every stick and stone of it, some impulse came, some sympathetic vibration that pierced direct to my heart and told me: This is home.

SO PASSED my first twenty-four hours in the company of the stenos. And, as so often happens, the great and tumultuous wave of feeling that passed through me as I watched the sleeping herd of stenos did not herald the beginning of some great new age of enlightenment and understanding. Rather the reverse. Forty hours later, when, still with reserves of food and power, but limp, exhausted, my brain gray with lack of sleep and the nervous tension of constant watchfulness, I released the signal that would bring me (God willing) Seminole Sam and his helicopter, I had learnt little or nothing more than I've already told you, and was in a state of deep depression which, though I didn't recognize it at the time, was anger. An anger that couldn't take shape because I didn't know what its target was, or because its only possible target was myself, the nature of my brain that would let me see but not understand, the nature of my body that rebelled against the trips my brain laid on it—and because there was nothing I could do to change those things.

And I was angry because I had to return to the *Farquarson,* and could not accept that anger, because it was unnatural. The *Farquarson* was filled with my own kind. After enduring hardship and loneliness in the wilderness, a man is supposed to long for the company of his own kind. To look forward with joy and relief to being with them. Whereas all I could feel, thinking of them, was boredom and impatience. It wasn't natural.

The means of my leaving was thus: I had first to fix, on a dorsal fin (I chose Duke's, it was the biggest after Bull's, and Bull's I thought might not stand up to it) a small radio beacon. It had to go into the dorsal fin because there it would be clear of the water for longer periods than anywhere else. The purpose of this beacon was so that the radio ops on the *Farquarson* would be able to keep track of the pod while I was away and give me a position to return to as soon as I had recuperated from my first trip. The beacon was very light but Duke must have noticed it going on, and any creature as finely balanced as the stenos were would have felt some encumbrance when he swam. Yet he didn't show any reaction at all, of resentment or even disturbance, something that would have puzzled me more at the time, if I had been less exhausted. Then I had to get some distance between myself and the pod. I had come to them out of nowhere, I would return into nowhere, if that was possible. And it turned out to be easier than I had feared, or perhaps hoped—could they be so indifferent to me? shouldn't they have stopped to find out what was happening to me? I simply, as the move to the morning's sleeping place progressed, allowed myself to fall further and further behind the pod. None of them seemed to notice. It was, I reassured myself, the business of the laggard to keep up with the pod, they probably wouldn't come back looking even for one of their own. Their sounds grew fainter, the last shape vanished in the dimness of the distant water, and I was alone.

Even through my fatigue I felt a numbing sense of loss.

I released the beacon and its balloon soared up, pulling out its reel of mooring wire. There was nothing to do now but wait for Sam. That was, if my signal had been heard. All kinds of thoughts went through my mind. There was nobody on watch. The signal was too weak for them to get a proper fix on it. Or my wanderings had taken me past the range of the beacon and they would hear nothing at all. I would never know the answer, whatever. I'd wait, and no one would come. My food would go, my strength with it. I'd sink helplessly, if my helmet was waterlogged; float helplessly, if it wasn't. Perhaps sharks would cut things short.

I wished I was back with the stenos.

I don't suppose I passed more than a couple of hours like that, though it seemed longer than all the rest of the trip. Salt crystals had worked through the grease that encased my body and come to rest in the folds of armpit and groin, so each time I moved arms or legs I felt like I'd been rubbed with sandpaper. I had a crick in my neck, from trying to look up, as I floated, and spot the helicopter approaching—which was crazy; if it came at all I'd hear it long before I could see it— and, since I'd figured it would approach from the southeast, my eyes ached from staring into the sun. And yet there was a sense in which I was lucky things took as long as they did, because by the time I did hear it—first faint, then clear, then drowned in gusty wind, disbelieved in, recovered, lost, heard fainter then as if already receding *the stupid bastard why the fuck can't he find me now he's got this far is he blind or something* and then firmly at last and descending—I was good and ready to show proper gratitude to my rescuer.

When I'd dragged myself, hand over hand, up the rope ladder, a black wrist smooth as a snake yet bulging with tendons like wire ropes under the skin latched onto mine and hauled me over the sill of the cabin. Just as well, I doubt I'd have made those last inches. I lay on the floor of the cabin. I tried to say something, even if only as banal as, "Thanks, buddy," I knew I should say something, I wanted to say something, but I could not. The words had dried right out of me. It wasn't just fatigue. I didn't know what it was. Even through the relief, and in spite of myself, I felt more captured than rescued, and I did not understand this and needed space and silence to interrogate myself before I could talk. But Sam was going to want me to talk. That was natural. It was his right.

"So the boy is saved," Sam said, not too loud, not to me, not even to himself—to the surrounding air and water, perhaps. "The boy is saved, Hallelujah, Lord, You done tooken him from the deep just like Jonah out the whale belly, him ye watch over, him shall not suffer objurgations nor no manner of untoward thing, nay, not even in the dark where no christen man goeth, world without end, Amen." And he switched the rotors to "lift" and threw on full power and didn't say another word until the lean gray streak of the *Farquarson* loomed up below us. I would never have thought of him as a tactful man. I was amazed and properly chastened.

BACK ON BOARD the *Farquarson* I was hustled down to the sick bay with a kind of impersonal solicitude, as if I had been some rare but unfeeling object, an anfora or coelocanth, perhaps; then after a quick and perfunctory measurement of my fluids and functions—samples of blood and urine, pulse and blood pressure taken—a medic with rabbit's eyes and a wisp of cornsilk mustache said, "Justholdstillasecond, yawontfeelathing," and slid the tip of a hypodermic under my left bicep. "Now take it easy, take it easy now," the other one, heavy jowls and a five-o'clock shadow at noon, kept repeating as he pinned me to the cot, needlessly, for I was too weak to do more than curse them and quick to realize I could have harangued them a hundred years and they still would have seen nothing wrong in handling every contingency with its appropriate chemical. The patient needs rest? Five cc's of rest coming up, zap! The sterile, white-metal box around me started to fog. Then nothing—not even dreams.

I was out eighteen hours.

Then it was bed rest with salves and nourishing soups; Stubblejaws played chess with me on one of those ratty little sets that have pegs you stick into the board. "What opening is that?" he asked me, first time out. I told him I didn't know. He made a face like I was crazy. He'd read books on it and knew all the grand-master gambits by rote. My kooky opening spooked him so bad he was mated in twenty-three. After that he could usually manage to beat me if he could only keep himself together. I played kamikaze style, on intuition, leaving myself wide open to forethoughtful counterattacks. But I took no more than seconds to consider each move, and shame at his own slowness made him hustle and slip. Silk Tash watched us occasionally with a kind of disapproving sneer. He was a kosher doctor, it turned out, Stubblejaws was just his go-fer temporarily transferred from some other go-fer duty, so it was beneath his dignity to fraternize with patients. Most of the time I was alone and grateful for it. Sam came in to see me a couple of times, but his spatulate nostrils wrinkled at the astringent odors, his big rump wriggled on the folding chair. You could see that, to him, anything resembling a hospital was a place all sane and healthy men instinctively fled from. And the Captain came, once, asked a number of questions, didn't listen to any of my answers, yet managed to suggest, even in his manner of turning and leaving, that he'd paid me an inestimable compliment by coming at all.

Or did he? Or did I, hypersensitized by my experiences, bored and resentful, anxious only to be strong enough to go back into the ocean, simply imagine all of this? I can't help thinking, now, that my reaction to the crew of the *Farquarson* was an unduly hostile and exaggerated one. Surely they weren't all that bad? Surely they were no more than ordinary men doing their ordinary jobs? True, and yet there was something else besides, something I think I had a right to react to, that was all the more vivid by the contrast with where I'd come from, and that turned me off them completely. Maybe it came out most clearly in the way they dealt with Sam. I don't mean they were racist. Oh no, far from it. No Jim Crow on the *Farquarson*'s roster. Indeed, everyone was supernice to Sam. Walked round him like on eggs, always smiling. But you know that smile: the one people smile when they catch you looking at them. There's no pleasure in it, no real friendliness, not even bitterness or disdain, precisely what's so lousy about it is that it carries no feeling for its object at all—it's just a message about the Self; it says, please accept this in lieu of an emotion, I'm much too self-involved to have any truck with you right now, but you're not to get mad at me on account of I'm really Mister Nice Guy somewhere deep down inside. Call it The Raincheck Smile, but don't ever try to cash it, because its user hasn't really seen you at all, might not even recognize you a second time around.

YOU COULD NOT imagine the stenos smiling that smile. Not even if their faces had the rubbery mobility ours have. I'm not suggesting that as a sign of superior virtue on their part. I leave that kind of thing to the Franks of this world. We are as we're made, and entitled to no special praise for it. But, for one thing, it would have been a waste of time for them. The Raincheck Smile is so we can hide our thoughts and feelings from others. Stenos can't do that, whether they wish or no. The sound impulses they send that can pass as easily through flesh as through water can tell instantly whether muscles are tensed or relaxed, whether the glands that control rage or terror or desire are functioning or at rest. So why fake?

And then there was the bondedness. Again I'm not claiming this as virtue, just as fact. There was no way they could not be bonded. It's different with us. We can forget about the way the web of humanity sustains us. There are people who claim to be "self-made men." "I did it all myself." "I'm an individualist." "I do it my way." "I owe it all to my own efforts." No steno could make that claim. It's only too obvious that he owes it all to his brothers. Without the pod he could not hope to survive. It's as simple as that. And nothing sentimental about it. I don't want to suggest that because of the strength of their feeling for one another they spent their time billing and cooing like in some Disneyland of the deep. Far from it. They fought, they got mad, they nagged and bugged one another, as much as any of us do and maybe more than most. Yet somehow they never lost sight of the fact that they needed one another. And it was because of that, perhaps, that there were no durable enmities within the pod. A pair of them would slug it out, snapping their beaks, hammering one another with tail blows, and then a few minutes later you'd see them nuzzling together or gliding in tandem, one pushing the other with his beak. But always the closeness, whether hostile or friendly. That was the difference, that was what was lacking on the *Farquarson,* and not just on the *Farquarson* either. You'd have to go looking for it a long way in America, or even in more remote places. Maybe we had it once, when we lived in tribes, when loyalties were clear, before there had formed the thought, "If I go to the aid of my buddy, *I* may get fucked over too."

It followed that there was no passing by on the other side for the stenos. If one was menaced, all responded. No questions, no hesitations, no enlightened self-interest. The first time I saw this was on my third or maybe fourth outing with them, on a brisk breezy morning of whipping whitecaps and cottontail clouds, when I heard (for the first time since my own first visitation, but once heard, it was unforgettable) the high curving alarm-whistle of the stenos. It was answered instantly, and weirdly, by a chorus of names. For, as I should have mentioned, the one linguistic fact about the stenos of which I was reasonably certain was that they used the distinctive signature-whistle all dolphins possess as their names for one another: thus, Mojo's real name was a plangent, level tone with a kind of downward hook at the end of it, Susan's an upswoop with a warble, Duke's a sharp zigzag of sound, and so on. It sounds crazy, in human terms, to keep shouting your own name as you rush to someone's assistance: as if, when someone fell into the tanks, back at the Station, all of us should have come out yelling, "Andy, Andy, Andy!," "Les, Les, Les!," "Frank, Frank, Frank!" But dolphins aren't humans. A human in distress is usually immobile; a dolphin in distress is either highly mobile or dead—and usually taking violent, evasive action in three dimensions, needing desperately to know which of his friends is coming and how fast and from which direction and how far they still are, all of which information he can read quickly and easily from the signature-whistles homing in on him; so it makes a lot of sense, for dolphins.

That time it was Hester calling, and the trouble was cookie-cutters. Cookie-cutters are the smallest of shark species, no more than about eighteen inches long, but what they lack in size they make up for in ferocity, and a great many of the bite marks on the stenos, which I'd originally thought to be the marks of giant squid suckers, in fact came from the round, gaping, cookie-sized jaws of these nasty little monsters. Within seconds the water around Hester was a boiling mass of foam, from which mangled fragments of cookie-cutter were violently ejected; three other members of the pod got bitten (I was lucky, that first time), an uncertain number of the minisharks got dismembered and the rest fled. It was over in a couple of minutes, and at once, as far as I could tell, the incident was forgotten, as if it had never been.

And there lay another difference between our two species. Figure what mankind would have done had he been afflicted by foot-and-a-half-long rodents that leapt out from behind rocks to take chunks out of him. Remember what happened to the Cave Bear and any other species that stood in our way (plus plenty that didn't). Imagine the plans, the traps, the poisoned bait and, more nauseating than any poison, all the self-righteous speeches and articles about the Cookie-Cutter Menace and the Anti-CC Campaign. Weren't the stenos smart enough to see that if they killed off all the cookie-cutters they wouldn't get bitten any more? True, they had no bait, no traps, but what was to stop them, most social of all species, from banding together and sweeping the seas of these vermin? Was it because they wouldn't, or couldn't? Or was that question itself, perhaps, meaningless?

The thought began to creep into my mind that I might wind up learning far more about my own species than I ever would about theirs.

FOR, TO BE HONEST WITH YOU, I was learning precious little about the stenos: after the elation of my first spell with them, each succeeding tour seemed to bring diminishing returns. It was a paradox that festered in my mind till I reached a point of almost hysterical rage and frustration, all the worse because there was no one and nothing on which to vent it with even the most specious pretense of justice. I could not even vent it on myself, for I was already doing more than a human could to solve it. And the paradox was this: although the whole workings of dolphin society were laid open to me, like the works of a watch, through the transparency of deep-ocean water it still did not mean anything to me. It was like watching TV with the sound turned off. Only the grossest physical incidents were interpretable. Anything subtler was at best five ways ambiguous, at worst totally opaque. And the key, as with the vision-only TV, had to lie in the means of communication they used, their language, as I thought of it. But I was no nearer deciphering that language than I had been the day I started. I needed a Rosetta Stone; but there is no Rosetta Stone between species.

And if I found this situation frustrating, how did the stenos find it? My greatest dread, that I would hardly admit even to myself, was that they would suddenly one day tire of me and break off all contact. There was nothing I could do about it, though; no court in which I could appeal that decision, should it come.

For the present, though, there seemed no sign of it. Though they had quickly tired of trying to teach me to communicate with them, there were other things which, perhaps, they felt were still within the scope even of so limited a creature as I.

One of these was leaping. Their power to leap out of the element that embraced them was one of the things I most envied them; only gravity, it seemed, kept them from true flight. Speed was important, but not speed alone; timing and angle were essential too. They worked with me on my leaping, far more than I had a right to expect; with Duke, who, after Susan, was maybe my most persistent teacher, I got the distinct impression that he simply couldn't believe I could be so inept and clumsy, and had had to be reminded of it on every new occasion. And at first, my attempts were indeed pathetic; just my head and shoulders would bob limply out of the water, nod and subside again. But they kept on nagging me, long after I was ready to give up, swam alongside me, nudged me, chivvied me with their beaks, and demonstrated their skills yet again for me, over and over.

Then they tried to teach me to catch fish. One morning we hit a school of flying fish—my fourth or was it fifth trip, that time, I don't know, they blur in memory, but there'd been a big storm while I was gone that left huge and sluggish green hills of water, up and down which we rolled, sickeningly. (You can get seasick without being in a boat, was one of the less enthralling discoveries I'd made.) Each time a wave came I'd be lofted up to what seemed an abominable height and then peep over the top of it at a nauseous welter of crisscrossing green valleys between me and the next looming, reeling hill—valleys into which, with gut-wrenching force, I would once more be pulled down. Then suddenly there they were, the flying fish, bug-eyed little freaks with a panic-stricken look and their finny wings trailing spray, flipping and skittering like those flattened pebbles that boys skim across ponds—dozens of them, right on top of us, in full flight from other predators, no doubt. Down one tumbling green wall they came and on up the next, and all the stenos had to do was snatch them from the air in toothed beaks as they fled by, and swallow them.

But they didn't swallow them whole; flying fish are bony and spiny, so they took those round heads with the lugubrious eyes in their beaks and slammed the bodies of the fish against the water's surface, over and over, till head, backbone and guts came out all in one piece—whereon they let go the head and grabbed the more edible portions before these could sink. The more fastidious even tore off the wings. At last, I thought, I've found something I can do better than they can. I tried to grab one, missed, tried again, then Mojo, nearest, saw what I was doing and instantly divined my purpose, caught one and flipped it to me. I snatched at it, treading water, forced myself to rip out bones and fins—revolted at so handling a living creature, yet desperate enough for approval to fight down this revulsion—and tossed it back to Mojo, all, I was pleased to note, far quicker than any of them could have done it. Within seconds, it seemed, half a dozen of them were catching for me and I, in turn, was hurling back the poor gutted bodies. Then Susan returned one to me. I pretended not to understand, and in a parody of politeness the fish was flung back and forth between us maybe half a dozen times. But then Susan sqwawked and chattered angrily at me, miming the act of eating while I held the thing, and then I knew I had to try—raw and disgusting as it was, sick as I already felt, I had to gag it down. It was nauseating—leathery on the outside, all rubbery flesh and squishy lymph within. But I managed it. Somehow. I think she knew I almost vomited. I think she was amused.

THOSE WERE THE high spots, my learning experiences. For the rest, like anything else, however bizarre or glamorous, that you do repeatedly, it was getting to be a chore. Dropping out of the sky into the wilds of ocean, consorting with an alien species amid the perils of the deep, being snatched back into the company of what was still, after all, my own kind, became, as the weeks spread into months, a commuter's routine. Even the Fighting Seminole grew blasé about it. Sam no longer praised the Lord on my safe returns. By the third or fourth repetition it had gotten to "You is the gentleman called Radio Cab, sah? Well, sah, heah *be* your Radio Cab, sah. So sorry for the delay, sah. Had us lil' bit trouble on Tenth an' Main, sah. Cops thick as blow flies on a dead DAHG, sah. Cops is blue, blowflies is blue, you gets the connection, well that'll be fifteen fifty *plus* tax *plus* gratuity *plus* . . . Plus what, sah? Why, plus whatever you be so kind enough to *do*-nate, sah!" And then he'd crack up, giving me five, on my hand, my thigh, anywhere in reach, and I'd have to laugh too, though I felt and recognized some undercurrent of meanness in it, and never could tell exactly where I stood with him.

Not that it was all routine, by any means. Strange and wonderful things still happened. Like, the last trip before I returned to Honolulu (though I didn't know it was the last trip, then) this happened: late one evening, down from the north, there came a shape, dark blue, enormous. A boat turned turtle? A nuclear submarine? No, it was a blue whale, vastest of creatures that ever sailed the waters of our world, and, thanks to us, now maybe the rarest. I don't know what it was doing down there in the tropics—blue whales are mostly subarctic creatures. Maybe it was just trading Poles. It came on at ponderous speed, ninety feet long, a hundred tons dead weight; its flukes were as big as the tailfins on a jumbo jet, it pushed ahead of it a bow wave like a schooner's, and I felt only awe at the approach of a creature that could shatter me with one flip of its tail and move on, not even knowing what it had done.

The stenos, however, showed no signs of awe. They headed straight for its bow wave.

That was nothing special as waves go: two to three feet at most around the whale's snout and tapering as it spread, and far from the critical point of breaking, but it was rideable, with a pure glassy shape, and one by one the stenos got up on it and rode it, Bull and Duke on the inside sections, closest to the whale, the others strung out in rough order of rank and size.

It was like no wave I'd ever ridden before, because a true surfing wave is always on the point of breaking, and all your maneuvers are conditioned by this fact, but the whale's wave would remain intact until the monster that made it sank back into the depths. However, I'd had more time body surfing than any steno, and I began to work inward along the wave, maneuvering round the stenos in my way till only Duke was between me and the whale. But Duke wasn't going to yield the primo spot without a struggle. There was no way around him; without effort he slid his ponderous bulk into a blocking position whichever way I came at him, and he was far too big and heavy to be simply forced aside. I tried, though. I guess it was understandable. I'd at last found something in which I had parity, if not an equal edge, and I was determined to go for it. We slid apart and slammed into each other again and again, forgetting exactly where we were in the heat of our competition; and then, all of a sudden, wham! We had skidded right into the whale's nose.

That was enough. The foolery of children he might abide, but gross impertinence . . . He went down like a stone, the wave coiled in on itself and I felt the dragging undertow of his bulk. The stenos, robbed of their ride, tossed aimlessly in the vortex he left behind him and complained loudly to one another. And then suddenly there came a roar like a thermal geyser, and a column of white spray, smelling incongruously of rotting pseudopods, soared above us and rained down over us; his tail like a huge blue-black delta wing eclipsed us with its shadow and then fell, lashing us with spray; and, finally, he breached, body following head into the air like the first slow, massive thrust of a space rocket—as if the whole gross mass of oil and bone and blubber would continue to accelerate until it was fully airborne and dwindling toward the stars. I suppose no more than the first thirty feet of him could have breached, but it was like an apartment block leaning over us, tilting, falling, as we fled in confusion, and then it hit, and I must have blacked out for a while, since the next thing I remember is the

Loving Couple, one on either side of me, swimming beneath me and forcing me up to the surface to breathe.

When I'd got my breath back, I turned and looked to the south, and there he was, hull down on the darkening horizon, heading toward his unimaginable goal.

THE BLUE WHALE has nothing to do with my story, really. He's not a character, he doesn't appear again. And yet perhaps he's everything to do with my story, a tangible reminder of huge things, obscurely glimpsed, beyond our understanding, perhaps forever.

It was right after the blue whale trip that Barry called me by radio from Honolulu. How was I getting on? I was guardedly pessimistic, remembering that Barry went by opposites: If I'd given him a gung-ho speech he'd have shot holes all over it. Indeed, he was sympathetic. "Sure, it's all confusing at this stage. That's a good sign. That means you've really got a lot of data, even if you don't realize it. It's when you've only got a little that it drops into place on the first go-round. All you have to do is quantify." *Quantify?* "Yeah, sure. Like that joke about, you know, 'Don't confuse me with facts'? Well that's what you are right now. Confused. With facts. You don't want facts at this stage. Facts are pretheoretical. You want *numbers* of facts. Categorize, quantify, then you'll see the Picture starting to come out . . . You'll need a computer of course." Well, there was a computer on the *Farquarson* . . . "And you can get unrestricted access to a terminal? Not if I know those boys! Listen, we have this new guy now, Fudge, took over your job programming. He's a lot better than you were. No, you were adequate, but you never had the real feel for it like Eric has. He can give you lots of tips. I think what you'd better do is come back to base for a couple of weeks or so. You could use the break too, I bet. You can get stale stuck out there. You'll get a different slant on things. Yeah, better come back to base."

Base! It was obvious when you thought about it, but it was the one thing I hadn't expected or planned for. Life back on shore just didn't seem real to me any more. Here I was with my Problem, and I could see no future but to go on grappling with it until either it or I ceased to exist. But I could think of no single argument to oppose the dozens Barry could muster. Base it was to be.

And at least I'd be with Keala again.

I can remember vividly the guilt I suddenly felt because, I only then realized, I'd scarcely thought of her during all the time I'd been away.

On the way to Johnston Island, Sam, suddenly paternal, explained to me the regulations under which service personnel could use civilian transportation between Johnston and Honolulu at the taxpayer's expense. A few joking words with a fat sergeant carrying a clipboard, and I had a seat on the regular Continental flight from Majuro. I cabled, and waited. The flight was overbooked and overdue. It was one in the morning before we picked up the lights of Oahu's south shore.

My feelings, as we came into land, were bizarre. It was not like a homecoming. I felt tense and a little scared, as if landing for the first time in a strange country. The words of stewardesses and fellow passengers were without meaning for me. Their movements were as uncouth as those of bears. The mechanics of landing and taxiing to the terminal held an icy menace. I almost did not recognize Keala at the arrival gate, my eyes sliding far over a drift of indistinguishable faces while, only feet away from me, she held ready for my neck the ceremonial maile lei. Then I saw her, we embraced, and suddenly all was real and normal again, like coming out of a dope rush; I was glad to be back.

"You hardly wrote."

"You neither."

"I never get time, they keep me so busy at School of Social Work. But you, you lolo, you get plenny time, out there on the O-cean . . ."

"Bull-*shit*. You don't know. You have no idea what it was like out there . . ."

"What it was like?"

Our footsteps echoed heavily down the long aisles of the

terminal. Well, what *was* it like? I knew then that I would never be able to make anyone who had not been there with me understand: and that meant no one. All of a sudden all that too began to seem unreal.

"Ah, what does it matter?" I said. "I'm back. We're here. That's all that matters." I believe I believed that, too, at the time. We embraced again. She put her tongue inside my lips, then broke away abruptly.

"Hey! Where Mousie stay? I wen' leave Mousie here jus' five minutes ago, hey, Mousie!"

A girl I remembered vaguely from the Kealoha's Sunday picnics came up, carrying a baby of, I guess, a couple months old. "Here, Vernon, meet Andy," Keala said with a wicked spark in her eye. "Andy, meet Number-One Son."

"Meet *what?*"

"Our baby. Wassamatta, you forget that last night already?"

I was so stunned that for a second I was quite taken in. I stood gaping at the pinch-faced little monstrosity—too dark, surely, a Mendelian throwback, perhaps?—unable to believe it was of the same species as me, let alone the issue of my own loins. Aware, perhaps, of my revulsion, it immediately screeched at me. The two girls cracked up. "He know you, you see," Keala got out between tears of laughter. "He know his Daddy." Realization began to dawn on me.

"But it couldn't . . . It's only three, four months since . . ."

The girls were falling about, clutching one another for support. Mousie almost dropped the baby.

"The great scientific genius," Keala gasped, crimson-faced. "Einstein finally crack the case."

"Christ, what a mean, sneaky . . ."

Then I had to laugh, too. You can't stand on your dignity with Hawaiians, unless you want to look pompous, even to yourself. But even laughing I had to glance down at her belly, to make sure.

"No worry," she said, intercepting my glance. "It never take, after all. This baby is Mousie's own, she get him for Woody, ah, Mousie? Or was my brother's?" And linking arms with me as naturally and easily as if we'd never been parted, she led me down toward the Baggage Claim Area, oblivious to the shocked protests of her friend.

WHAT WAS IT LIKE? was, predictably, the first question anyone asked, although I detected a strong tendency not to listen if the answer lasted more than about thirty seconds and contained any original material. With Les it was okay because he knew the background and had all kinds of technical questions to ask about the performance of my gear. I could get lost in these trivialities and forget the hole in the center of the donut.

"But what was it *really* like?" even he had to ask in the end.

"Les, honestly, I don't know . . . I feel I'm up against a wall."

"Do like Barry said. Run it all through the computer. *Something* may come out."

"You don't really believe that."

"No." Les tugged at his earlobe. He had had an ear pierced while I was away, I realized. Was he going gay on me? Then I registered the scrimshaw pendant hanging from the ear, and the mystery had solved itself. He had scrimshawed a pendant. Then found he'd nowhere to put it. Ergo, he'd pierced a hole for it. Simple. Direct. That was Les all over.

"I was just saying that for something to say," he said.

"Be my fucking guest."

"But there is one other possibility."

"Yeah."

"Only I didn't like to mention it on account of it's kind of a remote one. I don't like to raise false hopes."

"Naturally not."

"Right . . . You ever hear of a guy called Wayne Batteau?"

I racked my brains. The name seemed kind of familiar, but I couldn't place it.

"He was some kind of a crazy genius, used to work around here once. At the Oceanic Institute. With Bateson, Norris and them."

"Didn't he drown or something?"

"Right. Pity. Sounds like he was a real neat kind of guy. Ever hear of a machine he invented?"

"No."

"For seeing by sound."

"You're kidding!"

"Fact. He never really developed it. And the prototypes are lost for sure by this time. But there are descriptions. Enough so you could figure out how it worked."

"And . . . ?"

"I'm working on it. Should have something in, oh, a week, ten days, say."

"Holy *shit!*" For it didn't need Les to tell me the significance of this: if you could produce a machine that would replicate the dolphins' mode of perceiving the world, you might still be a ways from cracking their code, but you would have taken a giant step, as they say, out of your own skin and into theirs.

FUDGE, WHOSE NAME was Earl, not Eric, of course, turned out to be a clean-limbed, short-haired youth who, if he kissed ass (which he did), did so out of ignorance and conditioning rather than native servility; his was the kind of fresh-faced innocence that will spend hours searching for the left-handed Stillson wrench and still laugh with genuine good humor when it's explained to him. Though I would have died rather than admit it to Les (who had sentimental loyalties to "the old-time crew at the Station") and though I teased and tormented him as systematically as Les did, I found him an improvement on Frank, and certainly on Frank's replacement, Cheryl—Barry's belated and ill-informed attempt to affirmative-action the male-*haole* monopoly on the Station's staff. Moreover, as I had grudgingly to admit, Barry had been right when he said Earl could teach me things about computers. All I still doubted was that the things he taught me would be of any use.

Computers, Earl said earnestly (whenever he talked of their magic powers, there entered his eye the gleam of the true believer), are free from the bias endemic in all human thought. That bias is inevitable: we are built so that we *feel* about what we *think.* We actually have preferences, based on God knows what amalgam of garbled experience, about what lines of inquiry we should pursue in any given case, and what kind of solution we should hope to find at the end of them. Such preferences necessarily (though, of course, quite unconsciously) dictated our whole mode of research. We would persist in a futile approach long after its futility should have become apparent, simply because we had been conditioned to believe that an approach of that kind was correct: we would abandon or ignore promising avenues, simply because they failed to appeal to our irrational instincts. The computer was immune to such failings. Emotionless, it was totally neutral with regard to all possible hypotheses. Before its impartial frown, the most plausible and the most ridiculous hypotheses were equal. For a man, this would matter; a man could not work fast enough to test every hypothesis. A computer could. And amongst those "ridiculous" hypotheses, which we would discard untested, there might just be the one that would solve everything, the one we never would have chosen even to test, because of our cultural blinkers.

I've poeticized a little, I've got to confess. Earl's explication was a good deal more fractured and prosaic, but the gist is preserved faithfully. And the moral was this: I should take my raw data, my observations of countless pieces of dolphin interaction and putative speech acts, and categorize them in as many possible ways as I could think of, and then take every possible categorization of the two sets—the social interactions and the speech acts—and correlate them as many ways as the machine would permit, and at the end of all that, *some* significance, *some* statistical skewing beyond the limits of chance, would be bound to appear. And there would be the key to the solution.

Q.E.D.

I couldn't buy it. To me, every significant advance seemed to have come from some leap of the imagination that no machine could reproduce. I thought of Einstein, who realized that if you fired a revolver at an ascending elevator, the exit hole of the bullet would be fractionally lower than the entrance hole —an Observation the dumbest Mafioso might have made— and then went on to wonder just what were the implications of this fact for the laws that govern Motion, Space and Time?

But it was useless telling that to Fudge.

LES'S NEW TOY, when it emerged, consisted simply of a pair of opaque sunglasses attached to a small gray plastic box. The box rested against your forehead, and from either side of it wires with miniature receivers on the ends of them led down to your ears. The glasses fitted tight round your eye sockets so that, wearing them, you were functionally quite blind. The box, when you switched on its battery, emitted a high-pitched beeping noise. It was eerie, at first. You stood, blinded, in the middle of a familiar room turned suddenly hostile and uncompromising; a thorny forest of sounds hurled itself back at you as you milled aimlessly around, unable to orient yourself, unable to tell one sound from another. But with practice, enlightenment came. Sounds sorted themselves into reasoned classes: dull booming echoes of walls; sharper, clearer ones from tables and chairs; and from windows a sound like the crackling of thin ice. Scanning, you could begin to get the size and shape of objects by pinpointing where changes of pitch set in—crudely at first, then, once you'd got the hang of it, with swiftly sharpening definition. After an hour or two's practice you could even distinguish, say, an upholstered chair from a plain wooden one, and in two distinct ways at that: from the scanning pattern and from the quality of the echoes themselves.

Then you could begin to navigate. Cautiously at first, bumping into furniture. We had lots of fun with that. We'd get Earl to put on the machine and then, when he had scanned his surroundings and was attempting his first steps, we'd slide broom handles and similar obstacles into his path. He must have gone down a dozen times before he caught on to what was happening. He was very decent about it, more than either of us would have been. And of course, when it was our turn he knew better than to try those tricks.

I learned fast. In two days I could go anywhere in the Station without bumping anything or falling down. No great feat, really, I guess. The Wayne Batteau machine was, after all, no more than a sophisticated version of the blind man's cane tapping its way along a pavement; what I was doing was no more than what every blind person must perforce learn how to do. What drove me on, what made it magical, was simply the thought, obscure as yet but already powerful, of the new purposes to which this skill was going to be put.

It took about four more days for the idea to really connect, and it came about in a strange way, as follows:

Right then (I mean after the initial strangeness had worn off) Keala and I were really close, close as we'd ever been, and rather than have me drive her home in the small hours, as had been our custom, she would stay and sleep beside me in my narrow bed in the Station, which was okay, on account of Barry never showed up there much before ten. If you've ever slept double in a twin you'll know that, while romantic, it is also extremely uncomfortable, and really only possible under the condition that one of you never sleeps thoroughly but skims along on the brink of consciousness, always ready to adjust to the movements of the more dormant partner. Naturally, that one was me, not so much out of chivalry as that even then, unless I was heavily sedated, that was the way I had begun to sleep. So it happened that I was often awake while she slept, especially as the first light showed, and I would watch her while she slept, refueling my desire from that look of abandonment sleepers have; only, on that one morning, I also saw something that I must have seen a dozen times before, without reading any significance into it.

Under the delicate blue-veined skin of her eyelids, her eyes were moving, darting this way and that like mice under a blanket. Rapid Eye Movements—REMS, as they are known in the trade. REMS mean you are in profound sleep, accompanied by dreams, and I lay there for several minutes watching them in fascination. What could she be dreaming about? And then, usurping the Lover, the Scientist in me asked:

Why should anyone's eyes move about just because they're dreaming?

Answer: because they're following the movements of the creatures in their dream.

Q: But those creatures aren't really there!

A: Of course not!

Then it came on me in a rush, like an amyl nitrite hit, and I sprang from the bed and raced down the rickety stairs, naked as Archimedes from his tub, past the two tanks where Lei and Mele were still tirelessly circling, and hammered on Les's door, because Les was the only one who might immediately understand me.

Imagine a godlike creature with movie projectors for eyes. Would he need words to talk to you? Of course not. He would flash thoughts and visions directly onto the screen of your mind. There would be no boring narrator interposing himself between you and the events—it would be as if they were happening before your very eyes.

Now imagine that such a creature used audio instead of visual images. Pictures like the sound pictures that the Batteau machine made.

Les finally opened the door.

"What's happening? Streaking is back in fashion?"

"Shut up, let me in," I said. "I think I've got it at last."

STENOS, I SAID, saw the world by sending out pulses of sound and reading off the echoes. They had big brains, big as ours, that were largely devoted to this process, so that they could make minute distinctions with regard to the size and shape and even texture of objects as well as their distance, speed (if any) and direction. They had had twenty-five million years to perfect these skills.

"This is new?" Les yawned. "You broke my beauty sleep to tell me this?"

Okay, so these were things that anyone who knew anything about dolphins knew. But no one had thought through the implications of these facts, especially as they affected language.

It's hard for us humans to even conceive of a language radically different from our own. Surely all languages must, like ours, basically consist of a stock of distinctive names for both objects and actions and a set of rules for stringing these names together so as to make messages. But that doesn't follow from some Universal Law of Language—it's simply because of the way human beings are made.

We are made so we get most of our knowledge of the world from sight, but to communicate that knowledge we must use mostly sound (books being mere parasites on speech). That means switching modalities, and, in order to switch them, all the rich panoply of sight has to be hammered down into a few crude symbols, sound-shapes to which the visual images are somehow attached. Thus, if we wish to convey information about a shark very large in size that gives off radiation within a particular band of the spectrum, we call it a *great white,* and one with a head shaped very vaguely like one of our own common artifacts we call a *hammerhead.*

But dolphins didn't need to switch modalities: they perceived and communicated in the same medium, sound. So what would they need names for, *when they could use the distinctive sound pattern each thing sent back to them?*

"Wait a minute," Les said. "They're using the same kind of sound for echolocation, aren't they? Wouldn't the two things get mixed up?"

"How?"

"Well, when they got a sound picture of something, how would they tell if it was the real thing or just someone talking about it?"

"Maybe they wouldn't, all of the time. Didn't guys who can fake bird calls ever fool you? But remember, their hearing's much finer tuned than ours. They can imitate the human voice, well enough to have conned some experts into thinking they could learn English, but I bet they don't fool one another that often. And they would probably have tabus against things like,

oh, making a sound-image of a killer whale without some kind
of sign that it wasn't for real."

Les wasn't convinced entirely, and nor, to tell the truth, was
I, although as things turned out, and as is maybe always the
case with another species, I had in fact wildly *under* estimated
the dolphins' capacities. Echolocation, for the stenos, was neither a random nor a continuous process. I think I mentioned
already the way they would take turns, while traveling, in
standing guard on the pod, so at any given moment any steno
knew who was liable to be echolocating and who wasn't. And
you just didn't talk and echolocate at the same time; that, in
steno circles, was about ten times as disgraceful as talking
while you are eating is in ours. Other times, when you were
hunting or in some strange or potentially dangerous situation,
your senses—if you were a steno—were totally concentrated
on your own sonar impulses coming back to you: all other
sound was damped down, just as we damp down the myriad
voices of cocktail parties and hear only that of the person we
wish to hear. But again I'm anticipating; it was to be quite a
while before I knew all of that.

I HAVE SAID nothing of Lei and Mele in all of this, which may
seem surprising. You might think, if I loved the company of
the stenos so, I would leap at the opportunity to socialize with
them while I was deprived of the company of the pod. But I
didn't. If I loved the stenos it was mostly because of what I
then perceived as their freedom—freedom from all the con-
straints of the human condition. But Lei and Mele I still saw
as captives, as victims, locked into the human world of
schedules and restrictions. I might pity them from a distance,
but to associate with them was very embarrassing for me.
There was no appropriate role I could adopt with them. There
was no way I could tell them, look, I am not like the rest of your
captors, I have gone where they dared not go, I have lived with
your people in the open ocean, I bring you messages from
them . . .

Of course, if I *had* been able to bring messages, it might have been different. But for that, I had to learn to talk myself.

The next step was so obvious that I overcame my reluctance and, the same morning I had talked to Les, went into the tanks. Blind. With the machine. That was scary. Like I said, the tanks were only four and a half feet deep. I stood up to my chest in Mele's tank, closed out the king of the senses, and let myself sink immediately. The echoes were all wrong, quite different from those in air. I froze immobile at the bottom of the tank. But I couldn't remain there, Les and Earl were watching (supposedly to lend help if anything went wrong). I began to swim. Immediately the echoes changed pitch and began to come faster. I was swimming into the wall! I changed direction, but it was the same, I was getting echoes of my echoes all around the small circular tank. I put my feet down, kept my head beneath water and made what I hoped was a 360. In one corner of the tank, I remembered, was the small wired-off enclave that housed the Last of the Turtles. I began to get a kind of mushy echo from the wire, although I still couldn't sort the turtle from the background. No matter. I now knew, by the recurrence of the turtle-pen echo, when I had completed a circuit of the tank. I came up for air, bobbed down and shuffled my feet in a circle two or three more times. Now I could make out the soft bulk of Mele drifting on the opposite side of the tank (I'd picked her tank rather than Lei's to start in because I could be reasonably sure she wouldn't interfere with me). I was gradually getting a picture of the tank and my position in it. I tried swimming again. Immediately I began to move, everything went haywire, I lost all sense of direction. I stopped again, rescanned the tank. I had to do this several more times before I could move freely; at first, like the guy who couldn't walk and chew gum, the problems of moving underwater and echolocating at the same time were too much for me. But, by the end of the morning, I was moving fast across the tank, swerving inches short of the walls.

All this time, Mele had not shown the slightest reaction to the fact that I was emitting dolphinlike sounds and behaving in a dolphinlike manner. Later on in the other tank, Lei was something else though. The moment she heard my beeping, she rushed across to me, imitating it. Or was she trying to communicate? I'll never know, because my persistence in emitting these inappropriate sounds soon seemed to drive her into a frenzy: she jabbed, bumped, snapped and swatted with her flippers, giving me so hard a time that I was forced to go back to Mele's tank to complete my training.

BY NOW, OF COURSE, Barry knew about my changed approach, although the reasons I gave him for it were rather carefully edited: nothing about speech, a great deal about "improving my understanding of the stenos by perceiving things in the way they perceive them." He was politely sceptical but not opposed. His own work had now reached a point where he was almost ready to begin the teaching of an artificial language to Lei and Mele; he was too deeply engrossed in this to have more than superficial feelings about any other work. I sensed that if the entire ocean project yielded zilch, it wouldn't worry him, as long as his own stuff was hot. But he wouldn't cut it short (it gave him an in with the services, at least) unless I did something embarrassing—like reporting the existence of dolphin language. From now on, my research would have to keep two sets of books: one for Barry's inspection, the other for my eyes only.

For my eyes only?

What about Les, who had done so much to make the project succeed? What about Keala, from whom I had few, if any, secrets?

I can't, at this stage, remember exactly when it first occurred to me that if I did indeed succeed in communicating with the stenos, I should keep this knowledge entirely to myself. The idea seemed to have sprung fully formed into my mind, perhaps in the no-man's-land between sleep and waking where so many decisions are shaped. All I know is that, once conceived, it had too great a sense of rightness to be easily abandoned. After all, I thought, it's not that I don't trust them. I knew that neither Les nor Keala would deliberately betray a confidence. But who guards his tongue well enough to guarantee that no clue, no inadvertent hint will ever slip out? Merely the suspicion of what I was doing might be sufficient to destroy it.

And the ban need not be permanent, of course. Could not be, for sooner or later Man would have to know that he was no longer the sole intelligence of his planet. But for the present, silence. Lies, even, if lies were needed. At least until I was sure.

Although I had learned already that all knowledge worth having is only gradually and painfully acquired, I still thought of that moment, the moment when I'd be certain of the truth one way or the other, as a single point of light just over the horizon of time; and the hours that divided me from that point as burdensome interruptions, to be plowed through as swiftly as I was able.

SO IT WAS, when I finally returned to the ocean, after interminable days of search to relocate my adoptive pod, that I was in a fever of impatience to begin.

I dived immediately, shut my eyes (the dark glasses, for obvious reasons, had not been incorporated into Les's latest model of the machine) and started echolocating like crazy. I was not expecting answers—the pod was, as usual, still out of range, and I had thought that if there were no solid bodies in my immediate vicinity, I'd hear no echoes at all. I was, therefore, surprised to pick up, amplified by the headset, very faint ones that seemed not to vary at all, as long as the position of my head remained constant. At first, I thought of distant objects; then realized what I was hearing was not so much an echo as a change in the resonance of my signal. If you've ever heard the differences of your own voice in a small room as against in the nave of a cathedral, you'll have some idea what I mean. Aiming downward, it was altered by passage through water of increasing density; upward, it was distorted by the turbulent interface between water and air. The world of sound was subtler than I had believed; swimming below the surface with eyes closed, I was able not merely to orient myself but also to make adjustments in my course accurate to within a few degrees. I was so fascinated with this discovery that the first hard echo came as a shock, and before I could properly read it, it was swamped in the confused stream of sound that came pouring at me from the steno pod.

I suppose only someone who has been blind from birth and then had sight given him by miraculous intervention could really understand what the next few hours were like for me. I was stumbling like an infant through an unfamiliar world: each new experience was followed so fast by another, there was no time for digestion. My memories of that time are therefore so confused that I can't hope now to reconstruct them. I was only dimly conscious of the pleasure with which I was received—of Joker leaping and slapping at me with his flippers, Sexy Susan rubbing with her beak at where she supposed my genitals might be, and even Bull, with the rather lordly and distant air he had always adopted toward me, nudging me reflectively and allowing me to pat his grizzled shoulder for a while. I could not respond with the enthusiasm I might otherwise have felt, not because of any lack of feeling—far from it!—but simply because I was so preoccupied with my own adjustment.

I'm not sure that I helped matters by starting, right from the beginning, to try to signal to them. My attention became so divided between monitoring their signals and manipulating my own that for the first few hours, days even, my senses were locked in a vertiginous kaleidoscope of impressions from which I despaired of ever drawing patterns. Psychologically, though, it was the right thing to have done. Just as in a foreign country nothing will more delight the natives than your sincere attempts, no matter how clumsy or halting, to learn their tongue, so there was no way I could have pleased the stenos more than by my attempts to communicate with them. For I had no doubts that that was how they interpreted my signals. From the moment that I began, in their hearing, to put out sounds of a kind they recognized as potentially meaningful, the whole pod went into convulsions, bunching tight together around me, leaping and slapping the water with their tailflukes. But then almost immediately they fell quiet again and swam slowly alongside me, clicking and squawking at one another as well as at me. How I wished I could have understood the smallest fraction of what they were saying! ("So the dummy finally got himself a voice" is the most charitable guess.) I clicked back at them, meaninglessly, and, as I did so, flashed on yet another dimension of the enormity of my task. Suppose you speak to a foreigner, even if you are totally ignorant of his language you at least know whether he is answering you, or merely coughing, sneezing, or laughing. But there was no way, at that stage, in which I could tell whether their responses were meaningful or were merely the steno equivalents of laughter, cries, groans or grunts of disapproval.

If you read science fiction you know how badly this side of things is usually handled. When aliens meet they usually have some machine (specs unspecified) which instantly translates their English into fluent Centaurian or Aldebaranian, or vice versa. Or they just quickly pick up a few names of familiar objects, as tourists do, and then ten times quicker than any tourist they're yakking away to six-legged unicorns or intelligent blobs of slime like interstellar Dr. Doolittles. I suppose that's understandable: they have Plots to get on with, I only have to tell you what happened to me.

But that's hard. Try and remember the stages by which you yourself learnt anything: a language, a science, a trade, even something as simple as riding a bike or swimming. I bet you can't do it. You remember the finished skill or knowledge, and that's it, it's as if the complete thing had somehow just dropped into your head. You can't for the life of you remember how come you kept falling off the bike, why the simple algebraic formula kept on eluding you. There must be some circuitry in the head that shunts such things into the cellars of memory.

And at this time, you must remember, I still did not know —I had faith but not one piece of evidence—that the stenos used language at all. And I was only too well aware, as any researcher should be, of the danger that belief might sway my judgment, and interpret data along the lines of my wish. There are no facts in nature: a fact exists only through being perceived, but if the perception is biased . . . All of this had been drummed into me by Barry and others, countless times, yet how could I, out there alone with the stenos, break the vicious circle of subjectivity?

I think it was a joke that first told me with certainty that I was right.

LIKE I SAID, I was working on the assumption that the "name" for any object was the distinctive sonar-echo it gave. So the obvious approach was to familiarize myself with as many such acoustic images as possible. Unfortunately, those first few days our environment wasn't very rich—no rocks, no ships, no more blue whales, only occasional fleeting fish and the mushy shapes of the Deep Scattering Layer—so I was reduced to practicing on members of the pod, low though the practical value of that was (you'll recall that the names of pod members were their signature-whistles rather than their acoustic shapes). However, as a five-finger exercise it was good and demanding; differences between members of the same species are so slight and subtle that once you can reliably make them, not much else should be hard for you. In the early stages, though, there was only one steno that I could consistently distinguish from the others.

Pregnant Patsy was by now very near her time. The whole rear part of her body had thickened, and not only was her shape different from that of the others, the resonance from her swelling waterbags was, even to my ears, perceptibly different from that which the firm flesh of the other stenos gave. I worked on these differences until, with eyes closed, I could identify her ten times out of ten. Had I been less sure of this, I might have been ready to dismiss what happened as mere wishful thinking.

One day, milling slowly in the dawn water (I think on the second trip of that second tour) I found myself swimming alongside Duke and Susan. They were engaged in what I could swear was conversation: one would send out a string of clicks, punctuated by whistles, and then stop, and the other would seem to answer. Suddenly, after a brief silence, Duke gave a truncated version of Susan's signature-whistle, followed immediately by the peculiar click-train that was Patsy's acoustic image. Quick as a flash, and long before I could grasp the reason, Susan rolled over and bit fiercely at Duke's face, forcing him to take violent evasive action. At the same moment, Mojo, who was swimming nearby, and who had begun, I'd noticed, to free himself from Bull's dominion and develop a personality of his own, repeated an identical sequence of sounds, and Susan, lashing the water, turned on him in equal fury. And only then did I get it.

"Susan, you're pregnant!"

That must have been what Duke had said. And since it wasn't true and since everyone must have known it wasn't true, the whole pod was now cracking up, pouting out chirping, snorting sounds that could only be their laughter.

I wish I could report that from then on it was all plain sailing. In fact, it was days before I could even tentatively identify another utterance; many times in the frustrations of those days I had cause to doubt my own discovery, and wonder whether, after all, my imagination had tricked me. Besides, other and more urgent events were taking place.

First came the Storm. It began to build up on the evening of Duke's joke, and although I'd been with them, this time, little more than twenty-four hours, I ought to have read the signs early and called Sam for a pickup. I didn't. I felt on the brink of discovery; any moment the whole code might unfold; it was not so much that I said, ah, fuck the Storm, I'll take my chances—I would never have been that foolish—as that my obsession with my discovery made me systematically downplay and misinterpret the obvious warnings of sea and sky. No, it would be nothing much, no, it would blow over—and by the time I could no longer fool myself, it was too late and too dark and too wild to even think of calling for help.

I had never been out in the ocean under really bad conditions. I had been pulled out in time, or I had gone back into the aftermath of storms, but never the real thing, for there was some doubt whether I would be able to survive that. That, like the pitcher at the well, I'd sooner or later get caught, if I kept on long enough, was something I guess I and my handlers had always known at the back of our minds, but had preferred not to think too closely about. But now it was here.

If you could only go down and stay down, the maddest storm that ever shook the waters would be no sweat to you. Only the surface is enraged: twenty feet under, all is calm. But if you are an air-breather, you cannot stay under. Not for long. You have to surface into the heart of the turmoil.

The onset of the Storm was not truly gradual; it came about in a series of sharp increments. Going on toward dark, I was thinking, well; it isn't getting any worse; if it gets no worse than this, I can weather it; and then between one descent and the next rise, no more than a minute apart, the sea in the faint last light had risen in torment and slammed me with an avalanche of white-veined black water as I rose, sending me helpless for a dozen yards or more before I could force myself beneath it. I knew then that I could never make it, even if it got no worse; it would have to abate from that peak, if I were to live through the night. But it did not abate. For an hour or two it remained more or less constant, although it felt worse, being quite dark by then, so that, battered though I was, I caught some kind of second wind, and began to hope that after all I might succeed in enduring it. But then again, quite suddenly, almost incredibly (for I could not easily have imagined any further increase in the sea's violence) a mountain of water came crashing down on me as I surfaced, almost before I had had time to draw air, all but stunning me; and then I was really finally afraid, seeing my own extinction now only minutes away from me, and nothing (that was the worst part of it) nothing I could hope to do in order to save myself.

The stenos, too, were in the same plight as myself, but with infinitely greater reserves of strength to withstand it. With greater skills, too. Rising as smoothly and inexorably as submarines with blown tanks, they breached every time out of the back of a receding wave, just ahead of the trough, and were down again before the next could break over them. I don't quite know how I learned this, not being able to see more than inches in front of me, whether above or below the surface, but I did, and I think it was because, quite unconsciously, and in a halting manner, I had begun to read the sound patterns of the waves, just as they did. You could tell your depth from the time sounds took to bounce back off the interface of air and water; a long time meant the crest was directly over you, a short time, the trough. Time your breathing right and you surfaced at the point of least turbulence. That knowledge carried me through to the Storm's next increment, which may have been at midnight, give or take a couple of hours. But after that, the seas lost all shape, waves were hammered flat by the force of the wind and waters surged every which way; there was no longer a place of least turbulence to aim for. After that, it was a matter of strength alone.

They say drowning is the pleasantest of deaths; I don't know on what evidence: all I experienced was the terror and desperation of a trapped animal as I felt the last reserves of strength pouring out of me, knowing that the next time I surfaced would be the last, or the next to last. My life did not pass before my eyes. Whimpering in animal wretchedness I let the last energy flow from me, as it clearly wished to do, and merge its pitiful drop with the power that was engulfing me . . .

I would have died then and there, but for the stenos. They bore me up, even as I lay almost unconscious, taking turns, two and two; in staggered formation, one slightly ahead of the other, one left and one right flipper extended so I would not slide between them; bodies pressed either side of mine, sandwiching it into place, and the beak of the hindmost poised to prod me back into consciousness. I believed it was all a dream, at first. I was dreaming an interesting dream, which I would relate to Keala when I woke—quite soon, surely—a dream in which I had been at sea, in a storm, drowning, and dolphins had borne me up, not as in classical legend, singly, but two at a time, inflation having touched even this, no doubt. But how to get this clever insight into my dissertation? Dreams are not scientific evidence. In the waking state that I dreamed succeeded my dream, I cast around for expedients, and decided that a footnote, "personal communication, R. Moore, research mistress," would constitute adequate documentation. Then, obligingly, as if to confirm itself, the dream repeated. More vividly. Until I could no longer even pretend to distinguish reality from dream.

In fact they supported me through all that was left of that night and through the next day and much of the night that followed it, until the seas began to go down. At least, that is what I assume they did. My memories here are as reliable as those of high fever, but they must have done, or how could I have survived, for more than thirty hours, a storm that sank a cargo boat of eleven thousand tons?

Aboard the *Farquarson,* I was given up for lost. When my signal began to come through, on the third day, they would have liked to attribute it to some hardware malfunction. And afterward, when my miraculous return could no longer be questioned, the Raincheck Smiles grew brighter and more empty, the movements more deferential yet swifter, as if the temperature around me had dropped several degrees and they couldn't get away from me quickly enough. It was a long time before I recognized their reaction for what it was, it seemed to me such an absurd one. It was fear. As if I owed my survival, not to a social gesture of intelligent beings, but to the intervention of some diabolic power. I'm sure they never put it quite like that. They prided themselves on their hard-headed realism. Yet they felt there must be *something* pretty weird about me, and that it would not hurt to keep their distance.

AFTER THE STORM, the Birth.

No sooner had I rejoined the stenos than I became aware of strange new vibes. Movements had become more jerky and erratic; there was an air of tension. As we headed for the night's feeding ground, the formation tightened, and sonar-bursts from the flanking stenos grew more rapid and more frequent. Hester the Handmaiden pressed close up against Patsy, nuzzling her belly, pressing against it with her head. Suddenly, darkish fluids were expelled from Patsy's vent, and then, almost immediately, a pair of tiny flukes extruded. They waved limply, like a frond of seaweed. Hester continued to press hard from beneath. Gradually the body oozed out, and at last the head freed itself, followed by the coiled umbilical and the bloody mass of the afterbirth, which drifted away on the current. Hester snapped the umbilical with her beak, swung her head under the baby's body and hoisted it to the surface. There, it breathed feebly, and flickered into consciousness, feebly stirring flippers and tail. Hester guided it down, and pressed it against its mother's side; Patsy held it in place there with her left flipper, surfacing to breathe, then rolled onto her right side so the baby could breathe too. The baby stirred restlessly, as if seeking for something it knew it had to do; then nuzzled its way down to her teat and clung there, pumping milk into its beak.

Suddenly hard echoes were coming back from the flanker's sonar barrage. Something was out there. An alarm whistle went off. Tailflukes began to beat rhythmically, the pod picked up speed. I did not need telling what must have happened: sharks had smelled the blood of the afterbirth in the water.

Until that time, except for the cookie-cutters, we had not been troubled by sharks. Sharks aren't the vindictive creatures of our paranoid imaginations. Like other creatures, they attack only when they're hungry or if you provoke them. Even then, they figure the odds rather carefully. We'd seen them, a number of times, but merely sonar-scanned them and hurried on by, and only once one had trailed us, for maybe a mile, in the hope perhaps that some weaker member would drop out. But this one was more persistent. One? No, the echoes were coming from at least two directions. The stenos picked up more speed. It wouldn't worry them if there was more than one. They could outswim any shark; it was only if surprised, trapped or outnumbered that they were in trouble.

But I couldn't outswim any shark.

Already they were pulling away from me, and I was swimming at top speed and powering myself with the booster unit too. I had nothing left. Nothing except, of course, the CO_2 gun. So much had I grown into the habit patterns of dolphins that I truly never remembered this most human of solutions until the first of the creatures was, quite literally, breathing down my neck. I rolled over, and beheld a tiger shark, full-grown, not far short of twice my size. Lucky for me their first pass is an exploratory one, or he could have taken a limb right there. As it was, he glided by within feet of me, and by the time he'd turned and come in again, I had the gun aimed at him.

Sharks are unusual among fish in that they have no form of swim bladder. This means they literally cannot float; if they stop moving, even for seconds, they will begin to sink toward the bottom. But if you shoot a gas cartridge in them, the gas expands into their internal cavities and draws them upward, they struggle to counterbalance it, lose all control over direction and wind up rolling around helplessly—at least that's what the makers claim. And that's what happened, the first time. I got a direct hit just aft of the gills, no special achievement at a range of twenty feet. The shark did not undergo any dramatic change; its rush just carried it three feet above me instead of right on top of me as it had doubtless planned. It circled, but its circle too was out of whack. Try as it would, it could no longer go where it intended to go. And its pea-sized brain just wasn't equipped to handle crises of this kind. Within a minute it had gone bananas—lunging blindly this way and that, twisting and snapping at its own rebellious flesh, thoughts of dinner no longer on its mind.

But that didn't necessarily go for its two buddies.

They had materialized about eighty degrees apart, and the first thing they did was to increase that distance, as if to ensure that I couldn't keep them simultaneously in view. For the moment that was their only move. They were evaluating the situation. The behavior of their partner was a disturbing factor.

Go on, go for *him,* tear him apart, I mentally urged them as I rearmed the gun; that was what sharks were supposed to do, savage their own maimed kind, in the best adventure books. But they stubbornly refused to do this. They were more interested in me, they watched, curious, as I darted from side to side, trying to ensure that neither of them took me from the rear.

This time I didn't wait for them to attack. I was in fighting form now, all imbued with the spirit of my species: Get Them Before They Get You! I fired. And the goddamn thing didn't work.

Sure, the human way's fine, but the bugs are never completely ironed out of it, and when it blows, you're left with a lot of nothing in your hands.

I fiddled desperately to unjam the gun. That meant I took my eyes off the sharks. I doubt they had the wit to realize what was happening, but they must have sensed my attention lay elsewhere. When I looked up, they were both of them coming in fast.

There flashed through my mind something Walter Kealoha used to say to me: "You no watch om, you gon' end up sharkshit, Andy." And that was the truth: I had the sickening image, that was to haunt my dreams on many subsequent nights, of my head, arms and torso still swimming frantically upward while legs and guts were already in the monsters' maws, and of my mind knowing this for the interminable second before trauma shorted out the brain. Like the first shark's, my bodily mechanisms refused to obey me; the cerebral cortex shouted for rapid evasion, but the nerves, mutinous, froze me where I hung, just under the surface, clutching my useless weapon. Even my eyes were closed. If it was inevitable, I could at least spare myself the sight of it.

So it was that I didn't see Bull's first charge. I only felt it, felt the surge of water buffet me aside, thought incredulously, "they've missed again—both of them!?" and blinked open my eyes to make sure. By then already the whole scene had changed. Half the pod was swinging into action behind their leader; the wounded shark was drifting down and away; one of the others was already in full flight; while the third, perhaps feeling itself surrounded, was fighting back.

It was a short and unequal fight. The stenos slammed into it full force, one after another, their bodies driving their bills like a hammer drives a nail; you could see the shark jolt from each shock even as it continued to writhe, with eel-like agility, and slash back at its attackers with sickle jaws. But no creature could take such punishment for long. It bled from a dozen puncture wounds. Its movements were slower, weaker. They were beneath it now, forcing it upward, thrusting it out of the water—not, as they had done with me, to save life, but to destroy it, for sharks, like other fish, can breathe only in water; they were drowning it in air.

It convulsed a couple or three times and then went limp, and they dropped it. Stopped, immobile, it drifted downward into the darkness beneath.

I thought for a moment that we had all come through unscathed. Then I saw that Joker was wounded, a ragged hole in his back, just to the rear of his blowhole. It looked ugly enough, but I expected, or hoped, that over the days to come it would heal into one of those many scars that marked the older stenos. For some reason, it did not. Over the days, I grew so absorbed in my search for the secrets of their tongue that I did not, at first, notice the change in him. He no longer clowned and teased the others. His movements had grown listless, perfunctory. He swam slowly at the rear of the pod, the wound raw and open, its edges festering. Soon he ceased even to dive for food. The others fed him. Restricted in its movements, the pod no longer met with other pods for the daytime sleep. Its activities were centering more and more on its injured member.

When the time came for me to leave again, I knew that he was dying.

"WHAT AM I to do, Sam?" I asked.

Sam, as always when asked a direct question, took God's

own good time in replying to it. The skin above his nose wrinkled and his nostrils flared. He was studying hard. "You see, it's all my fault," I went on, too impatient to wait for him, "if it hadn't been for me, they'd just have swum away from the sharks, he wouldn't have been hurt. He got hurt saving me. And they saved me before, in the Storm, so am I just to leave one of them now, now it's time to repay the debt?"

Sam grunted, not answering the first question, merely noting this addition to it. "But then," I went on, "if I do anything, I blow my cover. Not that I give a damn about that, really, not against a life. But my whole relationship with them changes. I came to learn from them. Then all of a sudden I revert to the god, the healer. That's how all missionaries start, Sam. Not Preaching the Word. Healing the Sick. Something so sincere nobody can quarrel with it, and yet there it is, the thin end of the wedge that'll smash their world to matchwood. Manipulation. That's the name of the game. And I don't want to start down *that* route, even for the most exalted of reasons."

I had thought this argument would surely appeal to Sam, whose ancestors had defied in arms the might of Church and State combined. I forgot his rearing in fundamentalist religion. He rolled his eyes at me.

"You do just what you conscience tell you."

"It doesn't tell me anything, that's the trouble."

Sam snorted. "If you conscience don't tell you whuffo do," he said, "then don't do nothing."

"No," I said, knowing instantly. "That was a lie, Sam. It does tell me."

"Then go do it, boy, what you waste me time for?"

RIGHT AFTER the medics were through with me, this time, I requested an audience with the Captain. Simply and straightforwardly I laid out the situation. A launch could be dispatched, Joker netted and raised aboard it, he could be brought back to the ship, where a small holding tank could be erected, and shot full of antibiotics; subsequently, restored to health, we would return him to his grateful pod. The Captain listened with interest and, I thought, a perceptible lifting of the unease my presence had provoked ever since the Storm incident; here, look, I was no child of the devil, but a human being with all the warm, caring human responses. Therefore it came as a blow in the face when, at the finish, he shook his head and said, "No."

"But why not?"

"Logistics."

"There's nothing I said that we can't do!"

"Right. But not at the price it would cost. Not for just one dolphin. Look, what was the pod's last position, two hundred and fifty miles from here?"

"Nearer three hundred."

"That's a full day's sail in the launch. Two days' fuel. Four or five personnel tied up that long. Plus whatever effort was needed back here. More personnel tied up. Space. Space is at a premium. Where would you put a holding tank? And that's assuming you catch him. Dolphin's aren't that easy to catch."

"You wouldn't need to. I'd talk him into the net."

The Captain smiled. "Maybe. Maybe not. Even if it was a certainty I wouldn't feel able to authorize it."

But they'll be eternally in your debt, I thought. You'll have enslaved them a little. Isn't it worth it even for that, to enslave them a little?

"If it was necessary for your research . . ."

"No," I said automatically, then kicked myself, I should have said yes, then realized this too would have been futile: I'd have had to justify in detail. You could not talk to these stone faces about blood debts.

"I'm sorry then," he said. He wasn't in the least sorry. What he meant was, "It's not my fault, don't blame me, it's Vast Forces Outside of our Control." I'd have told him go fuck himself, if surprise had not so deflated me. It was ironic. There I was with all my qualms about manipulation, and for once the good old manipulators had refused to manipulate. Even when they had the technology, the motivation . . . but not, apparently, the money. That, after all, when you came to think of it, was typical. There was always something missing. Something that stopped the human solution from solving anything. It might be in the will or it might be in the works, like with my gun that didn't work when I needed it, but it was always the same with human solutions, they promised paradise and delivered shit. Then explained that shit was near enough paradise, if you had the gall to complain about it.

SO I WAS FORCED to be Mature, Responsible and Detached, in spite of myself.

Meanwhile, the pod had continued to move further and further away from the *Farquarson,* at a rate that made me think Joker must after all have recovered. When I rejoined them I saw how wrong I was. The others were taking turns to support him, in pairs, as they had done with me. All the time they were swimming steadily northeast, with some purpose, I felt sure, but one of which I remained in total ignorance.

I took my turn in helping to bear him along. It was the least I could do.

On the third day I began to hear unusual echoes coming from ahead of us, echoes that suggested some object much larger than any we had hitherto encountered. A ship? Another whale? Surfacing to breathe, I was amazed to see a white line of breaking surf.

Amazed, because the charts showed no land of any kind for hundreds of miles—no island, not even a reef or shoal. Yet there it was, a dark spine of rock, a few dozen yards long, a few feet above the waves, too new to have acquired even a blade of vegetation. The stenos swam toward it, uttering keening cries. Among the sounds they repeated over and over was one I didn't recognize until long afterward, when we met a shark, maddened by injury or disease, which tried constantly to bite its own tail: the acoustic image of a creature bent in a circle, end meeting end. Then Patsy and Mojo, who at that time were supporting Joker, drew away from him, and baby, who'd been swimming patiently in Patsy's wake, moved up to nuzzle her teats. Joker, swimming feebly, approached the narrow strip of detritus—you could hardly call it a beach—that had formed on the lee shore of the island's tip.

It was broad day, but a high, still ceiling of cloud gave a somber, northern aspect to the scene. Joker swam onto the desolate beach and grounded there. The pod swam to and fro offshore, and continued to call out, as if to comfort him. He himself remained motionless except for a kind of shuddering of his flesh around the blowhole. Dolphins on land die quickly from dehydration, and the kindly people who carry them back to the sea are saddened and puzzled when they immediately ground themselves again.

After a while, Hester, Susan and the Loving Couple began to surf the break where the northwesterly swells wrapped themselves around the island. From time to time, others would change places with them, so that there was always a small group holding vigil with Joker in the little bay. At first it struck me as indescribably callous of them to seek their own pleasure while Joker was dying. Later I understood their wisdom. They knew it wasn't their fault that Joker was dying and that there was nothing they could do for him, except comfort him with their presence. So, if they could surf and be present at the same time, why not? They did not visit there often, and it was a beautiful wave, hollow and glassy, breaking six to eight. You could get tubed in it, which is not easy to do, body surfing, unless the wave has near-perfect form. The way I know that is because eventually I joined them. I didn't want to. They nagged and chivvied at me until I did. But afterward I was glad. The clouds began to break up near sunset, and the sun's almost level rays turned the curl of the wave into a tunnel of iridescent green, down which we slid on our bellies with the thunder of the wave's breaking right in back of us. It was so lovely, I almost forgot about Joker. Almost, but never quite.

I think it was while we were still surfing that he completed the circle of his life, from darkness into darkness, and also the circle of his race, that had come from the land so long ago and now, in his person, returned to it. There was no change you could point to in his body, yet already it looked shrunken and disused. We turned south. Our numbers were now the same as when I had joined the pod—fifteen; only its composition had changed, having gained one member and lost one. A time would come when every member who now swam with me had gone, yet the pod would still exist, an organism greater than the parts that composed it. Perhaps it had existed before the first Pyramids were raised. Perhaps it would still exist when our species had perished, self-destroyed. Or rather, might have—if we hadn't destroyed it first.

THE EXISTENCE of the island is not so surprising, really. The sea in that region is not deep, as the Pacific goes, and its floor is studded with seamounts, knobs of old volcanic rock that reach sometimes to within a thousand feet of the surface. It would need no very great upheaval for one of these to emerge, briefly, before the sea set to work to destroy it again. Such processes must happen over and over without us knowing. Certainly the crew of the *Farquarson,* though Survey was the name of their game, knew nothing about it, and I took care that they should remain in ignorance. When they started telling me about dolphin communication it would be time to tell them about seamounts. Meanwhile, I added it to the growing list of private knowledge. I had no prescience, then, of the role it would play later in my affairs.

MEANTIME I WAS painfully acquiring what I thought were the rudiments of their language.

Now here, right away, I am on difficult ground. Rather like that of the guru who comes back from his psychedelic trip and says, "I have found out the secret of the universe." "What is it, what is it?" cry his eager disciples. "You cannot hope to understand it, my children," he tells them, "until you have experienced all that I have experienced. And then, of course, explanation will be superfluous."

I will try to be more helpful than that. What complicates matters is that, first, I only ever understood a small fraction of it, and second, the part that I did understand was by no means the most remarkable and important part. In fact, I didn't even know there was more of it, at this stage. So I'll content myself, for the moment, with the first things I learned.

One thing that threw me was that there were no nouns, as we know them. No names even for the classes or the species that they met with most often. No equivalent for "squid," say. In a human language, "squid" covers everything from monsters of the deep with arms forty feet long to the near-microscopic transparencies that the stenos scooped from the Deep Scattering Layer—anything with tentacles that isn't an octopus. General, then, if somewhat vague. The stenos had nothing like it. If they wanted to talk about a squid, they would project the exact sound-image of the squid they were talking about. There was no way in which they could say, for example, "All squids are invertebrates." In short, they could not generalize.

At first sight you might think that that was a crippling defect. Remember your Logic 101. "All Spartans are brave; Epaminondas is a Spartan; therefore, Epaminondas is brave." The power to generalize is the cornerstone of all thinking. Well, all *human* thinking. But the stenos weren't human and they didn't think human.

Why, after all, would a species need to say things like "All Spartans are brave" or "All squids are invertebrates"? You didn't have to say such things in order to know them. Any steno must know that all squids were invertebrates, because in not one of the thousands he'd scanned or had imaged to him had he detected the least echo of bone. The only reason you needed to say them was if you were parceling out the world, putting everything into its pigeonhole—the vertebrates here, the invertebrates over there—so it would be ready to be manipulated. For that was all our Science was, really. It masqueraded as a Quest for Knowledge but that Knowledge was just a blueprint for Manipulation. For making over God's Creation to what we thought was our better liking.

Dolphins didn't have nimble hands and busy fingers to make over God's Creation with. So they had no need of that kind of thinking or that kind of language. It was as simple as that.

They didn't have any verbs, either. They didn't need to. If you can project the sound-image of a squid receding, why would you need to say "The squid left"? Likewise they didn't need adjectives. They didn't need to say "a big squid" or "a small squid" when they could just show you the exact size of the squid. You might think this would lead to trouble when you got to abstract concepts, but it didn't. Like, one of the earliest things I learned was how to say, "I am satisfied," or "I am happy"—tell me the difference, without splitting hairs, if you can—which was to make your own signature-whistle and, at the same time, project the image of a dolphin with a bellyful of fish. In the same way, if you wanted to say that you weren't satisfied, you projected a dolphin with an empty belly.

And, if you're thinking such remarks could get mixed up with "I'm hungry" or "I'm stuffed," you're forgetting that the stenos could monitor one another's internal states and therefore knew in a flash whether the remark was meant literally or otherwise. For that's another way in which steno language differed from human language. You couldn't lie in it. At least, not about your feelings. You couldn't say you liked someone when you didn't or that you were contented when in reality you were madder than hell. Or, well, you could *say* these things, but everyone would know they were not true, so if you did say them they would be understood as a joke, like Duke's remark about Susan being pregnant.

But what I was still missing (though I didn't know it at the time) was the real purpose of their talk. When humans talk, it is true, it may often be to lie, or to bluff, or to put the other person down, or just to fill a social space, but there is always some communicative content. I know people will tell you that that isn't so, that when we say to someone, "Hi, what a nice day!" what we probably really mean is something like "Hey, you look like a real neat kind of person, gee, I'd like to get to know you better." True, as far as it goes. And true that the other person can see it's a nice day as well as we can, so we're not exactly adding anything to his world view. But it's also true that what we said communicates a fact about the day, and there is nothing we can legitimately say that doesn't equally contain some such fact: if we go around saying "ooga booga" to people we may be conveying nonfactual emotional states but we'll pretty soon wind up in the funny farm.

So naturally I was looking for a certain kind of content in all that the stenos said to one another and, when I failed to find it, attributed this simply to my continuing ignorance of their infinite stock of images. In which, as you will learn shortly, I was completely wrong.

MEANWHILE MY LEAPING improved, as did my diving. Under full booster power I could now breach my own height out of the water, which meant that if I drew my knees up and curled my mermaid tail at the moment of breaking surface, I became entirely airborne for a fraction of a second. That sounds like no big deal—anyone can jump higher than that, on land. But the difference between jumping from a solid surface and soaring from water into air is as great as . . . well, that between land and water. In the one, you thrust your soles against the flat of the earth, it's all conflict, striving; in the other, you have to flow cleanly and mold yourself to the elements. In the one, you feel all the time the stress of your muscles forcing you one way and gravity the other; but in the other, you float, for that fraction of a second, weightless, or so it seems.

Diving, I still could not reach far into the Deep Scattering Layer, but I could with ease plunge to the daytime schools of small fishes that the tuna preyed on. The stenos, like all dolphins, were always on the watch for tuna schools, knowing that where tuna are found there will be rich and easy hunting; they would spot a tuna school at maybe thirty or forty feet down and come in on them like dive bombers, snatching fish out of the tunas' mouths. But that was dangerous. That was how they got caught by purse-seiners. Just as the tuna showed the dolphins where the small fish were, so the dolphins showed the purse-seiners where the tuna were; they would watch from the masthead for the telltale swirls of dolphins breaching, some of the bigger operators would even put up helicopters to spot them with. Then they would encircle pod and tuna school both with their giant seine, and pull it in. There is a maneuver known in the trade as "backing down" which they can carry out, which (always in theory and sometimes in practice) enables the dolphins to escape the net. But it takes time, time they could use in bagging this tuna school and hurrying on to the next. It's more cost-effective to pull the dolphins in with the tuna, club them and throw them overboard. A practice circumscribed by law for U. S. seiners (who were told by Congress, no less, just how many dolphins a year it was okay to kill) but free for those who sailed under some other flags. And even more cost-effective (it was being whispered around in ecological circles, though no more than rumors had so far surfaced) to process the dolphins too and market them in areas where people could not afford to be fussy about what they ate. But that was still unconfirmed. All I knew for sure was that if I dived into tuna schools without first carefully checking the horizon, I might wind up in a rather unusual confrontation with those of my own kind.

And just what would I do if they then said, "Okay, fella, don't worry, you'll be alright; all humans are valuable; all animals are expendable; step this way and have a grog with the skipper while we dispense with these obstacles to commerce and progress"?

What, indeed, would I do?

Meantime I tried to explain to the stenos the risks they ran with tuna. I knew the kind of echo a boat's hull made, because I'd been down off the *Farquarson,* and had learnt it, and learnt to reproduce it, given the limitations of my apparatus, as clumsily no doubt as some Russian or Japanese might reproduce an English word he'd gotten out of a dictionary. They recognized it at once—far quicker, I thought, than we would have recognized some foreigner's mangling of our own words. I was ready, at this stage, to attribute to them, almost like Frank, nearly any powers in excess of ours. But I want to make quite clear that this was wrong, that they were not necessarily better than us—merely different. It followed from the nature of their language that they would understand: if you have ever struggled, and failed, to understand a small child's speech, and yet immediately understood his drawings, no matter how crude or distorted they might be, you will see what I mean. When Duke —who was the first I tried it on—signaled his understanding, I followed up with an image of a tuna, and then a dolphin, lying motionless, dead, and then boat, tuna and dolphin over again. I suppose it was childish of me to think they would understand. I did not know how to link the images together, and indeed, I suspect there was no way I could have linked them to give the meaning I wanted; to do that, I think now, I would have to have played the whole scene, as if on a recording machine, the ship first far then near, the circling and shooting of the net, the thunder of the winches, the growing medley of echoes as dolphin and tuna were forced closer and closer within the net, mounting gradually to a hysteria of sound . . .

And it would not have been new to them. Other stenos, who had escaped when the net was backed down, must have played that scene over many times. And it had made no difference. They continued to hunt the tuna schools. In humans, you would call that blind, ignorant folly. In them . . . I don't know. I was to learn, before the end, that they looked on life and death differently from the way we do. For now, that is all I can say.

RIGHT AROUND that time things were beginning to come to a head, forgive the pun, with Susan.

And here, maybe, I come to an even more awkward part of the story. I guess most of you will have read, some time or other, one of those book reviews that congratulates the author on his "delicate treatment" of incest, or foot-fetishism, or necrophilia, or whatever. But, I ask you, how are you ever going to have a "delicate treatment" of bestiality—last of sex practices to come out of the closet? It's unthinkable: not because bestiality is somehow specially obscene, but rather because it, and everything connected with it, seems to be hilariously ridiculous. One thinks immediately of the Basque shepherd counting his sheep, "One, two, three, hello darling, five, six . . ." Traditionally only cretins, sickies and folks gone nutty with lonesomeness would break the species barrier in this particular sphere.

I was raised in such belief, shared it, and for a long time it controlled my behavior. It made sense, from my angle. What was so bad about sex with animals was not so much some Mosaic tabu as the elements of coercion and exploitation in it. Just another use of creation for selfish purposes. But here, things were a little different. First, here were creatures intelligent as I, albeit in a wholly different way. Second, I was far from being the instigator. Susan took that honor. She was continually probing my groin with her beak, or trying to maneuver her ventral slit so that it would rub against me. And I got turned on by her. If you think that's weird, put yourself in my place: an active heterosexual, only just past the eighteen-year-old peak of my powers, away from females of my own kind for months at a time. I should have stayed faithful to Keala? Ah, come on! I was never all that faithful at the best of times, and somehow, with another species, it didn't seem to count.

But before I could finally weaken, the unthinkable intervened.

ALWAYS, TO ME, the most scary part of the whole business was the hours when, separated from the pod, I awaited my pickup. It wasn't merely a question of wondering what would happen to me if, for some reason, the *Farquarson* did not receive my call. It was also the fact that, alone, I was ten times more vulnerable to any predator. Naturally, when I thought of predators, I thought mainly of sharks. But the one that finally found me was vaster and more terrible than any shark.

I didn't see it till it was less than a city block from me, coming out of the face of a swell like some apparition from a nightmare: nearly thirty feet long and a third of that in height, black on its smooth upper surface and white beneath. *Orcinus orca,* the killer whale. Its mouth opened, and my blood congealed. The opening was like the entrance to a mine tunnel, only packed all around with huge ivory wedges of teeth.

It was shortly after dawn, with seas running high already as the weather worsened. I had had my beacon out for over an hour, burbling away from its balloon overhead, but there was no knowing how long it would be before help would reach me. I froze. There was nothing else left to do. Flight would have been futile. To fire at it with my CO_2 gun—even assuming the thing worked—would merely have driven it to a fury. All I could do was pray that the folklore was correct.

The folklore claimed there were no recorded cases of a killer whale attacking man. And it interpreted this fact, if fact it was, as a sign that Orca, being highly intelligent himself, automatically recognized the King of All the Species and treated him with appropriate deference. I could think of a better explanation. We only know of shark attacks because of the botched jobs, the swimmers who, mangled or merely scared, succeed in getting away. But who would get away from this monster? He wouldn't take just an arm or a leg; he was big enough to swallow you at a single gulp.

True, orcas have been captured, even tamed; Shamu the Friendly Killer has probably gamboled across your own TV screen; but that means nothing. Like I said about sharks, there aren't Nice and Nasty brands of carnivores, just replete and hungry ones. And this one looked real hungry. And even if, as Man, I did enjoy some special immunity, I was unlikely to use it now, since in my suit I looked more like a dolphin than a man.

Once they took thirteen dead dolphins from a killer whale's stomach.

In the time it took to think all this, the thing submerged, and swam around me with a kind of leisurely vigor. Sudden bursts of sound told me it was reading me on its sonar as well as watching me through small, shrewd eyes. Eyes so unlike a shark's. Eyes with the curiosity and intelligence of a creature perhaps my equal in brain power, perhaps my superior. Then it lunged.

I made no conscious effort to dodge it. Terror had burned out my neural circuiting like a power overload burns out an electric motor. All I knew was I was unexpectedly alive and floundering on the surface while my balloon with its radio beacon sailed away downwind. The creature's teeth must have sheared its anchoring wire.

It surfaced alongside. Glided abreast of me. And with a relaxed confidence more frightening than the most furious assault, slid in front of me and opened its jaws. I went down, under its belly; my back grazed its belly (it was very firm and smooth). And an incredulous hope was born in me. I had evaded it. Twice.

Evaded? A man lashed to a railroad tie would have as much chance of evading a locomotive. If it hadn't taken me, it was because it didn't want to take me. Yet. But it had all the time in the world. I was a novelty, a new toy. It was playing with me, as a cat plays with a mouse.

A cat plays with a mouse as long as it's fun. As long as the mouse squeaks, leaps, runs and does other interesting behaviors. When it goes limp the cat kills it. So I behaved. I screamed, I waved my arms, I beat the water with my tail, I bounced up and down. Interested, it circled. Then it made a third pass.

What was most awful, awful beyond any fear, was knowing that if anyone had come and said, "Do X and I will make the whale go away," I'd have done it. Whatever X was. Killed, tortured, betrayed. And embraced the one who demanded it as my deliverer. When you've known fear like that, you're never quite the same again. And there was no rational basis for it. What faced me wasn't a bad death as deaths go. Instantaneous extinction in that tunnel. Better than a shark mangling me. And at least I'd have been killed by an intelligent creature rather than some mud-brained automaton.

I don't know how long this lasted. Time had become a piece of elastic, to be stretched or shrunk as the whale pleased. I never heard Sam until he was almost on us. The Fightin' Seminole came in at wave-top height, downdraft from the rotor blades lashing the waves to foam, and then he was *below the crest,* I saw to my horror the waveface hanging level with the cabin, then he saw it too and lifted with only inches to spare, white water running through the skids and the engine screaming, all but stalling out, then pulling away sluggishly like a spoon from a honeypot. Away he went, under full power as the engine caught, skittering away over the waves, he was giving up, he was leaving me there, I shrieked, knowing he could not hear, but shrieking nevertheless, right out of control.

The whale, amazed, had plunged under the surface. Now it breached again, high, rolling its head—and Sam turned, he had the chopper under control again, he came straight down on the creature as if he would land on its head, then he veered toward me and the rope ladder came snaking out at me, I grabbed it, he didn't stop, I was dragged along, clean through a wave, another, another . . . Just as I thought I could hold on no longer he stopped, hovered as low as he dared, and with the last of my strength I drew myself up.

He was grinning all over his big face.

"I ought to left you there that time," he said.

I said nothing. I was vomiting out of the side of the cabin.

"Cause why?" he asked. "Cause Jonah!" he answered himself. "You was like to gone and relive biblical history. Prove that Bible story true. I tell you, man, when I see you down there, cain't believe my eyes, look like you waltzin' with that big bad motherfucker!"

"I'm not going back, Sam," I said.

"What that you say?"

"That was worse than anything. The storms, the sharks, anything. I'm not going back. Not unless they can give me something to take care of it."

Sam pursed his lips. "Ain't no way they can do that."

"How come?"

"That there was Leviathan. Ain't nothin' nobody cain't do about Leviathan."

Like I said, you never knew with Sam whether he was serious or not. Whether he believed what he said or whether it was an elaborate charade he sat back licking his lips and laughing at somewhere inside him. But, like most times, I went along with him. After all, but for him I wouldn't have been there.

"He's only flesh and blood, Sam," I said.

"Flesh and blood, sure. But he the most strongest flesh and blood that *be!* An' if they give you something to take care of him, you got to be stronger. You got to be the King of the Sea!"

He looked at me long and searchingly.

"And that ain't right! No, that ain't right nohow!"

WHETHER OR NOT it would reverse the natural order of things, I was adamant. The Captain relayed my position to his, and my, superiors, while I played more chess with my ill-shaven aide, listened to acid-rock tapes, and dreamed of strange minglings and matings in blue waters. Eventually, just when everyone was getting a little tired of my feet-on-the-table posture, orders came: I was to report forthwith to Lompoc in Southern California.

From Lompoc, I was taken to an unknown destination. I really mean that: no one told me where it was, and as I arrived at night by water and left at night by air, I really cannot say myself. There, I was submitted to days of testing, psychological as well as physical. It dawned on me, slowly—never having been drafted, the ways of the military mind were inscrutable to me—that all of this probably had nothing at all to do with my civil disobedience but had merely happened to coincide with it.

Fortunately, there were those there who were not entirely strangers. On the fifth day, the skull-faced spook who'd first interviewed Les and me in Honolulu showed up.

I knew better than to repeat my performance—it would smack of desertion-in-the-face-of-the-enemy to his ears. I simply told him what had happened, and asked if there wasn't, maybe, some up-to-the-minute gadgetry his secret arsenals could supply.

The Skull thought for a while, probably going over all the security regulations he might be breaching.

"Affirmative," he finally said (they really do talk that way) and I was just about to bust out and congratulate myself when I realized all he had said was, yes, they could supply such a thing, and not that they would supply it to me.

That took another hard half-hour's talking. It wasn't my own skin I talked of, naturally. Being eaten by a whale was all in the day's work. But look how valuable to the Nation this poor carcass must be if they were ready to spend a week and X thousands of dollars just finding out what had happened to it. And how rough on the Republic if its investment were to go down the tube. He nodded safely. Such things were meaningful to him.

"It's a laser gun," he said.

"Like some kind of a death ray?"

He smiled icily. "I'd hardly use those particular words." He didn't say what particular words he would use. "You must understand that killing whales is not what it was meant for."

"What was it meant for?"

"Classified."

"Come again?"

"That's classified information."

"Look, I have to know *something* about the goddamn thing in order to *use* it."

"There is a manual."

"Terrific . . . These bastards have a thick layer of fat, you know. You can guarantee your little dingus will cut through it?"

I had impugned the honor of his weapon. He came as close to a human reaction as I ever saw.

"Goddamnit, it'll cut through a steel hull!"

Instantly his mouth snapped back into its thin, turtle line; as if I'd somehow tricked him into saying more than he'd intended.

He brought one himself, though, a couple days later, just as I was getting ready to leave. It didn't look like much. A stubby tube of grayish metal with a kind of box on one end. I leafed through the manual, but it didn't tell you much more than where the on/off button was. "How does it work?" I asked him.

"You have No Need to Know."

I was about to say something offensive when I realized that this wasn't a personal remark, but a ritualistic formula; the President of the U.S., too, probably had No Need to Know, and would be told so in similar terms. "Well, thanks anyway," I said, picking the thing up.

"I'll have that back, thank you."

"Don't I get to keep it?"

"Negative."

"Why not?"

"Security. You'll be using civilian transportation."

This was the first I'd heard of it. I must have looked bewildered, for he said, "One will be crated up and dispatched to the *Farquarson.*"

"You mean I'm not going straight back there?"

"Affirmative. Dr. Levitt has requested you stop off in Honolulu en route." It was okay to dish the dirt on civilian fucks; I could almost imagine the trace of a frosty smile lurking somewhere in his eye sockets as he said, "He seems to be having some problems with his new research scheme."

I HAD TIME to call Keala from L.A. airport and tell her my flight number and arrival time. I knew from her voice over the phone that something was wrong, but the final boarding call was coming over the P.A. system so there wasn't time to ask.

She walked slowly up to meet me at the arrival gate, and this time there wasn't any lei or any embrace; she just kept her eyes down and said in a dragging, listless kind of voice: "Walter's dead."

"No! How?"

"Syndicate shot him."

I took her hand in mine, her fingers were very cold and limp as wax. "But what for?"

Nobody was too clear about that. He'd started work as a bagman a few weeks before; maybe his money was funny, maybe he picked the wrong side in a faction fight, maybe he shot off his mouth once too often. They found him in the parking lot at the Ala Moana shopping center, locked in the trunk of a '65 Chevy, his hands and feet tied with baling wire, a small-caliber bullet wound through his forehead. No witnesses, no suspects, no evidence, it had hardly even made the papers.

"What are your folks doing about it?" I asked her.

"Nothing."

"How you mean, nothing?"

"What you can do when it's the Syndicate?"

I can't tell you how much this depressed me. And it wasn't merely that I'd liked Walter, which I had, and regretted the waste of his life, which I did: another of my illusions had died with him. I'd always thought that the Kealohas—flexible, resilient, tight as a dolphin pod—could rise superior to anything life threatened them with. If their kids got in trouble in school they'd go punch out the teacher; if DSSH cut their welfare they'd hassle their Worker till they got back on the rolls; if anyone fucked with them, they'd gang up and beat the shit out of him, even if he was a cop. So, if one of them got murdered, they should have gotten out their shotguns and Saturday-Night Specials and gone the rounds of the clubs, cockfights and gambling dens, blasting down Syndicate guys wherever they found them. Absurd, I know; everything has its limits; the Syndicate was their *Orcinus orca.* But the whole thing still left me feeling sick and disillusioned.

Later, trying to get to sleep (which was now more and more of a problem for me when I was on land) I had time to grieve for the person who had, perhaps, started this whole story going. And to recognize that he was not, perhaps, after all just an innocent victim. But as responsible as anyone else for what had happened to him. Yet not responsible, since the way things are molded the way he was. Yet responsible, for I extend and close these fingers, and know that my will is free. Isn't it? Responsible. Not responsible. Responsible. This sleep comes to you courtesy of the makers of Valium. Thank you. Amen. Goodnight.

WHEN THINGS START well, they go on well, but when they start shittily . . . That's been my experience. That trip back to base was no exception. Keala couldn't spend much time with me because her mother had gone into some kind of psychotic break on the occasion of Walter's death and she, as the dutiful one, had to give most help and comfort; and then she had her MSW thesis to work on. Alone at night and sleepless, I made the bad mistake of reading newspapers and magazines to pass the time. Normally I had proceeded in blissful ignorance of what was happening in the world; now, the accumulation of its disasters broke over me like a tidal wave of filth. There was genocide in Cambodia, race war in Rhodesia, terrorism in Italy, torture in Iran; and at home, a steady drizzle of rape, murder, child abuse and madness. Nothing out of the ordinary; just the regular everyday fare of our species; but I could not help but contrast it with the peace and harmony of life among the stenos. I had, almost for the first time, an argument with Keala about that.

"You just sentimental about 'em, 'ass what."

"Sentimental!"

"Sure! If we do more evil than them, 'ass just because we get a bigger capacity. For good or evil. Look all the things they no can do."

"Like what?" I asked. "Fly to the moon? That's just gimmicks. Medical miracles? Malaria's back and Africa's got it."

"What about works of art?"

She had me there, because, ignorant as I was, I still believed the stenos had no works of art. "So what is art worth?" I asked her. "What are you saying exactly? A sonnet is worth six executions? A cathedral is worth a couple of dozen torture chambers?"

"I never say that!"

"Then what?"

But she took refuge in sulking; the claims of her own species were so obvious to her that to question them could only be a sign of willful perversity.

But it wasn't so for me. I'd been taught, like a good little liberal, to question everything, but had somehow failed to absorb the unwritten codicil that this process must never be applied to the assumption underlying all other assumptions: that Man is the Measure of All Things, the hub on which the universe turns.

BACK AT THE Station, as the Skull had intimated, Barry and his merry men were running into some deep trouble.

Barry's approach to teaching language to dolphins was based largely on what had been done with chimps, but substituting sonic cues for hand signs or cutout symbols. He'd already taught them cues for the objects they played with, "ball," "ring," "bucket," etc., as well as for "fish" and their own names, and a few simple action verbs like "take," "fetch," "put" and "give." Mele couldn't get fish now unless she said the equivalent of "Give Mele fish." Once they'd got that behavior patterned, the next thing was to determine whether, when they seemed to utter and understand sentences, they had really learned language or had just rote-learned strings of symbols more complex than, but essentially the same as, the cues animal trainers have used since time immemorial to make animals do tricks. But it was no easy matter to prove this, for, as Barry's earlier experiments had shown, stenos have long immediate memories, longer than humans have. You might think, for example, that if you taught a dolphin symbols for "put," "ball," and "ring," got him to put the ball in the ring by saying "put . . . ball . . . ring," and then got him to put the ring over the ball by saying "put . . . ring . . . ball," then he had learned that the same symbols in a different order mean different things—one of the most profound differences between animal communication and human language. But there was no way you could be sure that he hadn't simply learned the two sentences as "putballring" and "putringball," two ready-made vocabulary items that had only a coincidental resemblance to "put," "ring" and "ball."

So, Barry had taught them questions. First, a sound cue that means "Where?" Then you can say things like, "Where . . . ball?" and answer them yourself with "ball . . . bucket." Then you ask the question and the dolphin has to answer. At first of course he answers all kinds of crap, grunts, whistles, symbols for "bucket," "give," "fish." You don't give him any fish until he says "ball . . . bucket"; since his vocabulary is finite, it can't be too long before, even on the monkey-and-typewriter principle, that pair comes up. You then reinforce him with a fish. You're in business. Soon you can put their toys in three different positions and have them answer correctly "the ball is in the bucket," "the ball is in the ring" and "the ring is in the bucket," ten times out of ten.

But wait. They could still have learned these sequences as single words. So here comes the kicker. Without any prior modeling, you put the *bucket* in the ring and ask them, "Where's the bucket?" Remember, they've never heard the sentence "The bucket is in the ring" before in their lives. So if, straight away, they come up with the symbols for "bucket," "in" and "ring," in that order, you know it's either a fluke (which you can check by using further combinations of objects) or else they've grasped the basic principle.

But Lei and Mele had not come up with "bucket . . . in . . . ring."

"Think about it," Barry said. "We've been going round in circles here. Maybe we're stale. Maybe we need a new viewpoint."

"Maybe they're just dumb animals after all," I said, straight-faced. But Barry did not dig irony. Besides, now he had invested time and money in them, they just *had* to turn out intelligent. "No," he said, dead serious, "I don't think so. I think there's a flaw somewhere in the experimental design. With what you know about their habits, you just might be able to spot it. We're having a brainstorming session, ten tomorrow. Be there."

"Or be square."

"I beg your pardon?"

"Nothing."

"That's happening to me all the time lately." Barry, looking vaguely worried, thrust the tip of his little finger in his ear and made it vibrate like a road drill. I looked around, but Les wasn't in sight, alas; gross, we would have mouthed at one another.

"Wax. I think there's wax in it."

"Put olive oil in to soften it," I said, "then aim a showerhead at it. Or swim in a pool where there's plenty chlorine."

"Really? And does that soften it? Really. I'll try that. Interesting. Most interesting."

"SO HE'S ALREADY briefed you," were the first words Les said to me when we finally met up.

"Right."

"And he thinks you can bail him out?"

"Bail him out! How the fuck would I do that?"

"Oh, sure, you wouldn't tell him how, of course. But if you'd learned how to talk to them . . . *Have* you learned how to talk to them?"

It was on the tip of my tongue to answer, "Yes . . . Well, with qualifications . . . At least I'm beginning to." But I did not. In time, I remembered my resolve. I felt like the meanest bastard in the world, not leveling with him, when it was only through him that I'd made the small advances I had. Don't worry, Les, I swore speciously to myself, I'll make it up to you, after the Great Day on which Full Illumination Finally Dawns.

"Something's missing," I told him. "I keep feeling I'm right on the brink of it, but something's still missing."

He grinned smugly. "Think I know what it could be. After tomorrow's session, maybe I'll tell you."

TEN NEXT MORNING, there we all were: Barry, Les, Earl, Cheryl —the Japanese girl who'd replaced Frank—and myself. Cheryl's long lashes and creamy, delicate cheeks waged violent war with her voice, which was like a bandsaw, and her manner, which was that of a drill sergeant in boot camp. "I have an announcement to make," she said, straight off, before Barry could get a word in.

"Sure, go ahead," Barry said meekly. He was scared shitless of aggressive women.

"This is a joint announcement from Greenpeace, Save the Whales, Life of the Land, the Ohana and the Ecological Coalition. First I'll read the text of this U.P. release."

In a rapid and remorseless monotone she read:

> Reports from numerous sources over recent weeks indicate that the world's already threatened dolphin population is confronted by a new danger. Owing to the decline in the world tuna catch, certain tuna-boat owners operating under flags of convenience are believed to have adapted their ships for commercial netting of dolphins, and are allegedly canning dolphin meat, on shipboard or in secret canning factories, and selling it in Third-World countries under fictitious labels. The United Nations today appointed a special commission to enquire into these allegations.

"There's a special fund been set up called Save the Dolphins," Cheryl went on. "I'm asking for contributions from all of you. Yes, even you, Les."

"I'm broke."

"Write a postdated check. Just make it out to Save the Dolphins."

Everybody contributed, Les in small change, Barry with a twenty-dollar check, I don't know whether because of Cheryl or because he was developing a conscience. It seemed crazy to me, dolphin jailers giving money to stop dolphin executioners, but I threw in a five, partly because my money was accruing faster than I could spend it and partly so as not to stand out. Then Barry called us to order.

"Well, team, you all know the score. Any suggestions?"

There was some desultory chat for about ten minutes; then I said, as casually as I could, "Is it the same bucket?"

"The same bucket as what?" Barry asked.

"As you used before?"

"No, how could it be? It's got to be smaller."

"Why?"

With the labored patience of one explaining to a child, Barry said, "First we taught them 'The ring is in the bucket', so the ring has to be *smaller* than the bucket. Now we want to put the bucket in the ring, so the ring has to be the *larger* of the two."

"You could have used two different rings."

"Well, we used two different buckets. Earl." Earl sprang to attention. "Earl, bring the buckets."

"Yes, sir," Earl said, scurrying off for them.

"They may be confused about the meaning of 'in,' " Cheryl said importantly. "They may think it just means, 'inside something hollow' . . . like a bucket."

"No, because they do 'The ball is in the ring' okay," Les said.

Cheryl gave him a look that marked him down for annihilation on the day of the Amazon Takeover.

Earl said, "Here are the buckets, Dr. Levitt."

"Well, Andy?"

"One's twice the size of the other."

"Of course. But both are buckets."

"To us, naturally . . . But to them?"

Barry knit his brows and flickered his tongue over that one. After a moment he said, "You realize what you're suggesting? That they can't generalize? That they name each individual object and nothing else?"

I was wise enough to say nothing to that.

"No," he said, shaking his head, as if answering himself. "No, that's not possible." For it made nonsense of his whole research plan, if it were true.

"We can easily check it out," Les said.

"How?"

"Will the ball go inside the small bucket?"

"Yeah, it'll kind of wedge into the top of it. Yeah."

"So we know they can do 'The ball is in the bucket' with the big bucket. Let's see if they can do it with the small one."

Barry looked round. Nobody had any better suggestions.

"Okay," he said. "Let's go. We can use the old program."

We went out to Lei's tank. Earl switched on the Wavetek and it began to put out sound cues just as it had done in our earlier experiments—only now the sounds had meanings. First on the program came "Where is the ball?" Les dropped a red rubber ball in the tank and, as the sound cues—a beep and a kind of curly whistle—came out of the machine, Cheryl slipped a red rubber ring over it. Lei swung her head, not bothering to sonar-scan, since she could see quite clearly, and repeated the second sound, the whistle, followed by the kind of blatting noise that stood for the ring. "The ball is in the ring!" Les threw her a fish and #2, "The ring is in the bucket," followed. Lei got it right, and the next one, and the next. Then came #5, "Where is the ball?" "The ball is in the (small) bucket."

Lei lifted her head from the water, lowered it, lifted it again, swam a little way toward ball and bucket, turned sharply away and let out a string of angry squawks.

"Switch off, Dr. Levitt?" Earl asked.

"No, no," Barry snapped. "Keep it running." He looked worried. Lei successfully answered three more questions. Then the ball in the bucket came up again. Again Lei hesitated and moved off, her blowhole puckering.

"You said she gave no response," I said to Barry.

"Right."

"Well, she's responding now."

"I meant no *meaningful* response."

"I think it *is* meaningful. She's saying 'Why ask questions I don't have the words to answer?'"

Barry looked like he was about to say something cutting, then pulled a wry face and walked away. The program ran through to completion. Sometimes the ball was presented in the large bucket, sometimes in the small one. When it was in the large bucket, Lei responded correctly; when it was in the small one, she behaved in the same disorganized manner as before. When the small bucket came up twice running, she sulked, swam to the bottom of the tank and remained there, surfacing only to breathe, and refusing to answer any more questions.

We sat down again in the office.

"It's pretty obvious," Les said. "She doesn't generalize 'bucket.'"

"We'll have to give every object its own name," Earl said.

Barry was so mad he beat the table with the heel of his palm. "No we won't," he said. "That's the null hypothesis. If she doesn't generalize buckets, it doesn't follow that there aren't things she *can* generalize."

But what might such things be? Nobody was prepared to answer that question.

"Tomorrow," Barry said at last, resignedly, "we'll have to start over from scratch. Find out what things are different for her. Start with different buckets. Same size, same material, different colors. Then, same size, same color, different materials. Then, a range of sizes each a little different from the next. Cindy—"

"I'm Cheryl."

"Cheryl, I'm sorry, Cheryl, do you think you could look around the toy shops, see what you can find?" With an air of reproach, he added, to the rest of us, "Someone should have done this in the beginning."

Nobody was tactless enough to point out that on the assumptions he'd started with—that dolphins were just like chimps until proven different—any such procedure would have seemed a complete waste of time.

"WELL?" I SAID to Les after the meeting.

"Well what?"

"Well water . . . okay, okay, well, what was The Answer To It All you said you were going to come up with?"

Les looked genuinely puzzled. "I said that? Did I really say that?"

"Uh-huh."

"Yeah, well, that was kinda . . . 's not an *answer,* really. More like another question. Like, if they do talk, what would they talk *about?*"

"Sex," I said. I was in no mood for riddles.

"Ah, be serious. Let's think what they would *not* talk about. That we do. Now, they wouldn't talk about each other's feelings because they always know what the other one's feeling. They wouldn't talk about possessions because they don't have any possessions."

"They make jokes."

"All the time? And maybe they give warnings, information like that, but never that often."

"That would leave a lot of talk-time unaccounted for."

"Right. Now suppose they weren't actually *saying* anything."

"Ah, come on, Les!"

"No, I'm not saying what you think I'm saying. I'm not saying they have no meaning. Does something have to be *saying* to have a meaning?"

"Yeah, sure."

"Think a minute. Is a blueprint *saying* anything?"

"Well, it—"

"Yes or no?"

"Okay, it's not *saying* exactly. It represents something."

"Fine, it represents something—"

"Will you can the Socratic shit and get to the point?"

I don't know why I popped off at him like that. My nerves were getting worse all the time. But he only smiled reproachfully.

"I *am* getting there. A blueprint is what, exactly? It's like a picture. It isn't *about* something—in a sense, it *is* that thing. So if you had a language like the stenos, one that made pictures in sound, you'd be that degree closer to the reality of things . . . Listen, you remember the first way you thought of it, you were raving about godlike beings with movie projectors for eyes?"

"Something of the sort."

"Well, what would such a being project—fact or fantasy?"

"Uh . . . both, I guess."

"So, fantasy . . . pictures in sound of things that aren't there. Don't we have a name for that kind of thing?"

I'm ashamed to say how long it took me to get it. "Art," I said at last.

Les smiled beatifically. "That's what they're doing when you think they're gossiping. They're creating art."

SOMETIMES, EVEN BEFORE you've had time to think about a solution, you know it's right. So with this. Once you put it into the steno frame of reference, it made sense. If you're any kind of intelligent creature, what's the way you'd first struggle to penetrate and understand the universe around you? The cave paintings of Lascaux antedate all religion, all science, all philosophy. They were a feeling one's way into the world while that world was still distinct, fearful and other, before there was born the terrible ambition of warping it to one's own ends, what one thought were one's own ends. Stenos, freed from this by their handlessness, had never arrived at that stage.

So they would have entered into the world by representing it in terms of their own choosing. But here another difference from us. All our lives we accrete things. We come naked and leave with cars, furs, mansions, trunkloads of documents, Old Masters. Our art is built to endure, a pathetic dream of permanence. Stenos have nothing, accumulate nothing. Their art could only be like shadows in the wind, cloudshapes. Gone even as perceived. Never repeatable twice the same. But none the less rare and beautiful for that.

I HAD A DREAM that night. I was lying in my bunk in the *Farquarson* listening to tapes of stenos, only they weren't like any audio tape you ever heard, the sounds transmuted into shapes and back into sounds again—no, they were both shape and sound, or something beyond shape and sound that merged the properties of both in a slow-shifting torrent of images . . . but here was something strange: I was myself actor as well as watcher/hearer, I was in the heart of the pod, and not just the pod, but the whole daytime herd, and the herd was rotating like a wheel, and round the perimeter of the wheel, round the hundred-strong herd, rode a school of killer whales, like Indians round a wagon train—and snap! a steno vanished into a tunnel mouth, and snap! another. But it was me they sought for. They would swallow the herd one after another until there were none left for me to hide behind. And then from above there was thunder and shattering light and the helicopter was there and Sam calling to me, "Come up!" "No!" I called back to him. "You'll die!" "I know! But we are one kind." One kind? Yes, I was changing, my body growing rounder, deeper, my legs no longer merely pressed together but welded into a single limb; my arms had grown shorter and stubbier and the hands were almost fingerless. But I was not yet quite one with them, nor as helpless as I feared, for in those stubby fingers was the smooth cold metal of the laser gun. And instantly, without effort, I had vaulted over the herd and fired on the nearest of the monsters, which shriveled under my fire into a wizened wrinkled creature half its original size, in shape and consistency like a half-collapsed party balloon, that burst and flew into ragged pieces— whereupon every killer vanished simultaneously, like the blips of UFOs leaving a radar screen. And I was left with the decimated herd, Lord and Protector of my chosen tribe, but alone, reigning in solitude, without my mate.

My mate?

Yes, for Susan too had been engulfed by the black jaws. But not before I had known her—known that strange fierce forbidden contact, the feel of smooth, cold, salty and alien flesh. Yes, my seed had pierced the species barrier; my organs knew the mystery of another kind. I dreamed the memory of that coupling, fleeting and vague, yet darkly satisfying, even while I mourned her loss. It was still there, that memory, in my mind as I awoke and reached out for Keala's warm and familiar flesh.

MY RETURN to the stenos was less sensational than the dream, yet not without a certain low-key drama of its own.

As soon as Sam had dropped me, after I came back the second time from base—as soon as I heard the familiar babel of the pod, and saw them leaping toward me, with Duke's familiar scarred forehead up front, Bull bringing up the rear, the baby and his mother at the pod's safe center, all the shittiness I had felt on shore fell away from me as if it had never been. And then the relief and gratitude of reunion was suddenly submerged by something much stronger.

Now I knew what to listen for; it was as if a door had been opened onto another world. With all the will in the world I can't open that door for you: it opened for me, I realized, not just by virtue of Les's insight but because of countless thousands of impressions that I'd been accumulating, quite unconsciously, over all the months I had spent with them, that had meant nothing to me at the time but that now, given the key, fell miraculously into place like the pieces of a huge and bizarre jigsaw. Imagine you have been listening for many hours to the cacophonous music of some savage tribe, and then suddenly you grasp the principle that turns your dissonance into their harmony, and imagine that at that moment too the music begins to generate pictures in your mind—no, more than that, that the music somehow *is* the pictures, that you know these are not just idiosyncratic images like you may get when listening to any old music, but the true heart and essence of the music itself, objective and untransmutable . . . that's poor, but it's the nearest I can get.

They were reviewing my life with them. I saw again my first descent among them, the blue whale rising against the evening sky, waves soaring and plunging in the storm, the sharks attacking, but I saw it through their eyes, not my own, saw myself as a character in their lives, odd, pathetic, even pitiful at times, and yet strangely endearing in his comical persistence. I don't wish you to suppose that I grasped all of this immediately—some of my memories may have come from later encounters (for this saga of my experiences with them was repeated, albeit with many variations and embroideries, at every subsequent reunion) and even at the last of these there was still much that was quite beyond my understanding—but enough of it at least to marvel at what had been so close yet hidden from me so long.

That side of their creating was like a picaresque novel; there were others that were more purely like painting, or music, a flowing of forms unlike any beings we had encountered, which moved me from the start but which I could not understand so readily. And there were more routine, everyday exchanges. Mojo was soon alternating images, both perceptibly of me, yet different in detail. "How is Andy now different from Andy as he was then?" he was asking.

Quick as a flash came Susan's answer, again the image of myself but this time with a smaller version, shaped like me, swimming alongside: "Andy's having a baby!"

Then steno laughter echoed all around me, and Hester threw back an image of something being extruded from my belly—only this something was hard, metallic, and I realized for the first time what they were talking about: the bulge made by the housing of the laser gun strapped to my side.

I unfastened the gun and held it out for their inspection; they converged on it, scanning it swiftly, then ran off into joke-fantasies of metal men, metal babies suckling metal teats. All of this part was like an animated cartoon, and I think I got most of it, since it relied heavily on one of their simplest devices—the creation of novel images simply by superimposing the sound-image of one object's outline upon the sound-image given off by the substance of another; that way you could have metal men, wooden fish, flesh-and-blood boats, whatever. Underlying it I sensed a kind of good-humored mockery. It was weird, to them, and rather ridiculous, that I should appear among them with mineral accoutrements. Perhaps indeed I was revolting from the animal kingdom, their images slyly suggested—aspiring to the permanence and deadness of minerals. Or did I read too much into what was merely play? Remember I was thirsty for philosophic overtones, and judge accordingly.

One thing I did notice: some of the images in their cartoon had bifurcated legs and some had not; and from this I deduced (what I should have guessed long before) that they had no illusions about my nature or my provenance—that the elaborate charade of my arrivals and departures had been a waste of time. Nettled more by this, perhaps, than by the more obvious assaults on my human complacency, I thought to myself, "Right, I'll show you mothers." And I began to broadcast something that was all too easy for me to recall—the shape of *Orcinus orca* coming in for the kill.

I should have remembered my own guess, made long before to Les, that to broadcast *orca*'s image, with no prior warning or disclaimer, would be tabu among them. The next thing I knew, Duke hit me across the back of the head with his tail-flukes, just as I was surfacing to breathe—I blacked out for a moment, came to choking, and took another massive blow from I don't know who, not as heavy as the first but enough to send fiery orbs pinwheeling through the night of my vision. When I could draw air again, Duke was pouring at me a stream of sound, the precise meaning of which was opaque to me, but the gist of which was crystalline: "Don't do that again—*ever!*"

I felt the need to explain to them, show them that what I had done was not a gratuitous assault, even if it earned me more blows. There was a sound which, I now realized, probably signaled a transition from factual to nonfactual remarks: a kind of low, interrupted whistle. I made it, as best I could, through the tubes of my helmet. Repeated it, until I got what looked like signs of recognition and assent. Then I made the image of the laser gun, then of *orca* approaching, then the gun again, then *orca* floating, limp and lifeless. What I was trying to say, in my blundering pidgin of their tongue, was something like, "Okay, so I may look comical to you, but with this grotesque metal gadget I can kill your deadliest enemy, *orca.*" But I was far from sure of the precise tone of the whistle; perhaps what I had really said was, "Don't take seriously what I'm saying, it's all in play."

I tried again. Projecting *orca*'s shape, then the image of a dolphin voiding its bowels—which I knew from earlier was their symbol for fear. "Are you afraid of *orca?*"

They all gave their affirmative whistle, and yet somehow gleefully, as if still joking. Their attitude seemed quite irrational, in human terms. If any being threatens us, the proper response to fear is hatred and implacable enmity, not laughter. I tried over and over, in every way I could think of, to show them that I now had the power to destroy their destroyer. But, somehow, the point would never get across.

OCULAR DEMONSTRATION might have helped, of course. But it so happened, on that trip, that no *orca* appeared and no shark came within range of me. I therefore field-tested my laser off the *Farquarson,* swimming out off the stern ten minutes after they dumped the day's garbage. Four or five sharks were there already. I lined up on the nearest of them and depressed the firing lever for a fraction of a second. Something like a lightning bolt of microscopic thinness seemed to leap between myself and the shark's head—extinguishing so fast that it might have been merely the trick of an eye blink. But the shark jackknifed, straightened out and began to drift downward, lifeless, through the fog of decomposing matter that clouded the water. I fingered the lever again, this time traversing the center of its body. The shark fell apart in two halves, as neatly as if cut by a cleaver, and its guts slipped slowly out of it to join the rest of the stuff that was in the water. Two of the other sharks went for the guts and wrangled over them like two dogs fighting for a string of sausages. It was a sickening sight, and I was sorry I'd done it, but at least I knew the thing worked.

I MENTIONED EARLIER that Susan had been pressuring me, but that had been on a purely physical level—or rather, I had been deaf to the accompaniment. Now I knew that the sounds she hurled at me, as she rubbed against my groin, were monstrous images of couplings natural and unnatural; dolphin with dolphin, whale with whale, whale with dolphin, dolphin with human, human with shark. Their effect was monotonous but massive, cumulative in time. The waters around me became saturated with desire.

One early morning was very calm, I had never seen the sea so calm in mid-ocean, the sun was just up and blazed reddishly through a fine mist rising off the waters, rising and dissolving into a sky without cloud. The whole pod idled, drifted, occasionally one would leap and fall with a resounding smack. As Susan swam at my side I sensed their attention focused on us, not pressing, kind of a relaxed interest—doubtless, scanning through my suit, they were aware of my arousal. Duke and Hester swam past us, locked together, bodies swiftly pulsing, as if to provide me with a model. Their image was reduplicated in Susan's sound-sketches as if in a maze of mirrors. She squawked and whistled above the hail of images: "Look! Look! Yes! You and me! Now!"

The suit was a problem. There was no zipper in the front (it not having been designed with such an end in view) and I had to unzip the back and draw my legs and the lower half of my body clear of it. The loose tail flopped around, hampering my movements, but the water was sharp, chill and invigorating on my naked flesh. Susan came at me in a rush; instinctively I covered my groin with my hands, I didn't trust her beak, but sensing my nervousness she checked, turned and rolled over on one side, presenting her ventral slit. I rolled to face her, threw one arm over her smooth body and, after several misses (for she was squirming in delight and her skin was slippery as glass) thrust inside her.

Remember those fairground rides that start by accelerating down a steep slope, then go up and down and up again at vertiginous speed, with stomach-wrenching force, so even if you wished you hadn't gone on it or wanted to get off there was absolutely nothing you could do about it? That's as near as I can get to how it felt. The instant I entered her she took off, driving forward with great thrusts of her flukes, and I was dragged with her through the water. Her huge muscles gripped and sucked at me, relaxed and then gripped again, in rhythmic spasms, so that any movement I might have made would have been superfluous. Indeed, it was all I could do just to hang on to her and still keep breathing. For when she rolled over to breathe, I was upside down beneath her, and in my distraction I had forgotten to breathe deeply enough; I'd almost blacked out before she rolled belly-up and it was my turn.

And all the time those great muscles were pumping at me so that for all my fear and confusion I couldn't hold back. I wanted to hold back, from habit maybe, or some atavistic fear of sowing my seed in alien flesh—there flashed through my mind, absurdly, the thought that in all my study I'd never read or observed whether female dolphins have orgasms, was there a paper for *Nature* in it?—but there was no way I could have held back, I was there, without warning, it was like a jet of liquid fire leaving me, volatile as the foam that burst round us as she braked violently, her body contracted, and her tailflukes beat heavily, once, twice, three times, before her tension relaxed. I had gone limp, I was sliding out of her, it was over. I let go of her, half stunned.

Her beak rubbed my shoulder, as she projected the image of a steno crammed with fish. Was she saying I'd satisfied her? No, there was a question-whistle with it. Was *I* satisfied?

That wasn't easy to answer. I felt drained, exhausted, yet at the same time filled with a wild exhilaration, like no feeling I'd ever had before.

I struggled back into my suit; she circling me, miming my clumsiness in sound—then she flipped spray into my face with her tail and, laughing, swam away from me.

ON THOSE TRIPS I spent a lot of time with the baby steno. I had figured that there was a lot they would have to teach him, and while he learned I would be learning too. Of course it wasn't quite as easy as this suggests. Each species has a mind that's built to accommodate what it will need to survive. Rats may seem simpler than you, but that doesn't mean you can learn all that rats learn, or think and feel as a rat does. So right from the very start they were feeding him stuff that was already hard for me to follow. Partly because there were not just real objects and creatures with it, but things that I suppose were their equivalents of dragons and unicorns. It seemed to me at first that this must confuse him, until I realized that we presented things in the same way to human children—mixing dragons and unicorns with dogs and horses, and giving both sets, indiscriminately, our own powers of speech and reason. And this doesn't confuse kids. They don't get mad when their doggy won't speak to them; they know that a unicorn, like a horse or dog, might be okay to pat, but a dragon not. Somehow and without much trauma they grow into the realization of what is real. Same with stenos.

But that similarity apart, there's not much resemblance between our nursery tales and what the stenos told Baby. What the stenos told was much richer, or so it seemed to me, and infinite in its diversity, not bound, like the nursery tale, to a few conventions of princesses and castles, but ranging over all possible and impossible worlds. I remember a giant seaweed tree, every trembling branch of which was a shark; I remember coral shapes that danced; I remember creatures like sentient whips in a thin and gaseous ocean.

These were not mere idle visions. Often the story-telling steno (who quite often now would be Bull, Bull in the beginning of decline now and slowly yielding leadership to Duke) would stop in the middle of an image and Baby would be required to complete it. In this way they trained not merely his discrimination but his power to communicate. Only gradually did they begin to bring in lessons. To show the despair and fear a small steno would endure if lost and isolated from the pod. Or to envisage possible ends for him in the maws of monsters. But these aspects were played down; incidental, almost, to the learning of the art that filled their waking lives. They did not need to acquire the vast mass of information and moral precept that we needed to survive in our world. A few simple rules of loyalty and watchfulness were enough.

But there was one story, or legend, or blueprint—all these categories, or none of them, seem to fit—that gave me, I guess, as much insight into their minds as I could ever hope to have. This one, which I heard in varying forms many times, always began with the sounds of immense numbers of dolphins churning together in the ocean. Then the finest, minutest echoes—the small invertebrates of the Deep Scattering Layer. Then images of small squids, small and then larger fishes, a hierarchy of creatures gradually growing in size until once again there resounded the full-bodied echoes of the dolphin herd. But at no level of the hierarchy were the other creatures as numerous as the dolphins.

Then there came images of a smaller number of stenos moving across the ocean, moving fast and far, and then, approaching, echoes of shoal water, rising land; and then the echoes of the stenos ceased to move, became welded to the land. One by one, their images flickered out. Leaving rest, peacefulness, satisfaction.

The tapestry of sound was complex and it took me a long while to sort out. Once that was done, understanding came in a flash. The food chain! The story had begun with a portrayal of the food chain, beginning from amoeba, on top of which the stenos stood—a balanced system in which each species served to give sustenance to that above it. But something had gone wrong with the chain. Those below had grown too few; those above, too many. As happened many times in nature. Among the beasts, predators suffered at random the pangs of starvation. Man, head of *his* food chain, manipulated the world— grew crops, fattened herds and, mostly, survived. The dolphins alone, without the power to control fate but with the wisdom and feeling not to let suffering fall blindly upon all, chose the way of sacrifice. Decided, in some way unimaginable to me, who should survive and who should die so that others might live and the great wheel of nature be readjusted. So that the chosen would swim to shore and there offer up their lives, refusing rescue, even if our species offered it to them.

I would be joking and playing with Susan or Duke or Mojo and it would seem for a while that we were all mammals together, with only trivial and accidental differences, and then something like this would fall between us and I would feel, with a shiver of awe, the vastness of the gulf. My species wore itself out battling against its fate; theirs resigned itself, yet not passively, like fatalists—rather joined with it in an act of voluntary triage that boggled the mind.

Boggled mine, anyway. I could see, in principle, the beauty of it, yet how could I really hope to feel it inside—I who would fight for life even if life were worthless and the fight without hope, how could I see yielding up life for those I might never have known? And yet it followed that in a truly intelligent being the bonds of love and union would not stop at the family, the pod, the tribe, but would proceed to embrace the entire species and perhaps others besides. In us too there was that desire, but every time it fucked up: our prophets and revolutionaries preached universal brotherhood, but all that issued forth were bloody crusades and iron dictatorships.

Why?

How come we could fly to the planets, dive to the depths of ocean, bind round the earth with our webs of steel and concrete, yet be utterly powerless in the face of our own crimes and injustices—able, at most, to mend one hurt by making another, as if human misery were a fixed sum that could only be humped from one place to another and back again, like in some ridiculous make-work scheme? Big questions. Too big for a kid in graduate school, wait till you grow up, Sonny, then you'll have sense enough not to ask them, because all the sages of the ages haven't been able to answer them yet.

No way you could answer it because to do so you would have to stand outside of yourself, outside of your species, and see it as it would appear to another race.

But if there was another intelligent race, you could stand in *their* shoes and see yourself whole at last.

LET'S BE REALISTIC. At this stage I knew about as much of their language as a two-year-old child. A *foreign* two-year-old child. I wasn't just lacking in words, I was almost totally ignorant of their mind-set, where they were coming from. Though not so ignorant as to suppose that questions such as I'd put to myself, even if they could be translated, would necessarily have any meaning for them. So how was I even to start?

It would take time, a long time, to learn to ask questions. And another long time to get answers. And perhaps even as long again to understand those answers once I got them.

One obvious and immediate problem was that they must know even less about us and how we worked than I knew about them. So I asked Duke (question-tone whistle, fork-legged sound-picture), "What do you know of Man?"

Duke positioned himself directly in front of me, lifted his tail and slapped me twice, lightly but firmly, on the top of my head. They had taken to doing this whenever I said anything fatuous; they were annoyed that I didn't learn quicker, look, there was Baby, just a few weeks old, and *he* learned quicker. So I must have framed the question too vaguely.

I tried again: question-whistle, coils of a steno brain, and old fork-legs again. "What do you think of Man?"

Duke leaped in the air, came down splat, gave the fork-legged sound-picture and, superimposed on it, a shower of soft, decomposing matter—

"Man is a heap of shit!"

Susan joined in, sending out a picture of a long, curly-limbed creature—

"Man is a heap of octopus shit!"

". . . whaleshit . . ."

"Man is a whale's penis!"

That was the next problem: how did you ever get them to take anything seriously? Or—I thought, as they gamboled, chortling, around me—impersonally? For I had suddenly remembered that they did not generalize; that if I pictured a single member of my species, this could not possibly stand for the whole, but could only refer to the nearest (and only) available member. So what they were saying was *I* was octopus shit and a whale's penis, since I'd been stupid enough to ask.

I tried again, this time producing images of a number of blurred, anonymous fork-legs, rest of the picture as before. This earned me only another slap upside the head. Too vague, too meaningless still.

I cast around for another way of approaching things. I thought of their food-chain story (alas, none of their stories seemed to have names, so you could never just refer to one without telling it all over again). That, after all, was the key to what I was seeking. That highlighted the gulf I was striving to bridge. I sent out, again, pictures of men, and then of what I hoped they would interpret as men's food. That was a problem. I could hardly broadcast Big Macs and French fries. But, never having practiced in the country, I didn't know what the acoustic images of steers or ears of wheat would be, either. I settled for a four-legged mammal somewhere between the size of a rabbit and a sheep. Hoping they would dig the connection; to do one creature eating another, as they could, was hardly within my competence yet (it was like the two images, first one, then the other, alternated faster and faster until they merged smoothly into one and then the blend sort of resolved itself back into the first image—tough enough to read, let alone produce). I made the food sources far fewer than the men, as in their story. Gave the men as empty- rather than full-bellied. Then whistled the variety of the query-whistle that I had come to know better, perhaps, than any sound the stenos made: the one that meant, "Did you understand?"

"Yes! Yes!" Duke and Susan and Patsy, who had joined in the conversation—stenos never had any qualms about butting in on anyone's conversations, unlike us—squawked back at me.

Double underline question question: "Are you *sure* you've understood?"

This was asking for a repeat, and asking for a repeat meant more head slaps, pokes in the ribs from beaktips, and more of the blatting, snorting noises that meant "Dummy! Cretin! Oh all right, if you're such a jerk, here goes." And, playing like instruments in an orchestra—Duke and Susan the men, Patsy the rabbit-sheep—they gave me back my story, only sharper, brighter, a hundred times clearer, and then merging their parts perfectly in the eating routine until Patsy faded her instrument into silence and only the pictures of puffy, satiated men filled the scene.

I SHOULD HAVE mentioned that all this was happening by night. Late in the night, when everyone had eaten, when the diving had become sporadic, and really all they were doing was lounging around waiting for the dawn. That I never thought to mention it, at first, shows how near I got to them, at the apogee of my flight. You'll recall that, so far, most of the things I've thought worth mentioning happened in the daytime, but that just reflects my own limitations; for me—until I began to use and understand their language—night was just a period of numb hanging on, waiting for my key sense to be restored to me. But now I was beginning to hardly even notice the transitions from day to night. Once I'd begun to take a sizable portion of my sensory input in the form of sound rather than sight, it just didn't make that amount of difference.

And in this I was really diverging from my kind. There's a tribe in Africa that has a saying, "Come into the light of the fire so I can see what you say," but this could apply to any of our species. We all feel acutely embarrassed at being addressed by somebody we can't see (unless the speaker is loved and the language of touch comes with it); so much of what lies between humans can't be passed in words, we have to read the stance and expression and movements of the other, or the words alone can easily betray us. But with the stenos, all this, too, is gathered in the form of sound, so sight wasn't needed. Even, for that matter, it didn't seem so dark any more, as my eyesight had gradually adapted itself to the phosphorescence of plankton that floated always its webs of ghost radiance under the surfaces of night. I could perceive them, the stenos, as dimly outlined shapes against this radiance, if I needed to. Now, as the images of men faded and blipped out, I began again to project my own pictures of men. But this time of men, empty-bellied, fighting other men. Killing. Dying.

Because that was the other thing that happened if *our* food chain went awry. If we couldn't expand the food source by technology, we fought one another over the diminished resources. War. Technology. Two different-seeming things, but not all that different really, just two ways of dealing with the crisis that recurred, over and over, in the life of every species: it got too numerous; and there wasn't enough food to go round. So, if you can't grow more, breed more, you fight one another, kill off plenty, enslave the rest and put them on short rations, put them out to work to grow more food for you. Slavery is just a form of technology. Crude, maybe, but quite effective.

My picture of battling men was so bad, so mushy and vague that I never really expected them to get it. But once more I had underestimated them. The next thing I knew, Patsy was projecting a weirdly beautiful image that I couldn't read at all until it dawned on me that it was the figure of a drowning man turning over and over as he sank. Then all of the pod that were in range joined in, and there was a wild babel of sound, from which I fleetingly extracted more drowned men, the hulls of boats, and suddenly a long, hard, rounded metallic shape seemed to speed by me—

A torpedo!

They were playing a naval battle. I doubt if any of them had ever witnessed one (although Bull might be old enough to have been present at Leyte or Midway), but they must have heard of them from others, perhaps dead now, who had, who had been caught, perhaps, in the night when it was too late to flee the rage of man's self-destruction, but who had lived to tell of their experiences later, in the circling day-herd. And now the sound waves surged back in shattered echoes of themselves—there had been an immense explosion, a shipload of ammunition blowing up, perhaps, and again the limp bodies rained down from above.

I had expected from them, knowing this much, some expression of, I guess, outrage or horror at the scene, so typical of my species, enshrined in how many thousand of its pictures and movies, which they had just displayed for me. But I was wrong. Once again I'd projected my own reactions onto them, and once again they demonstrated their independence. They were not horrified. Their reaction was rather one of fascinated interest. It was as though we had put on a gigantic spectacle for their benefit. Yet their interest was not curiosity as we know it. They never asked why such scenes occurred (not that I could have answered them if they had). Indeed, I realize now that I never learnt any equivalent of "Why?" in their language. Maybe they didn't have one. Things just were. They were the way they were because that was the way it was.

And then Mojo projected another string of images. A man. A shark. Shark and man overrunning, merging. Then no more man, only a swollen shark. The shark had eaten the man.

Instantly I felt their recoil from those images. They almost turned on Mojo for having shown them. It was like someone had loosed a string of f-words on a church picnic. They all pretended it hadn't happened but there was a stiffness and a sense of awkwardness about them that I'd hardly felt before. And there were no more battle pictures. Duke made a rather forced joke about Mojo being sexually attracted to squids— some of their jokes, I have to admit, were puerile even by high-school standards—and when I tried to get back to the original topic, I was clipped over the head again.

I THINK I UNDERSTAND, now, the significance of that little scene. I say "think" because I was never given time to find out. About that, or about countless other mysteries that bugged me, like whether their dawn-leaping was really a ritual and if so of what kind, or how they set up and navigated to the meeting places of the herds. I would have found out, I'm certain, if I'd been given time. But on the next pickup, no sooner had we turned to head for the ship than Sam said, "Well, hope you told 'em a good goodbye."

"You hope I told 'em *what?*"

Sam turned the edge of his hatchet face in my direction, made balls of innocence out of his eyes, and said, "Goodbye. Addy-oss. A river durchy. Sayonara, as them Chinese say."

"And why should I have done that?"

"Cause you done seen 'em for the last time, is why."

FOR SEVERAL SECONDS I was completely speechless. If I'd heard that all my kin and everyone I knew had just been annihilated in some natural disaster, I don't think I could have been any more overwhelmed. Then I began to rage and curse at poor Sam.

"Hey, ain' no use cussin' me, man!"

"You could have fucking told me! Before! When we were going out! But no, you're a two-faced lying sonofabitch like the rest of your fucking tribe! All that shit you gave me about never surrendering Florida! Fighting fucking Mexicans!" Because, out of curiosity, I'd looked up the history of the Seminoles the last time I was on shore. "Whitey whupped your ass in Florida! You marched out as prisoners of war to Arkansas. You ran from Arkansas to Mexico 'cause you was scared they'd make slaves of you again. You came crawling back when Whitey asked you to help him root out the *real* wild Indians from Texas." I said all this with as much venom as if I'd thought Sam had personally done all these things. And instantly, seeing those dark orbs turned reproachfully on me, wished I'd never said any of it; those hands steady on the controls of the machine had saved me from death in the mouth of *orca*. But no sooner are things said than it's too late already.

"I ain't know about it, before," was all Sam said.

All he needed to say. I had no answer.

"They get orders," he went on, not looking at me any more, "they get orders las' Wednesday. Return to base immediate. Account of the economy cuts this new feller makin,' is what they say."

I clenched my knuckles and, too, looked straight ahead.

"I shoulda knowed you was gon' take it bad. I shoulda put it more tac'ful."

"Sam," I said. "Sam, I'm sorry."

"Ain't no hurt to me. My skin t'ick enough. I just sorry you think so bad of my people."

I did something I hadn't done since I was a little baby. Burst out into weeping.

RIGHT AFTER we landed, the *Farquarson* upped anchor and set course for Honolulu. They oiled and sedated me as usual, but this time I was so mad it didn't take. I was out of it in five hours. I demanded to see the captain.

"Believe me," the captain said, "I'm no more pleased about this than you are. We were still two months off completing the survey. It's ridiculous, of course. Next year or the year after they'll decide it's essential for national security, only by then it'll cost twice as much to finish it. Politics. What can you do about it?"

"What can *I* do about *my* thing?"

"Listen," the captain said, leaning forward across his desk, suddenly confidential. "I have no orders whatsoever about your thing, as you call it. You seem to have slipped through one of their bureaucratic cracks. Far as I'm concerned, I'd have been within my rights to have steamed off and left you. Far as they're concerned, you can carry on your thing as long as you like. Only you don't get the services of the ship."

"Thanks!"

"You're welcome. Only, I thought it was hardly okay just to take the ground from under your feet, so to speak." He had a kind of very dry sense of humor sometimes that made it hard for me to hate him as much as I felt I ought to.

"Fair enough," I said, my mind running fast, now the initial shock had worn off. "So, if I'm not on the rolls, how about letting me off on Johnston Island, rather than sit on my ass till this tub makes it to Pearl?"

He shrugged. "See no reason why not."

I had nothing more in mind at that stage than avoiding another forty-eight hours in the company of him and his crew. But no sooner had I left his office than I flashed on the big bonus.

During my spells on the *Farquarson,* all my sea-going gear—the suit and its appendages, the Batteau machine, the laser gun

—were kept stowed in a locker in one of the storerooms. The locker wasn't locked, neither was the storeroom. They probably should have been, by the regs, but when you're in mid-ocean months at a time, you get careless, no one's going to rip stuff off out there unless it's like booze that you can hide in your belly, and they always kept the booze well locked. But now, bound for shore, any minute they'd start locking things up.

I tiptoed down the corridor. Not a soul in sight. Tried the door. Still unlocked. Went inside the storeroom and tried the locker. Unlocked. Took my gear in a big bundle, not worrying to be cautious now, knowing that speed and confidence pay better than funny business in scenes like this. And made it to my cabin just as the first blue suit turned the corner.

I still had no very clear idea as to why I wanted the stuff. After all, the captain's words had left me the loophole of hope that it was only his, not my project that was discontinued, and that all I need do was ask for some other floating platform to do my thing from. In which case my gear would be made available to me. And if not, it wouldn't seem as if I'd be needing it. I won't deny that some childish fantasy of selling it for vast sums to a Foreign Power may have flipped through my mind. But the real reason was that I felt, psychologically, it was mine—I'd earned it through countless hours of hardship and danger, I had moral title to it, somehow. And I was damned if I was leaving it for those bastards.

I crushed it into my sea bag along with the rest of my possessions. Or I should say "instead of," since I had to throw a lot of stuff out to make room for it. It made some ugly bulges. Surely everybody could tell what it was. Surely I'd be stopped, searched. What the hell. I'd just try and bluff my way through.

When it happened, my departure was nothing like that. Several people I hardly knew came to shake my hand. My scuzzy old chessmate shyly thrust something into my hands that, when I opened it later, turned out to be the set we had played with, with a note that said, "Just a souvenir, I got a better set at home so won't be needing these." I felt bad about that, afterward. Maybe I never gave them a chance. Maybe I was just a snob after all. I looked everywhere for Sam, but couldn't see him. He was hiding out. He must have been hurt. I felt still worse about that.

No matter how I felt—good, bad or indifferent. The guy at the bottom of the gangplank gave no more than a glance at my sea bag and shined me on. I was home free with all I needed to be a dolphin once again.

AT THE AIRPORT there was no one to meet me. Naturally, for I had told no one. I'd been too tied up in salvaging my gear to give Keala even a thought.

I phoned her from the arrival gate. Someone at the Kealoha household whose voice I didn't recognize told me she didn't live there any more, she'd moved out, she had her own place up St. Louis Heights, this was the number. I took it down, feeling my world slipping away from me . . . Moved? And not told me? *Moved in with someone?* A *haole* voice answered. No, she wasn't home. She was at work. (At work!?) She'd be back sometime that evening. Was there any message? No, I said, curtailing the desire to ask, "And who the fuck are you?" With my last dime I called the Station, got Les, and asked him to pick me up.

While I waited for Les I had more bad thoughts. I felt my karma catching up on me. I'd ploughed ahead with my own life, granted not for the usual selfish goals—for the Advancement of Human Knowledge and all that—but nonetheless without any consideration for others, just using them as instruments and yet still expecting them to come running when I'd gotten myself in the shit. And some of them would still do it. Look at Les now, racing up in his clapped-out Chevy van, bouncing toward me with shirttail flapping and a hairy grin.

I said, "Les, you were right and I was right and I knew enough to have told you so last time but I didn't. Okay, tell me I'm a son of a bitch."

Les shrugged. "Why should I do that?"

"Because I didn't trust you."

"So?"

"Whaddaya mean, so?"

"You trust me now or you wouldn't have told me. Who cares about last time? All that matters is you found out!"

"Yeah," I said. "I guess you're right. I did find out."

"So tell me. All of it. Right from the beginning."

"No, wait. I have a couple things to do first."

"Tight bastard."

"No, wait'll you see this." I gave a quick glance round the parking lot for cops and then opened my sea bag just enough for him to catch a glimpse of the laser gun.

"What the fuck—"

"Shoots holes in killer whales. And ships. Top secret, ol' buddy."

"You trying to get yourself in jail?"

"No. If they're discontinuing me, I just mean to look out for Number One."

"What'll you do with it?"

"I don't know yet."

"Best stash it someplace."

I threw my gear in the back of the van and we got rolling. We stopped at Omar the Tent Man and I bought a big waterproof haversack. Further on we stopped at a garden supply store and I bought a cheap shovel. Then we drove up to the top of Tantalus. Tantalus is a big hill, or small mountain, no more than a couple miles from downtown Honolulu, but get up near the top of it and a dozen yards from the road you're in rain forest with not a sign of humanity in sight. We hiked for maybe a quarter mile until we came to a big stand of bamboo. We squeezed our way into the center of the bamboo, well away from the trail, and I dug a hole, put all my dolphin gear in the haversack and buried it under two feet of reddish-brown topsoil. I made a few marks on the bamboo shafts so I could find the place again, then we walked back to the van and I told Les pretty much all I've told you here.

We sat in the van on an overlook with a view of the city and the Pacific to the horizon over which, somewhere, my stenos were playing, or maybe sleeping, it was a little shy of noon. It made you dizzy, almost, to think of that whole other life going on, out there, and then this life here, the city pullulating with stoplights and traffic, both lives sentient and aware but each totally ignorant of the other. Only theirs had been going on unchanged for twenty-five million years, while less than two centures ago this city had been a swamp, and in less than two more would probably be a black smear taken out in a Chinese first strike against the Pearl Harbor atomics. At least that's what Les thought.

"So you've got to go on," he said.

"I've got to go on, but why the so?"

"Because they're the only chance we have of learning how an intelligent species can live without tearing itself apart."

"I can answer that for you right now," I said. "We can stop changing. We can fix everything so it just stays the same way a million years at a time. Come on, Les. You sound just like Frank did."

"Maybe Frank wasn't so far wrong."

It was on the tip of my tongue to say, Fucking typical! All man can think of from another species is to get bailed out of the shit he's in. Like all these science fiction stories where an alien species, just like us only smarter and with no hang-ups, comes down from the skies and presents us, free of charge, with the cure for cancer, and war, and the solutions to philosophical paradoxes, and a saner sexual ethic. But I stopped myself in time, partly because I had learned, from the incident with Sam, to keep a better guard on my tongue when with friends, and partly because what I was seeking from the dolphins—not answers to questions, but questions, questions for us to ask ourselves—sounded so like what he was proposing that we'd only get into a stalemate over it.

"Well, whatever," I said. "I'm going on."

But how?

MY MAJOR HOPE—that I had been omitted from the economy drive that had cut short the *Farquarson*'s survey—lasted no longer than the first five minutes with Barry. "I have the order here," he said, groping around in his papers and waving a Final Overdue Book Notice from Hamilton Library at me. "No. No that's not it. No matter. I have it somewhere. And there's an official letter thanking you for your services."

"No decoration?"

He let that one go by him. "Frankly, Les—"

"Andy."

"Andy, could you blame them for giving it up? Even if it wasn't for all this fiscal nonsense? I mean what have they got out of it? Basically, a pretty expensive equipment test. And some physical studies. Oh, and before I forget, they want you to report to Lompoc for further testing. End of this week will do."

"In a pigskin valise."

"What was that?"

"I'm not going. Period."

"They'll pay your travel and per diem."

"I'm still not going."

Barry sighed, swung his feet up on the desk, steepled his fingertips and regarded me over their spire. "Andy," he said, "I've been putting this off as long as I could, because it's very unpleasant for me. But now I see I really can't put it off any longer. I have to talk to you about your Attitude."

"My Attitude."

"Yes your attitude!" he snapped like a whiplash. Then with a sudden swift change of gears he said, "You know, I do understand in a lot of ways how this feels to you. Don't think I don't. I mean you've done things that, well, if a quarter of them could have gotten known, why, I guess you'd be famous, rich, have everyone running after you . . ."

"You think I'm pissed because I'm not into that kind of circus?"

He blinked. "Well, that would be very understandable."

"Not for me."

"Well, in that case I'm at a loss to know why you're behaving like this. Have *been* behaving like this, for several months now. As if nothing were good enough for you. As if you were a law unto yourself. Well, that won't do if you're a team member. If you're a team member you play for the team. Not yourself. If you want to play for yourself, you must quit the team."

I tried staring at him but his gaze wouldn't budge and it was I who had to break contact. I was going to have to eat crow, I could see that, and this knowledge made me all the madder, but I kept it corked and said, "Are you asking for my resignation?"

"No," he said. "Your work has been satisfactory, what little I've seen of it lately. I just had to warn you that unless you Changed your Attitude . . . Well, let's leave it at that, shall we?"

I said nothing, and he took my silence for assent.

"So, you'll report to Lompoc."

"If they've discontinued the project, I don't see—"

"It's very important for the Station if we're going to get help from the Navy in the future." If you're a team member, you play for the team.

"Oh, well . . . okay."

"Then after that you can resume work on the language project."

"*Your* language project?"

"Is there any other?"

I said nothing. "Unless you have any cogent alternative," Barry went on. "But, frankly, as I was saying just now, your own work, fascinating though it was, doesn't seem to have turned out all that revealing. I mean, although you've added plenty of facts on steno behavior—enough to still get a dissertation out of, I'd think—nothing really turns out to have very much bearing on the problems of teaching them to communicate with us, which is what's of paramount importance to us here and now." And he shut up and smiled, over his steeple, as if to say, "Well, that's wrapped *that* up nice and neatly."

I had one card left to play. I played it.

"I have a confession to make," I said.

"Yes?"

"I lied to you. The reports on my research. They're pure bullshit. What actually happened was, they have a language, already, I'm learning it, and I've got to go on learning it, somehow."

Barry demolished his steeple, swung his feet to the floor, wheeled his chair up close to the desk and sat, gripping the edge of it, staring at me with a wild surmise. Neither of us said a word for a full minute by the clock.

IT WAS A PRETTY desperate gamble, I knew. But I knew also that I was never going to get back to mid-ocean unless I could show some powerful reason for putting me there. And I had no reason other than the truth. It *was* the truth, too, goddamnit. And we are taught that the Truth is Great and Shall Prevail.

Maybe, somehow, I could convince him.

Barry broke the silence by saying, "Andy. Please explain to me. Is this some kind of a joke?"

"No."

"I know I have problems sometimes with your generation. Understanding exactly what your generation is saying. I am aware that this is a weakness, and Cheryl is helping me to overcome it." I groaned inwardly. "So much of what you say seems to be hyperbole, or parable, or something, I suppose I should thank God you're not radicals like the last lot, but . . ."

"I meant what I said. Literally."

"You expect me to believe it?"

"Why not? It's the truth."

"In that case, why did you lie about it?"

"Because I knew you wouldn't believe me."

"Then why tell me now?"

He had me there. Again, there was nothing that even might work but the truth. "Because I have to get back out there, finish what I started. If I can convince you, maybe you can help put me there."

He said nothing for quite a while. Then, "You've got to admit that your way of going about this hardly inspires confidence."

"I know it."

"In the first place, what you're saying is so inherently improbable, one's first reaction is just to write it off then and there. So much so that one's next reaction is to say, 'Well! What motivation could Andy have for telling me this story?' And lo and behold, the motivation's right there, you gave it yourself. It's very sustaining for the ego to be alone out there, king of the sea, responsible to nobody, doing your thing with *Steno bredanensis.* You wouldn't want it to stop. You want to go on doing it. But you can't go on doing it unless you can dream up some super-duper discovery that would make it all worthwhile. The idea of talking dolphins has been floating around in the counterculture for God knows how many years now, so that's a natural. Your obvious first choice. However, one's third reaction is: 'Now, Andy isn't a complete fool, far from it, he must have thought of these objections and he presumably wouldn't have tried to put such a corny idea over on me if he didn't have some kind of evidence.' "

Barry stopped so abruptly that there was another period of silence while I strove to collect my thoughts. They remained scattered. He had overestimated my foresight.

Barry flickered his tongue. "Some tape-recordings, let's suppose. With transcription. And translation."

I shook my head.

"No? Well really! Just what have you got? Aside from your say-so?"

Of course, the answer was "Nothing," because I had never anticipated being put into this situation. Fantastic though it may seem to you, I had simply never thought about the day when I would have to face the scepticism of organized science. Perhaps I hadn't really cared. I had determined to make no disclosure until I had truly mastered the stenos' tongue, and that time still seemed so remote as to make it futile to prepare for. And then I saw the flaw in Barry's argument and said, "All right, suppose I had got tapes and transcriptions? What would that prove? It wouldn't prove a thing, because there's no way you could check the translation. I could tell you anything I pleased."

"H'm," Barry said. "Stalemate. No, wait. It isn't. Not necessarily. We have our own dolphins here. Mele and Lei. Okay, if you say you can talk with dolphins, all you have to do is talk with them."

It was so obvious I wondered why neither of us had thought of it before.

"Would you accept that?" Barry said. "As a legitimate test?" He said it with a kind of crafty eagerness, as if expecting I'd chicken out and the whole absurd episode would be done with, and we could all get back to Real Science again.

"Sure I'll accept it."

"Okay. When do you want to do it?"

"What's wrong with right now?"

I SHOULD HAVE foreseen it. A little thought would have given it me. But I was too full of confidence to think; anything less than Barry throwing me out on my ear was a victory, and he had actually agreed to a fair test!

Barry agreed that Lei was better to test out on than Mele, because Mele had been reared in captivity and therefore might never have fully mastered her ancestral tongue; whereas Lei, who had been captured as a young adult, should have no problems understanding me, and vice versa. I took Les's spare version of the Batteau machine and entered her tank.

Lei turned, even before I hit the water, and came toward me, squawking a welcome. My first problem was to establish some distance between us, for she came nuzzling me so hard I was being pushed against the side of the tank. Then, as soon as we were properly separated, I broadcast a simple image—that of a tuna, swimming around at the far side of the tank.

Her reaction was weird. First she braked sharply, veered in a swirl of foam and rushed as far from me as she could, as if I had terrified her in some way. Then she swam to the side of the tank where I had imaged the tuna as if she thought there might really be one there. She hunted half-heartedly for a few moments, and then broadcast a string of clicks of her own.

If it was an image, it was of nothing I could recognize.

For one awful second I thought, hell, she's from a different region, she must speak a different language! Then I realized that this was impossible. You can only have different languages if you are limited to the oblique, left-handed way we humans communicate. Since, with us, there's no necessary link between name and thing, we can call, say, some animal *dog* or *chien* or *perro* or whatever we fancy, given enough of us agree to call it that. But with the stenos, the name is the thing's own sound-image, and that you can't change, any more than you can change the dog's bark or its skeleton. True, the few abstract things in steno language, like the question-whistles, were arbitrary and could, in theory, differ from region to region, but Lei hadn't whistled—just fired off a click-train that should have been a picture of something.

Could be—since my vocabulary was so limited still—that it was just something I'd never encountered. No matter. We were bound to hit some shared item soon.

From the side of the tank, Barry called out, "Tell her to pick up the ball that's lying on the bottom and throw it out the right-hand side of the tank."

That was a breeze. I broadcast the request-whistle (no steno ever commands another to do anything) and the image of the ball shooting up and over the side of the tank. No response. Lei continued to cruise back and forth, back and forth at the far side of the tank. A horrible premonition began to grip me. I repeated the image, embroidering it, adding a steno that dived and pushed the ball where it was supposed to go, adding Lei's signature-whistle to the request-whistle. It could not have been plainer. It was so plain, in sea-steno language it would have been downright rude. Because, if I'd framed a request and it wasn't honored, I'd have gotten *some* kind of reaction from them—one of the annoyance-squawks, if I'd asked for something they didn't want to do, or a request for amplification, if they simply hadn't understood what I said. But I got nothing—no response at all. Except, when I paused a while to think of some new strategy, Lei began broadcasting what at first sounded like pure garbage—dolphin sounds, with some of the sounds she had been taught in the language program mixed in with them—but which then, I suddenly realized, was in part at least an attempt to imitate what I'd just said.

Then I knew for sure what had happened.

I kept on trying, though; went through other routines, asked her to do other things, but the result was always the same: blank indifference, or chains of sound that had neither relevance nor meaning, mimickings or just sound-salads.

I climbed, dripping, from the tank.

"Well," Barry said, with a smile so smug it was all I could do to keep from hitting him, "it didn't turn out too well, did it?"

"You fucking bastard," I said. "You've driven her insane!"

LIKE I SAID, I should have figured it.

We are social animals, but the stenos much more so. "Individualism" is something they just couldn't dream of—everything they had derived from their interaction with one another. And these two had been placed in solitary confinement for years—unable to see or scan one another, unable to exchange images. We know that solitary can drive *people* mad—then how much more so a dolphin? And how would we even know? How could we know if a member of another species is mad? How do we know if one of us is mad? By behavior, partly—but put any creature in a cage or tank and its behavior is going to be odd. But mostly we know by speech; if a person's speech is disordered, or incomprehensible, or inappropriate to the situation, we say that they are mad. If you can't speak to them, how can you know? But I could speak to Lei, and I knew that she was stark raving crazy, and that probably all dolphins held under those conditions were crazy too.

But there was no way I could prove that.

"It's too easy, you see," Barry, who had taken my outburst far more calmly than I'd expected, said to me. "You claim dolphins have a language, but you can't communicate with captive dolphins because they've all been driven insane by their cruel captors. So in fact there's no way of proving or disproving your claim. It remains just what it was to begin with —an article of faith."

"Try it yourself, in the ocean."

Barry sighed, and ran his fingers through his stiff brush of hair. "Andy—be realistic for a moment. At least I'm sure you're not faking anything, now. You really believe what you're saying. But just think about it. You've been out there, alone, with the dolphins, for weeks, months on end. A very unnatural situation. Enough to make anyone, well, lose his sense of balance. Maybe start imagining things. I think you've come through it all remarkably well, considering. There's not many people would have stood up to it as well as you have. But when all's said and done, there you are—were—listening all day and all night to the sounds these creatures made, and they do make a lot of sounds, let's face it, they're very noisy creatures. And alone, out there, like that, what would be easier than to start imagining that the sounds *meant* something, even to imagine they were talking to you, and you were answering them. On top of which, you decided to keep the whole thing to yourself. In fact, now I come to think of it, that's very significant, that you kept it to yourself, it suggests that maybe at some deep subconscious level you knew, all the time, that the whole thing was some kind of hallucination. Anyway, whether or no, you contrived to keep yourself insulated from any kind of comment or criticism that might have strangled this . . . this fantasy of yours at birth. So that it grew and grew until it dominated your entire thinking, and whatever happened now, whatever I or anyone else did to prove you wrong, you wouldn't accept, you'd just try to argue it away like you did with Lei's performance just now. And since your distorted thinking is limited to just this one—"

It had taken all this time for me to realize what he was saying.

"You think *I'm* crazy, is that it?"

"I don't like that word," Barry said, "and I deliberately didn't use it. Even if it were justified in some cases, it obviously isn't in yours. Apart from this . . . *obsession,* you seem perfectly normal. It hasn't affected your functioning because it's environmentally induced, and if you just remain in a more natural environment for long enough, it'll disappear of its own accord. Although I'm sure counseling would help. So what I'm going to suggest is the following: you'll be relieved of all duties for the next two months, and I'll fix for you to attend a very good clinic here, none of this Freudian nonsense about what your subconscious did when you were two, they're all good behaviorists who stick to the presenting problem—"

"I'm not going to any funny farm."

"This is not a 'funny farm,' " Barry said in quotes of distaste. "You'll go there for an hour a week or whatever they decide is appropriate."

"No."

"I can't force you to go, I'm well aware of that. But you must realize that things can't go on like this. If you won't agree to what I suggested I'm afraid I'm going to have to ask you to leave the Station. Permanently."

IT TOOK ME no more than half an hour to pack my gear and move out. I'd gotten through to Keala by this time, she came down with the Bug and got into a shouting match with Cheryl, who was sniffing around making sure there was no Station property mixed in with my stuff. Les helped me load up the Bug while the two women insulted one another; he looked wretched and embarrassed about the whole thing.

"You shouldn't have come on strong like that," he was saying. "You should have led into it gradually. Why didn't you tell me you were going to do that? I'd have argued you out of it."

"Do you think I'm crazy, too?"

He looked genuinely shocked. "No way, man! How can you say that?" And yet, sincere as he seemed, I knew that always, somewhere in the back of his mind, a tiny worm of doubt would dwell, and perhaps grow.

And why not? The scariest thing about my interview with Barry was the way reality took on a completely new twist when he handled it. You've seen those trick pictures that look like a jug at first, and then when you look again it's the faces of two old women confronting one another, and you wonder, How the hell could I have thought it was a jug? And then suddenly, click, it's a jug again. So it was with Barry's view of my experiences. As strongly as my soul might rebel against the idea, I had to admit that it had a frightening plausibility. Could it have been so? Could all I had experienced have been self-deception? Even as I ran to and fro with clothes and books and boxes of records—for having decided to leave, the sooner I left the better—I was asking myself these questions, quite sincerely, going over and over in my mind the events of the last months and asking myself if they would indeed bear the interpretation Barry put on them. And it was not until several hours later that the realization came to me: if I were really crazy, would I be so calmly and rationally prepared to face the possibility?

Barry appeared just as we were finishing.

"I'm sorry it had to end like this."

I ignored his outstretched hand.

"Well, it was your decision. Oh, by the way, what became of the suit and all your other gear?"

"It's still on the *Farquarson,*" I lied. "If you want it, you can argue with the Navy about it."

"Oh. Oh."

IN THE BUG, Keala and I hardly said a word. An almost palpable depression lay upon us, and it did not lift until, back at her new place, we had put down the best part of a half gallon of California red. I don't drink, as a rule—dope is more my scene—and I guess I was moderately bombed. I got rather noisy, and I think pissed off the people she was living with, though they were too polite or too timid to say anything about it.

Keala had graduated from the School of Social Work, and had a job downtown with a private agency, reclaiming alkies. So she'd moved into a beat-up old frame shack on St. Louis Heights with a bunch of other kids straight out of the school or in their first year on the job. It was all rather self-consciously hang-loose and let's-show-we're-human-even-though-social-workers. (There I go being hypercritical again—maybe I was just jaundiced, maybe I just resented Keala building a life for herself, though in my long absences, what was she supposed to have done?) Anyway, nobody objected when it was announced that I was to share Keala's room.

But what was I to do the next day, or the next?

By eight in the morning the house was empty. By the time I got up, it would have that sluggish, exhausted air a house has after a series of whirlwind departures. I'd go and look out the window, out over Waikiki and Diamond Head, and see the sets coming in like bunches of ruled lines on the expanse of velvet blue. That was too painful. I played the stereo but I soon got bored with that. I started to read the piles of old magazines and newspapers that were littered around the house, but that was a mistake I'd made before: the catalogue of human horrors just depressed me still more. I went surfing a couple of times, but even that wasn't like it had been before. I could feel all my anger just under the surface, waiting to break out. At Ehukai, a big moke tried to drop in on me and I elbowed him off his board, cussing him and ploughing over him with my own. That was bad news. He and four of his buddies came for me as I walked out of the shorebreak. A lot of mokes I knew, through the Kealohas, and was okay with, but not these. I made a kind of jab at the nearest one, not so much to do damage as to clear my way for a run, and to my amazement he went down in the sand. I thought it must be a fluke. So did the other four, they kept coming. I swung on the second, desperate this time, and he went flying heels over ass, all two-twenty pounds of him. The other three stopped dead, then backed slowly off, giving me stink-eye and cursing horrendously.

I was amazed, more than they. I'd never been that much of a fighter. But when I looked down at myself, which I normally never bothered to, not being into all that Phys-Ed shit, I realized that all those months of swimming and diving had developed my chest and arm-muscles till I was a positive Schwarznegger. And now I'd picked up on it, I saw people were looking at me in awe and envy of my big ugly build. That should have pleased me, but it didn't. What use was it all to me? A career in body-building? Yech! I felt creepy, like a stranger, a prisoner in my own body.

And there was at least one department of the physical in which I was well below par.

The first night I made love to Keala (actually the second night of my return, we were both too juiced the first) I was impotent. It scared the piss out of me. It had never happened in my life before. All was well, I was hard, thrusting into her, and suddenly it was like humping a mist, there was no contact. I couldn't believe it. Me? Soft? And then I made things worse by trying to make all kind of stupid excuses, my nerves, and the strain, and terminal fatigue, and I don't know what else. Keala was very good about it. Took me in her arms and told me not to worry, it didn't matter, it would pass, it was just temporary, and she hadn't wanted to make love all that much just then, anyway. And I, like a real mean asshole, had to say, "Is that your regular Masters and Johnson routine for impotents?"

She didn't answer me. Her eyes flashed, she was on the point of saying something hurtful back, and she should have, what I needed right then was someone to come along and say, "Watch it, you're on the way to becoming a first-class prick." But I guess her training had taught her to refuse gambits like mine, she just looked hurt and looked away.

Two nights later we had a rerun. Only this time she was human enough to say, "Andy? You get somebody else? If get, tell me, ah? I no gon' get mad with you."

"You lolo, how could there be anyone else, I've been at sea for months and I ain't gay."

But that wasn't quite true, was it? I mean that there couldn't be anyone else. Because I knew what it was all right—had known, from right after the first moment of shock and shame, although I'd forced the thought from my mind as monstrous, unthinkable. A woman's body just didn't feel right to me any more. It was too warm, too soft, too yielding—it hadn't the grip of those mighty alien muscles, our sweaty cavortings on the bed were not, somehow, to be compared with the frenzy of those wild charges through the ocean, spray flying through the air, sun flashing through the spray. Human love seemed a pale, insipid thing, after that.

For a time anyway.

But in time the present eats away the past; and as the memory of Susan's flesh faded and the demands of my own youth asserted themselves, I began to recover my powers. Not without relapses. I would be deep in Keala, rock-hard, and somehow, unbidden, an electric touch of salt coldness would fire through my memory like a rocket trail, and I would feel my member weakening and thrust the memory from my mind until I was restored again.

So my sex life recovered, and I had become strong and dangerous. But none of that answered the question that was asking itself daily, more and more insistently:

What are you going to do with your life?

THAT HAD NEVER been any problem to me before. Why should it have been? I had everything going for me, though I say it myself: courage, charm, brains, good looks, everything but money, and money you hardly need, with that combination—or, if you need it, you should have little trouble getting it. So I'd gone on, taking what I wanted from life, doing the next thing that came up to do without giving it another thought. I had run on rails, rails that seemed to go on infinitely into a vaguely shining future. Now, suddenly, the track had vanished; and that future, become the present, shone no longer, was a cold arid desert with leaden clouds. All that there was to strive for in the human world—power, wealth, fame, honor—now seemed stale and trivial beside the goal I had come so close to and lost. Maybe, given time, I would have realized that with enough wealth and enough power I could pursue that goal without need of assistance, and would have set myself to achieve them; although wealth and power on that scale tend to come only to those who seek them, not as instrumentalities, but for their own sake. But I was not to be given time.

. . .

IRONICALLY, IT WAS Barry who tipped me off. He phoned up one morning, when I was alone in the house, and said, right away, without any preamble, "You told me that you had left all your dolphin gear aboard the *Farquarson.*"

"That's right."

"No it isn't. You lied to me. They have no trace of it."

"They're crazy. You know how things are in the Services. They lose stuff by the ton. Some crooked quartermaster probably fenced it off."

"Did they give you a receipt for it?" crafty Barry asked.

"No, of course not. Why should they? It wasn't my gear anyway."

There was so long a silence I thought we'd been cut off. Then, "Andy, I think you're in a lot of trouble."

"How can I be?"

"I think you took that stuff with you. I can't think why or what you hope to do with it but if I were you I'd get it back to them. Fast."

"I don't see why you assume—"

"Look, I'm not arguing with you! I'm telling you!"

And this time the phone went dead for real.

Even while he was talking to me, little things I'd noticed but paid no heed to began to drop into place in my mind. Like the red Pinto I'd seen in my rear-view mirror a couple of times the previous day. Like the plastic hippy with the idiot grin I'd kept bumping into on the beach or at discos for nearly a week. I was under surveillance by the Feds.

And it was obvious why. It would never occur to them that I would steal top-secret equipment for merely private purposes. I must be part of a conspiracy. A bunch of radical extremists or even a full-blown Russki spy ring. Pointless to lift me and leave the cell unsquelched. So they were checking out my movements, where I went, who I saw.

It would only be a matter of time before they found there was nothing to find out. After that it would be a simple larceny bust.

Hawaii is a bad state to draw heat in. Any other and you can fade into the vast land mass of the Americas. Here you had to fly, and airports are the easiest things in the world to watch. About the only other way would be to find a yachtsman short of crew, but that's not easy at short notice, even when you're not being watched. I called Les (from a call box, I was sure Keala's phone would be tapped) and asked him to see what he could do. He said to call back in a couple of days. I knew that he knew a lot of the characters who hang around the Ala Moana Yacht Basin, but even I was surprised when, two days later, he said yes, there was a guy leaving early the following week for Palmyra, the Tuamotus and points south who would take me along. Thinking quickly, I had him fix up a meet at Shari's, a fast-food joint just off campus. I chose there for two reasons. First, they have tables outside under the trees from which you can spot people approaching before they can spot you, and second, because Feds would stand out like a sore thumb in the campus crowd.

I had no premonitions on the morning of the meet. Keala kissed me and left while I was still half-asleep, and even her Hawaiian second sight did not tell her that she would never see me again. An hour later I was up, washed and shaved, ready for action. First I checked out the window. For several nights now they'd had a surveillance vehicle, a small green van with no name on it, parked half a block up the hill. It never followed me; I guess they simply radioed ahead to a pursuit vehicle a mile or so down at the bottom of the hill, since there's only the one road out of St. Louis Heights. But this morning it wasn't there. That should have warned me, already, but I only thought, well, about time they switched vehicles, although Jesus, what a waste of the taxpayers' money! The real business would come down below, where I wheeled into the parking lot between Chico's and the corner gas station, got out and surveyed the scene. Nobody drove in and parked after me. I went in the supermart next to Chico's and bought a cold 7-Up. Nobody came in after me. I went out and drank the 7-Up on the sidewalk, monitoring the morning shoppers. Nobody looked awkward or out of place. But there was the chance they already had a stakeout in the lot, since it was so near home. So I drove slowly down Waialae to Beretania. Between Beretania and South King there are several alleys so narrow that only one car at a time can get through. I kept circling the block, down one alley to King, along King and up the next to Beretania, and so on, looking in the rear-view mirror all the while. Nothing. All my elaborate precautions had turned out to be unnecessary. And *that* should have warned me. But I'm rash and full of optimism, as you'll have seen by now, I throw myself in first and worry how to get out afterward, so I thought merely, what luck! I parked on University, and crossed the avenue to Shari's.

Two men in suits stepped out from under the trees, looking like fugitives from Hawaii Five-O, and one said. "You are Mr. Andrew—"

That was as far as he got. I ducked under the arm of the other and doubled back into the avenue, against the light. Brakes screeched. Through the racket I heard someone shout faintly, "Freeze, mister!" but I took no notice, jumped into the Bug and fired the motor. I saw him out of the tail of my eye just as I shifted into second, on the highway divider, down in that FBI crouch that looks like a dog crapping and with both hands steadying his piece. I couldn't believe it, even when something went "clung!" and a ragged hole magically appeared in the hood in front of me. Insane! Slinging .357 magnums around in a street full of cars and students! I jammed up the hill with all the power the Bug had in it.

They were out after me before I made the turn at the top, in a souped-up Mercedes convertible that had been parked two spaces below where I had parked. Even as I drove, at top speed, with most of my mind on how not to hit someone, the parts were coming together. That parking spot had been left for me, deliberately, I should have realized, there's never a space there, ever, during the day; the whole thing had been set up, they hadn't needed surveillance because they knew in advance exactly where I was going. For a second I cursed Les, thinking he'd shopped me, and then I realized they would have had the Station phone tapped, too; he had blundered into it as innocently as I. Shit! Nothing to do about it now, but try and shake these bastards.

I swung left, and it was Kraut against Kraut in the back streets of Manoa. Here there's a tangle of narrow lanes where I thought the Bug's maneuverability would give me the edge, but the driver of the Merc must have been to Spook Driving College and I couldn't shake him. Desperate remedies! If I was on the freeway I could shake any sonofabitch by hanging a right from the center lane into an off-ramp when I was already almost past the exit; scary, because the Bug's center of gravity's none too high and you could flip over, but sure to work provided you yourself didn't wipe out. Once on Punahou, there were only three stoplights between me and the Punahou on-ramp, and if I hit them all on green . . .

The first one, at Punahou and Nehoa, went red when I was fifty yards from it, coming downhill like a bat out of hell with the Merc another fifty in back of me. I would have shot the light if a red Pinto, coming uphill on Punahou, hadn't swung across and stopped, dead in front of me.

I shifted into second, practically stripping the transmission, leaned over hard, and made the turn into Nehoa on two wheels —thank God there was nothing in the way, because I hadn't had time even to look. If my stars had been right that day the Merc and the Pinto would have totaled one another, but miraculously they missed without even a fender-bender and were after me two abreast. And then, from the direction of downtown, I heard a police siren. They'd called the regular cops. They had me boxed in.

I hung a right at Nehoa and Makiki. It was my only chance, and it gave me a breathing space, because the road is uphill all the way from there and that Bug could climb and loop like a bitch, the way I had it fixed. Three bends up, they'd lost fifty yards; six up, they were out of sight.

As well they could afford to be.

Because I was on Tantalus Drive, and Tantalus Drive is a

loop road with no side turnings. They had me. They only had to block both ends and wait.

When I got to the highest point on the drive I stopped, parked and said a fond farewell to my trusty four-wheeled friend. From here on, it was Feet-don't-fail-me. I could walk into the Ko'olaus and stay there forever, they'd never find me. Trouble was, there was nothing to eat but lilikoi and strawberry guava. Sooner or later I'd have to come out and steal food, and sooner or later I'd get careless or unlucky. No future in that. Just a breathing space.

I walked up through the forest to the summit of Tantalus. On the summit there's a kind of big stone table I guess surveyors use. I hunkered down on the table and began to collect myself. It was a glassy day, so insanely clear you could see way over the ocean to the other islands, Molokai and Lanai and even West Maui. There was even a ball of cloud low down on the southeastern horizon that could have been the summit cloud over Mauna Kea, two hundred miles away. All the light in the world seemed to be focused on that table, and as I crouched there, brooding, everything started to come together in my mind.

If I went on the way I was going, it was jail, nothing but. I wasn't scared of jail, the shape I was in I could smear any ass-bandit onto the wall, but I had only so many years to live and I didn't see why I should lose any of them for this craziness. I knew though that to go to them now and say, "Hey, fellows, sorry about the confusion, I meant no harm, here's your gear back and let's say no more about it," would buy me nothing. They'd thank God the case fell out so easy and thank me by throwing the book at me. So perish all naïve idiots. I was made of sterner stuff. I was going to get out.

But out of what, into what?

I sat there in the appalling clarity of that light and looked around at a world that my species was slowly turning into nightmare—so slowly and so patiently that most of us aren't even aware of it. Those who knew, those who were aware, were all helpless, shaking the invisible bars of the prison that held them. For that was the second and stronger reason why going to jail was no big deal: we were already in jail, all of us, imprisoned in our own species, and there was nothing we could do about it. We wanted to do good and the good turned to evil in our hands. We wanted to save and in our hands the surgeon's scalpel turned into the assassin's knife. It had always been so, I guess, but right now, in my century, with all the power we seemed to have, the paradox had grown more appalling, the gulf between what we could dream and what we could do loomed absurdly immense. And that was why people blew out their brains with every kind of drug, and that was why people sought refuge in silence and madness: they were trying with all they'd got (which was never enough) to shake the bars of the cage, to loosen the bars, to break through them, to become all we could dream of being but never be, to be other than what we were. Sitting there, I could almost hear it, the way you can hear the roar of ocean in the whorl of a seashell: the strange longing, the new and terrible need the vision brought with it, roaring through the dreams of a million acid-trippers and echoing from the cries of the incarcerated in ten thousand asylums:

To be other than what I am!

I, and I alone, could break out of that prison.

I had gotten halfway out already. I had gone halfway toward meeting a species utterly different from our own, toward feeling and understanding how they were in their differentness. Why stop halfway? Why not go the limit? People had abandoned their countries, their faiths—changed them for others. Why should I not do the same with my species?

Once an idea like that grips you, there is no resisting it. Fantastic as it might seem. Because all that was needed, once you made the mental leap, was what all our species were good at: figuring out practical problems of technology and logistics. And on that level, it was nothing like as impossible as it looked. Within minutes, I realized I could have done it any time during these days I had been wasting. All I'd lacked was the motivation and the will.

And Keala?

Les? My friends? My family, such as it was? Everyone I had ever cared for? That was over. I had one momentary pang of regret for Keala, and that was all, I'm sorry now to say it, now that I know I shall never see her again; and after that I forced her and all the others from my mind. You have to make some sacrifices, if you take as heavy a path as the one I had just chosen. To become truly other, I would have to purge myself of all that I had ever been.

NO NEED TO GO into details. How I exhumed the gear that, as if gifted with prescience, I had buried less than half a mile from the summit of Tantalus. How I descended—at dusk, with infinite precaution—to the city, and hot-wired a pickup. How I then, with the money I'd drawn out ready for some rather less radical move, bought gas, bottled water, waterproof containers, medical supplies, dehydrated foods, vitamins and God-knows-what other bits and pieces, even (thanks to my long-time grad student's habit of making notes on anything and everything) the water-resistant paper and indelible pencils on which and with which I am now inscribing this history. And, with a full load, made my way to the small-boat harbor by the Station and the forty-two-foot Chris-Craft Commander that some fish-loving playboy kept moored there. By then it was ten-thirty with hardly anyone around; and if there had been, who would question a man taking gear *onto* a boat? By eleven, everything was stowed and the engine was firing, and the nearest I came to getting stopped was when I'd already cast off and was running for the harbor entrance—and then this boat came in right on top of me, one of the yachts that take tourists for romantic moonlight cruises, only they're not really yachts, the sails and rigging are pure decoration, they run on inboard diesels. The clown at the wheel was zonked is a good guess, and though I yelled at them they couldn't hear me over the *hapa-haole* guitar music and the drunken singing; I thought they would plow right over me. Somehow I got the Chris-Craft's head around in time, and we passed within feet of one another—"Power gives way to sail!" some asshole had the effrontery to shout—while all along the side the tourists shrieked and waved and cheered at me. I shouted, "Fuck the lot of you!" and gave them the finger, but most were too bombed to see or understand me, or they took it for some form of native greeting they hadn't mastered yet, for they kept on waving cheerily until I was out of sight.

It was a fitting farewell to my species. Who'd want to belong to *that*, in his proper senses, anyway?

Then suddenly I was over Shark Hole and felt the first swell from the open ocean lifting the Chris-Craft's keel. My heart leapt. I was home free! I checked that everything was in place, put the motor on full power, and set course for the seamount, twelve hundred miles to the west.

I HAD LUCK with the weather, at first. The Chris-Craft sped on smoothly over long oily swells. There were no other vessels in sight. After some hours I hove to and slept, or tried to; what sleep I could get was racked with strange and horrible dreams. Great monsters with lamped heads and needle teeth swarmed round me; eels involved me in their slimy coils; I was sinking irresistibly to bottomless depths; it was as if, resenting my betrayal, the souls of my species and all its ancestors were reaching out after me and trying to drag me back—reaching out from the vast shadowy tree of phyla and genera that seethed with the fear of the alien element.

Then the weather worsened and there were real fears to contend with. Hour after hour the Chris-Craft wallowed through the seas, only inches away from swamping and sinking. At first I lashed myself clumsily to the wheel; then I thought, how crazy, if we go down, I'm dead for sure, whereas free of the boat I could still hope to survive! I untied myself, suited up, and awaited the worst, hour upon weary hour.

At last, on what may have been the morning of the fourth day, the storm blew away to the east, the sky cleared, steam rose from exposed surfaces, sunsparks danced on the waves.

I had no instruments but a compass and a chart of the

Central Pacific with the seamount's approximate position pen-
ciled in. It might lie just over the horizon, or the storm might
have swept me hundreds of miles off course.

I was already low on gas, so I cut the engine. The Chris-Craft
rolled sluggishly. How was I to get my bearings? And then
almost immediately, as if in answer to that question, I heard
a loud splash to starboard, and turning, saw the high sail-like
dorsal fin of a steno plunge under the waves. Others surfaced
after him, there was a whole pod come to look at whatever
strange object the storm had washed up for their amusement.
I hoped for one moment that it was my own pod, but I recognized none of them. But then, as they circled me, I thought,
what's the difference, couldn't they still direct me? I strapped
on the Batteau machine, scrambled over the side and plunged
into the midst of them, whistling question-marks and making
the sound-image of the seamount's underwater slopes.

One or two of those nearest me recoiled, and there was a
moment of anxious conversation, in which I caught the familiar image of my own sound-shape. They had heard of me;
maybe their pod had joined mine in the daytime herd. I repeated my question, and this time it was answered: "Away,
over there, to the southwest, far, far!" I sprang back into the
Chris-Craft and we were off, the boat's keel slamming through
the swell-crests so hard I was scared it would shatter, and yet
I didn't care now, I was among my chosen kind, nothing could
go wrong for me, I was racing along in the sunlight with stenos
riding my bow wave, six either side of me, like an imperial
guard.

FOR TWO HOURS we traveled thus, or maybe longer, I had lost
all sense of time. Then there were breakers on the low horizon,
and soon afterward the stubby, eroded crown of the seamount
loomed through their spray. The stenos left me then, leaping,
saluting me, going about their business. I beached the Chris-
Craft on the lee shore, lay down on a rugged bed of detritus
and it was soft as feathers, I was asleep within seconds, this
time dreamlessly.

I did not wake until near dawn on the following day. At first light, I took everything from the Chris-Craft, stashed it in crannies of the rocks, filled the boat with boulders till it was near sinking, pushed it into deep water and stove a hole in the fiberglass hull. It sank until the white hull was only a glimmer on the shelf beneath. Then I swam back to the seamount.

I now had a secure base that would see me through the period of transition, where I could return, at progressively longer intervals, to recoup myself, until I became fully adapted to the stenos' world. With any luck, my supplies should last me till then. I rested the remainder of that day and the night that followed; then I set out on my search.

It never occurred to me to doubt that I would find them—impossible as that might seem, in the immensity of ocean, with no radio beacon now to guide me. But I knew, or thought I knew, that the seamount represented the northernmost limit of their territory. If I zigzagged south from there, sooner or later I must meet them, or at least some pod that shared their herd.

Two days and nights passed, in growing anxiety, loneliness and boredom, and I saw no member of their species. I was not afraid. On the second day a rogue barracuda tracked me half the afternoon and then rushed me, but I extinguished it in a microsecond with the laser gun. Sooner or later I would tire, I knew, but all I had to do then was return to the seamount, rest, and resume the search. Sooner or later, I was sure to find them. Meantime, I kept going.

It was an hour or two after dawn on the third morning when I saw the outline of a ship—just the superstructure, at first, it was hull-down on the western horizon. I had every reason to avoid contact with my own kind, but the stenos loved to surf bow waves, and it would be foolish to pass up this chance without a cautious look from a distance. Accordingly, I began to swim on a course that would intercept the ship. Would *have* intercepted it, if it had been moving. But it wasn't.

Stenos would soon get bored with a motionless ship. So, I was on the point of turning away, when it hit me: *why* would a ship be hove-to, on a calm day in mid-ocean? Could it be a tuna boat? I approached more closely, and indeed, there was the ugly tackle of the purse-seiner thrusting up at stem and stern. It was a big one, and it was working. I saw a sheet of spray fly up from one of the motorized skiffs, what they call pongos in the trade, that they use to round up the tuna herds and head off escapees from the net as the net closes. But the mother-ship being stationary meant that they had already shot and closed the seine-net and must be hauling it in. Sure enough, as I drew closer I saw puffs of blue smoke from the auxiliary engine and the faint rattling of machinery was brought to me on the breeze. And then the lines grew taut, the ship listed slightly to starboard under the weight of the loaded net, the net itself was coming up, in smooth, alternate rushes, on the twin Puretic power blocks, it was full, and it was loaded *with stenos, only with stenos,* it wasn't a tuna boat after all, but one of those conversion jobs like in the news item Cheryl had read to us, greedy heartless bastards who were massacring dolphins for their flesh.

I swam at full speed toward the ship. I had, as yet, not the least idea of what I would do when I got there, just the certainty that I had to go, that these were my friends who were being slaughtered and that I must help them somehow. But already stenos were being spilled out into the bowels of the ship, some dead already, drowned from being held under too long by the net or the weight of bodies above them, some still moving feebly; they must have surrounded a whole herd as it lay sleeping and cut it off. Then, there in the midst of them, I saw a familiar shape with the great weal of a squid's tentacle across its brow: *Duke, it had to be Duke, it was my own pod in there with the rest of them,* and then I made out others, or thought I did—Susan, Bull, the baby, all pouring helplessly into a pit like Hell Gate in a medieval picture, from which now I could hear the voice of different machinery: the grinding of the steel jaws and teeth that would reduce them to an anonymous powder, to be packed and sold to people who might have recoiled in horror if they had known what the tins contained.

I went mad with rage, I beat the water, but it was useless, I was too late; long before I could reach the ship the net was empty, coiled on the deck, already being wound onto the drum in readiness for the next shot, while below the terrible grinding and clanking went on.

I didn't recognize the ship's flag; doubtless it was a flag of convenience merely, belonging to some country too weak and poor to worry about what was done in its name. But I could make out the letters on the bow: COLON. Colon? The name the Spanish called Columbus, I guess that's who it was named for, but all I could think of was the colon, the greedy gut of mankind straining to swallow the world.

In fairness to myself, and in view of what happened afterward—the part you all know already, that must have flashed across all your TV screens, sickening you with its horror even when told second-hand—I should make it clear that at this stage I had not the least thought of violence. Preposterous as it sounds, I was convinced that if I could only talk to them, present them with the truth of what they were doing as only I could know that truth, I could get them to abandon this slaughter. It was too late now to save those I loved, my own pod, my new family, but that would matter less if others could be saved as a result of it.

A rope ladder hung down the side of the ship, with two pongos, empty now, moored next to it. I swam to the foot of the ladder, and then, on a sudden impulse—I was, after all, on a peaceful mission, that would hopefully end this one-sided war between species—I unslung my laser gun and fixed it by its magnetic clamp to the ship's hull, just below the water line. Then I clung to the foot of the ladder until my heart had ceased pounding. Rage and indignation, natural as they might be, would not help my case. I must be calm, lucid, logical; must present unanswerable arguments.

When at last I felt ready, I freed my legs from the lower part of the suit and climbed the ladder.

Nobody saw me till my head and shoulders were over the rail. There was a small cluster of men on the narrow strip of deck between the rail and the open hold, straightening the last folds of the net as it wound onto the drum. One who was facing my way cried out in surprise, and the others turned, straightening up, to stare at me. Hooking my leg over the rail, clumsily gathering up the tail of my suit, I must indeed have made a bizarre spectacle. They came shuffling hesitantly toward me, a motley crew, all races and colors. "Spik Inglee?" one who looked like a half-breed Melanesian asked. "Wheah you boat?"

"I don't have a boat."

They exchanged pitying and incredulous looks.

"You shipwreck marinero? Wheah you from? Wonem boat?"

They must have thought I was some poor castaway gone crazy from loneliness and exposure.

"Take me to your captain," I said.

"Okay, okay! Disside, disside come. We go take you cap'n." They led me toward the stern, and I followed them. I did not look down, to my right. If I had looked down, at the pulverized remains of my former comrades, I don't think I could have controlled myself. We descended a gangway, passed down a short corridor, and I was thrust forward into a small, crowded cabin.

I don't know quite what I'd expected: what monster of drooling tongue and Dracula fangs. What I saw was a hale, ruddy giant of a man, in his fifties maybe, but still smart and vigorous, bowed awkwardly over a desk, writing. He stopped abruptly as I came in, raised a craggy head barely touched with gray and gazed at me with blue eyes of a sunny, almost impish innocence. Slowly, dramatically, his thick brindled eyebrows raised, his hand reached out slow and firm and clamped the pen into its rack as he said, with a Scandinavian accent, "Oho! And what have we here?" Oh, he was a ham all right. And he was also everyone's father, the father anyone would have chosen, if he'd had the choice, whom I'd have chosen over the stooped scholar who'd somehow managed to generate me. And he was also the master of this hell-ship. For a good few seconds I'd forgotten that.

He stood up. "And from where have you sprung?"

"From the sea."

He laughed indulgently. "So much I could guess. I mean which ship, how do you find yourself here?"

"No ship. I live in the sea. Look." I indicated my suit. "This has all I need to support life. I don't need a ship. Ask your crew —have they seen any boat, any wreckage?"

He sat down very slowly, motioning me to sit also. He remained seated, silent, for the best part of a minute, his gaze turned inward; abstractedly he massaged his jaw with his hand. I had time to look about me. His desk, with its pens, pencils, papers, ledgers, was arranged with an absolute symmetry, save for a picture which stood on it at a forty-five-degree angle: a picture with a background of mountain and fjord, himself ten years younger, a drab, dumpy but cheery-looking wife, and three gangling adolescents who must be his children, grown now, all smiling shyly and awkwardly at the camera.

"Incredible," he said at last. "Quite incredible. The wonders science has today. Tell me, how do you live?"

I gave him a brief, highly edited version of my life and how I came to be there. He nodded, thoughtfully; he must have seen enough strange things in his time not to be easily fazed. Then he brightened: "But I think you come not here only to tell your story, no? How is it, you were bored with the fishes, you wish to talk to human persons again. I would think it is some time since you taste the alcohol, is it not so? You would care to join me?"

He was reaching into his desk drawer when I stopped him.

"Please hear what I have to say, first."

He leaned back, puzzled, his brow wrinkling.

"I've come here to protest your slaughter of the dolphins."

For a few seconds his face became blank; then, without changing expression, he began to emit a hissing, sputtering noise, like the burning of a fuse; then he exploded in titanic laughter. "What?" he spluttered, when he had recovered the power of speech. "What? You're one of *them!* These—these crazy people? What will these people think to do next? Look,

I am in Mazatlán harbor, they picket my boat, the Mexican police beat them but still they come back . . . they are crazy children! And even they try to infil, inflin—how you say it?—inflintrate my crew. To make trouble for me. And now you follow me all the way out here." He was laughing again, without any real malice, just a comic outrage, as if it was all part of a game in which I'd just pulled a clever trick on him—but one he was still well able to counter. "What have they done with you, dropped you from an airplane?"

"I told you how I got here."

He waved this brusquely aside, with a gesture that said, that particular charade is over. "Tell me, just what is it that your people try to accomplish in all of this?"

"Stop you from doing what you're doing."

"Why?"

"Because these are intelligent creatures you're killing, as intelligent as you or I. They have the same right to live as we have."

"As intelligent as you or I." He fingered his jaw reflectively, his eyes twinkling. "Tell me something. What kind of intelligence? Intelligence to build this ship, perhaps?"

"Why would they need ships?"

"To go upon the land, of course! Landships!" He rocked at his own humor, while I had a crazy vision, Hieronymus Bosch crossed with Rube Goldberg, of a wooden colossus filled with water staggering across the landscape while dolphins peered from its portholes.

"They don't have hands. They can't make things. What does that have to do with intelligence?"

"Everything! Intelligence is to make things. To make houses, and cities, bridges that join the lands, hospitals for sick people, all! And to make the great cathedrals, for the worship of God, and the pictures of Christ and all his angels—"

"They can make pictures, too."

He pounded on it. "Oh yes? And where are they seen, these pictures? In the Neptune Gallery, perhaps!" Again his own wit cracked him up. I could see it was no use trying to explain to him, but I had to try. "Come, you cannot be serious! They have nothing, nothing! They are animals."

"They have language. They converse, just like we do, they have ideas, they—"

"Please." He held up his hand. "You become angry. In anger is no use. Let us pretend you are correct, and it is true, they are not like sharks, not stupid creatures. But look at the world as we discover it in our time. Right? What do you see? Starvation? Yes, in some places is starvation, in the Sahel, perhaps. But in most places is not the starvation, is something worse than the starvation, most peoples have little to eat, but not enough. Just not . . . quite . . . enough. So what happen? In India now, in South America are growing children who never in all their life have enough to eat. In days before science and its miracles they are dead by disease—now not. They grow, but weak and thin, and their brain cannot grow. The food not rich enough for the brain to grow! So is coming a generation with the brains less than human—in shape they are like us, but in the brain they are animals! How a civilize can stay civilize when this happen? How long? No time! It finish! And if it finish—"

"If people are so stupid they overbreed—"

"True, true! But they *have* overbreeded, and so now what is to do? They are here, on this earth, these lives, these children. You will let them grow tall with their cripple brain? I see them, perhaps you do not but I see them, in Calcutta, the arms and the legs like—like—" He picked up the ballpoint he had been writing with and snapped it in two. "Like a firestick."

"Matchstick."

"Matchstick. You are right. I am always forgetting. They live to steal, this is all they understand. I say this not from prejudice, I am seaman, I love all races. Simply, they have not the responsibility . . . So. You say I am not to feed them. You prefer I murder these children more than those dolphins? Say! Speak out!"

"I have no solution."

"Say! Speak! You are afraid?"

"I have no solution. I just know that what you're doing can't be an acceptable solution. No way. We've made mistakes. We have to solve our own problems. We can't just slaughter other species to bail ourselves out. We don't have that right."

His eyebrows arched, stiffened. "Right?"

"No."

"You are wrong!" He stood up. "I will show to you that we have that right." He turned and pointed to the shelves behind him. "See, here I have the Holy Bible. In four languages. Norwegian, English, German, Spanish. I will take your own Bible, it is the old Bible, not the new-fangle kind. Here, here it says, Book One of Genesis, verse the twenty-six: 'And God said, let us make man in our image, after our own likeness; and let him have dominion over the fish of the sea, and over the fowl of the air, and over the cattle, and over every creeping thing that creepeth upon the earth. So God created man in his own image, in the image of God created he him; male and female created he them. And God blessed them, and God said unto them, be fruitful, and multiply, and replenish the earth, and subdue it; and have dominion over the fish of the sea, and over the fowl of the air, and over every living thing that moveth upon the earth.' " He closed the worn volume reverently and laid it upon his desk. "Everything that moveth upon the earth," he repeated. "Dolphins, too, is it not so? God's own words."

"No," I said.

He gazed at me, blankly.

"Those are not God's words. They're the words of some verminous little scribe sitting in a sand dune in Palestine. With delusions of grandeur. Writing his shoddy little program for taking over the world. A man like you or me, faking it as God, judge and jury in his own—"

He had turned as white as paper, standing there shocked, stricken. His lips moved. "That's . . . that's *blasphemy.*"

"I don't give a shit what it is, I—"

"Blasphemy. How dare you—"

I don't know what would have happened if, at that instant,

a man in a leather jacket hadn't run in on us and, with only a startled glance at me, begun to speak to the captain in a low murmur from which I could catch only occasional words.

"Well do it! Move!" the captain shouted. He came out from behind his desk. "I will come to the bridge."

"What we do wit' him, sir?" the man asked.

"Do what you wish with him, only get him out of my sight!"

The man grabbed my arm. I made no effort to resist him; what would have been the use? I was hustled on deck, where they all swarmed round me, shouting and arguing in half-a-dozen languages. Some were for putting me in the ship's brig; others, over the side. "Echale en la machina!" someone cried, and my blood turned cold. Throw him in the machine! With my companions who had preceded me there. Fitting, in a way. But the fuzzy-haired part-Melanesian who'd first spoken to me pointed out that my flesh might then be eaten by humans, and that was cannibalism, and cannibalism was illegal. The argument was tipping in favor of the brig when suddenly I flashed on what Br'er Rabbit had done in like predicament.

"Don't throw me in the sea!" I cried piteously. "Please, I'll drown, anywhere but in the sea!"

I had not underestimated the meanness of my species. Firm hands grasped me, I was lifted high, hurled outward; the sea came rushing up, glittering in the morning sun, my briar patch opened and took me in.

I WENT DOWN like a stone, leveled off and rose to breathe. There they all were, leaning on the rail and laughing at me; two of them began to pelt me with empty beer cans. I don't know what was in their minds; I expect they expected me to plead with them, after which, if my self-abasement had been humiliating enough, they might relent enough to haul me in and incarcerate me. I was still shaking from the aftereffects of powerlessness; I was too shocked, yet, to feel rage or indignation. Then the engines of the *Colon* began to beat. I knew why; the leather-jacketed man had brought news that another dolphin herd had been spied, and they were setting out to capture it. The boat shuddered into motion, began to draw away from me. From above, I heard the hoarse shout of an officer, I guess, sending them about their business. I swam alongside, keeping pace with the ship. I had to recover my gun.

My gun! You'll believe how numb my mind was when I tell you that I already had it in my hand and was swimming away from the ship before the words of Old Skullface blazed, as if on a giant projector, across the visible universe:

It'll cut through a steel hull!

Then it was like a dam inside my head broke, all my rage at the stenos' deaths and my own humiliation came pouring through, and I thought: All right, you fuckers! You and your fucking *Colon!* I'll give you a red-hot colostomy like you wouldn't believe!

For was I not the King of the Sea?

I'VE OFTEN WONDERED, since, what would have happened if I had not had that thought but had simply swum away, as I was about to do. It's a futile exercise, I know. We believe we have free choice; but I feel now that there could have been no other outcome. From the moment the dolphin project was conceived, my feet were set upon a spiral staircase that wound inexorably down to this moment. This moment of glassy, lucid calm, in which it was so simple and apparent what I had to do.

I swam parallel with the ship, a shade faster than it, for it had not yet picked up full speed, until I was almost level with the bows. There, angling below the surface, and only a foot or two from the encrusted hull, I flipped the lever and began to swing the gun slowly, through a great arc. At first I thought it was malfunctioning, for nothing seemed to be happening; and then slowly, beautifully, ineluctably, like a giant metal leaf, a whole chunk of the *Colon*'s side began to part, bend, fold and roll inward under the pressure of the water streaming against it.

So fascinated was I by this spectacle that it all but killed me. I felt the tug of the water just in time; just in time turned, limbs threshing, pulling clear of the jagged hole itself but still thrown by the pressure against the hull with a force that nearly stunned me. I inched along the hull, clinging to it, tearing my suit, my skin on its jagged fauna, until the pressure eased and I was far enough from the hole to kick off and swim clear. Then I breathed once, quickly, kicked down deep and swam hard, as far from the *Colon* as I could.

When I surfaced there was half the length of a football field of water between me and the *Colon*. At first I felt only a mixture of disappointment and disbelief. Nothing visible had changed. The decks were empty, the crew going about their tasks. The *Colon* steamed onward at a good clip, her lines level and unchanged. She was drawing away from me fast. Had I hallucinated the whole thing? A phantom vengeance in the mind? I did not dive again. That was stupid. I stayed on the surface, waiting, watching. Something had to happen. Soon. At the lick she was going she must be shoveling water into her gut by the ton. If I wasn't dreaming, she had to start going down by the head, now, any moment, surely . . .

It was so gradual that, especially with the angle at which she was drawing away from me, it took a long time before you could be certain. But, yes, there was something odd about her bows, and she was losing speed, no doubt of it . . . A bell jangled. A whistle blew; once, then repeatedly, with a note of urgency. Men ran out of one companionway and into another. Two men going opposite ways collided, slipped and went down. I was too far to hear their curses. And then there, on the bridge, was the captain, sweeping the sea with field glasses. No fool he. He'd tumbled to it, bizarre as it was, right away.

And reacted with instant war. It's funny, in retrospect, the shock, and even indignation, that I felt when I saw him signaling to a clutch of sailors beneath, and caught the glint of sunlight on a rifle barrel. If I'd thought about it at all, I'd assumed that they would be too caught up in self-preservation to worry about me. But when I surfaced, again, as much further from the *Colon* as one breath would carry me, lead tore past my ear and ripped a white hole in the glassy blue-green hillock in back of me. And I caught, before I could dive again, a fierce sputter of sound, like an angry bee, higher and sharper than the *Colon*'s engines. They were sending the pongos out after me.

It's a scary thing, in a fight, when your opponent reacts with several times the speed and violence you were prepared for. You need time to escalate to the new level of combat; but time I hadn't got. When I next surfaced, the nearest pongo was right where I had last dived, and there was a man in it standing, pointing, shouting: "Po ya ta!" Pidgin Spanish: "There he is!" I went down, knowing I had no chance at all, knowing that this is the last thing you should ever think in a fight—you might as well give up right away once you think that—but what if it were so? I beat the thought down, swung straight toward the pongo but fifteen feet beneath it, saw its wavering shadow run by overhead, then surfaced, where the tossing water in their wake might hide my head for a moment . . . I was right, the pongo swung in an aimless, sputtering arc, they were all looking the other way—but I'd forgotten the second pongo, that one was coming straight at me. I heard its crew's whoop of triumph and then I was down again, so close that its nose grazed my tail; if its own displacement hadn't forced me down I'd have been torn open by the propeller of its hundred-horse outboard, and now I was boxed in, both pongos circling the sea above me, I hadn't a chance, unless, unless . . .

Why didn't I think of it before? That will clue you in to how little bloodthirsty I was, even then. I hadn't wanted to kill, even though they had killed those dearest to me. It would have been enough to have destroyed their ship, giving them time to radio for help, and then scuttle off ignominiously in their pongos, an awful warning to any who should afterward think of threatening my elected species. But they weren't up for that. Manlike, they would seek to savage their enemy even in their own death throes. They gave me no option.

I surfaced. The nearest pongo swerved and came for me. I went down, slowly, leisurely, lifted the gun, depressed the firing lever. The laser split the aluminum hull from end to end, right down the middle. Even through feet of water I could hear them screaming, and then I had to move fast as it all came down around me, the two halves of the boat, all the junk that was in it—a shotgun, going end over end, just missed my head —while above, on the surface, white limbs threshed, and from them came curling . . .

Blood.

Masses of it. One of the limbs wasn't a limb any more. It was a ragged stump, pumping arterial blood. The poor bastard must have had his leg across the middle of the hull.

Dimly through the water I heard the second pongo decelerating, and then its motor cut out. I surfaced. The men in the second pongo were reaching out to rescue the men from the first. All except one of them. That one was pivoting slowly, his rifle at the ready. His head turned until it was pointing directly at mine. He fired.

The slug missed me by inches.

That, for me, was the finish of limited warfare. If even while trying to save their own they could spare the time to kill me, then fuck them. I dived, I drew down on the quavering underimage of their hull, I hit them dead center, not bothering to slice this time, one good hole should be enough. By the time I came up again they were half-submerged, struggling to keep afloat, those just rescued slipping back over the side. There was no gun to be seen anywhere. Sounds of confused shouting floated across the oily swells. Not from the pongo, though; from the mother-ship.

All the time I had been evading the pongos I had given neither thought nor glance to the larger vessel. Now I saw that the *Colon* was stationary, its engine stopped, bows down and stern up, screws almost clear of the water. Even as I watched, a third pongo, laden with men, pulled away from her side. More men were trying to lower a lifeboat; that was what the noise was about. They'd fouled the davits and the lifeboat hung at a jaunty angle. An ax flashed. Someone trying to cut it loose.

I don't know how it was that I never heard the helicopter. True, when you're listening intently to something, you can tune almost everything else out. Plus I wasn't expecting it, though I should have been; many of the bigger tuna boats carried spotter machines, and it was hardly likely they'd found another herd so close to this one with just a masthead lookout. Even when I did hear the thing, I couldn't see it; it was coming at me right out of the sun. And when I did see it, a mean metal dragonfly with blue plexiglass bubble for head, it was too late, it was right on top of me.

The man next to the pilot reached out and something black like a short stick came tumbling toward me. I was watching it like a dummy, open-mouthed, when all of a sudden it hit me what it was—

Dynamite!

I crashed. Almost too late. The blast of the explosion slammed against me like a steel door. For a moment I thought my ribs were gone. I felt as if all the air had been forced out of my lungs. I'd have to come up. There was no way round it.

He was up there, circling. Waiting. The guy was priming another stick. Bastards! They probably kept the stuff for atolls where they could toss a couple sticks in the lagoon and pick up maybe a tenth of the dead fish left there. That would be a typical trick. The copter swooped toward me, but before they could throw again I was down, down deep, twenty feet, thirty, with a good lungful of air to carry me . . .

No explosion came.

Who was I fooling? They had me now, no mistake. They were hovering up there, waiting for me to surface. The water was so clear they could see me, for sure, no matter how deep I went, just as I could see their lean shadow wavering on the huge flawed green mirror of the surface way over me; all they had to do was wait till the moment before I surfaced and let go, and that was it—nothing I could do about it, nothing at all . . .

Unless . . .

I aimed my head at the wavering shadow and struck out for the surface—hard, fast; as hard and as fast as I was able, driving with every muscle in my body, blending the thrust of each muscle into the smooth driving flow that the stenos had taught me, when they were teaching me to leap, and the mirror came down on me, and the shadow on the mirror, and then with a shattering explosion of light I was hanging in midair.

I had breached, breached as never before.

Right under them, in the thrower's blind spot. Even as I hung there, at the apex of my leap, the machine side-slipped and heeled over, and *he was on the wrong side, the thrower was on the wrong side;* in that instant of time I saw his face go tense with annoyance and his hand lift to lob the stick over the cabin— heeling, tilting, they were not more than ten feet above and to the side of me—and in that same instant, already beginning to fall, I swung up the gun and aimed and fired.

Not at the man. They could get another man. At the gas tank.

One second there was a shiny blue metal dragonfly humming through the air; the next, a rolling ball of orange fire. I hit water as it blew. I felt the first wave of heat sear me, then I was down, safe, in the cool below. When I came up again, it was a spidery twist of scorched metal, smoking, sinking with a prolonged hiss into the waves. I smelt burned oil and scorching flesh, and then the sea wind blew away smoke and smell and there was just a greasy slick to mark where it had gone down.

A wild shout came from behind me. I turned, to see the *Colon* perpendicular, balancing with its stern high in the air, then with a smooth rushing motion going down, vanishing. A dull, muffled explosion came from beneath. The waters heaved, subsided. The lifeboat, badly overloaded, began to move slug- gishly in my direction, oars rising and falling in ragged time.

It was then that I heard the screaming.

For a moment it bewildered me. I couldn't figure out where it was coming from. Not the lifeboat, the faces in it were grim and frozen. Not the helicopter, not the *Colon,* anyone left near them was past screaming by now. I'd completely forgotten the two pongos I'd sunk. But their crews were now only some thirty or forty yards from me, four bobbing heads barely visi- ble in the dazzle of sunlight. Four round black blobs. Four? Shouldn't there be more than four?

And only then did I realize that it was the round black blobs that were screaming.

A high black triangle cut the water; another, at an angle to it; the water swirled. When the swirl subsided, there were only three black blobs. But the three kept on screaming.

Now the men in the lifeboat had seen me. They had no weapons. But they cursed me and shook fists and oars at me. They were a hundred yards from the round blobs, and they weren't going to make it in time. Even before they could make another stroke, the waters seethed again, another head was gone; there must have been a dozen sharks at least, and with the smell of blood and the tremors of terrified limbs spreading further and further through the water, soon, very soon, there would be many more.

It was then that I did something that to this day I can't properly explain. I can only say that I had been half driven out of my mind by rage and terror, forced into a killing frenzy as mindless as that of the sharks. The men in the boat were no danger to me, they were unarmed, I could easily have outdistanced them. Instead, blindly, without a thought, I swam toward them and burned the lifeboat in half.

The two ends stood almost upright in the water and the men in them were spilled out, in a heap, a heap that writhed and shrieked as they struggled to climb back clear of the water, scrambling on top of one another, dragging one another down. And the reverberation of their struggle drew in like a magnet the sharks that were now sweeping toward us on all sides.

There was a roar away to my left. It was the third pongo, leaving fast, skittering away over the wave tops. Still gripped by the frenzy, I began to swim in pursuit, and had covered twenty yards before I realized the futility of it. Anyway, let them go, I thought. Someone had better bear the story to the world. To let them know that dolphins could no longer be slaughtered with impunity; that they now had a protector mightier and more deadly than any creature of earth.

Behind me, the shrieks were rising in pitch. It seemed inconceivable that they could rise higher, but they did. Fins were slashing the water all around the two halves of the lifeboat, which still showed a few inches above the surface. Some clung to them desperately, some struggled alone in the water. Water that was already streaked with great smears of blood. I could not count the sharks, because there were so many; I could not count the men, for at each blink of the eye another of them had vanished. And still the shrieks of terror and despair went on.

THEN, AND ONLY THEN, a wave of horror and nausea rolled over me, and I began to swim away, anywhere, I no longer cared where, any place where I could block the sound of that screaming from my ears. Sharks passed me, approaching the feast; one or two turned to examine me more closely, but fled when I merely lunged at them, knowing there was easier game ahead. At that stage, I think, I would hardly have cared if they had attacked me. And, even when the sounds had died in the distance, I kept on swimming mechanically, my nerves unable to give the command to stop.

Suddenly, way off and to my right, I heard a faint whistle. I thought at first that my senses were playing tricks on me. But the whistle was answered, from two different quarters. A dorsal fin flipped over, arching in a way no shark's could. Stenos! Some at least must have escaped the carnage, remaining on its fringes in the faint hope that other stragglers might have survived.

Well, one had. And here he was, come to rejoin his own, to reap the gratitude he had earned as their defender.

The cloud of horror lifted from me, I swam joyously to meet them, calling to them in my stumbling version of their tongue.

A whistle answered me. I swam faster.

But something was wrong. It wasn't a call of welcome: it was the alarm whistle. I plunged below the surface, and saw them, six or seven of them, all turning, heading away from me. Somehow they had misunderstood me. I swam after them, repeating my call. Their flukes pulsed as they increased speed. Through a fog of panic and exhaustion I drove myself on at maximum speed, calling and calling to them. They increased speed again. They were pulling away from me.

Magnificent in their flight, with a beauty that wrung the heart even in the moment of their betrayal, they fled from me, at a pace I could never hope to equal, their smooth silhouettes dwindling until, one after another, they flicked out like so many candle flames, and the water ahead of me was bare and empty. Yet still I swam on, long after they had disappeared from sight, babbling incoherently, praying that they would return to me.

But they did not.

Not then; not ever.

WHAT IS THERE LEFT TO SAY?

I persuaded myself, at first, that they had been afraid, not of me but of the horrors they must have witnessed; my sudden appearance had spooked them, that was all; once they had recovered they would accept me as they had done before.

In that faith, I somehow dragged myself back to the seamount, where I lay for two days or more, recovering my strength. Then I set out once more on my search.

Since then, I've met three different steno pods. Each time it's been the same. The moment they picked up my image, they fled from me. They could not all have witnessed the scenes with the *Colon;* the tale must have been passed from one pod to the next, must now be on its way to circle the earth.

What tale, that could bar me from them forever?

I think I know. I remembered, too late, that time when Mojo had projected the image of the shark eating the man. I remembered their shock and horror. I'd never really dug the reasons for that. But now I thought, if the whole thrust of your life is to reconcile yourself with the universe, if one of the keys to that universe is the food chain in which the lower creature feeds the higher, then the most terrible thing is to reverse that chain, and the most evil being is he who deliberately reverses it—who causes the lower to eat the higher, who condemns his own kind to destruction in the throats and bellies of sharks. That was the ultimate blasphemy. And I had committed it.

I AVENGED YOU! I cried before the invisible tribunal.

We do not recognize vengeance.

You, the scourge of tuna and flying fish, set yourselves up to be so virtuous?

We do not recognize virtue. There are those who preserve the law, and those who break it.

Those I killed had wantonly destroyed you!

That is immaterial and irrelevant.

But I loved you more than my own kind!

That is immaterial and irrelevant.

And is this the friendship for which you're so famous?

We do not understand what you mean. Perhaps you never saw us as we really are. Perhaps you saw only the image of yourself reflected in us. We fulfill our purposes and preserve the law. But what is it that you do? Perhaps that is what you must answer before you can know us.

Yes, I should have remembered Mojo and the shark. And I should have remembered my father, not despised him, when he warned me against trusting another kind. I had believed that I could pass beyond the bounds set for humanity. But I could not. None of us can. In the depths of ocean, on the moon or at the last planet of the farthest star, we remain ourselves; breaking free from all other bonds, we cannot break from the bonds of our species, bonds that are written into our genes and the circuitry of our brains—without which we would, already, be other than what we are.

So be it.

THEY FOUND ME three days ago. An airplane went over high but must have photographed me, for this morning a helicopter, a big Navy one, circled low over the seamount and some asshole with a megaphone called upon me to surrender. I ignored him. I'd been expecting that, of course; mankind would never let me get away with such an act of effrontery. I may not have been able to join a new species, but no one could have made a more thorough job of leaving the old one.

Soon the ships will be here. I still don't know what I'll do when they come. I could give up, sink to the bottom of the ocean, but my mind revolts at that thought while I still have a mind to think and hands to struggle with. I could flee, but where would I flee to? I could fight, but all the navies of the world will be arrayed against me.

There's only one thing I know: that I'm alone and will remain always alone, for whatever time remains to me on earth.

ABOUT THE AUTHOR

Born in England and educated at
Cambridge University, DEREK
BICKERTON is one of the world's leading
experts on pidgin and Creole languages.
He has lived and taught in a number of
remote places in the world. His
published works include a couple of
thrillers and a textbook on the *Dynamics
of a Creole System.* Currently he lives in
Honolulu where he is a Professor of
Linguistics at the University of Hawaii.
He is married and has three children.